# FOREVER PEARL

Claudia McKay

New Victoria Publishers
Norwich, Vermont

© Copyright 2004 Claudia McKay

Published by New Victoria Publishers Inc., PO Box 27, Norwich, VT, 05055. A Feminist Literary and Cultural Organization founded in 1976.

Cover Design: Claudia McKay

Printed and bound by Capital City Press, Montpelier, VT
1  2  3     2006  2005  2004

Library of Congress Cataloging-in-Publication Data

McKay, Claudia.
   Forever pearl / by Claudia McKay.
   p. cm.
   ISBN 1-892281-22-8
   1.   Mines and mineral resources--Fiction.   2. Life on other planets--
Fiction. 3. Women Scientists--Fiction.   I. Title.
   PS3563.C3734F67  2003
   813'.54dc21

                                                      2003008971

For Beth

## Acknowledgements

My thanks to all those who helped and supported me, especially John and my children, Matthew, Steven, Aaron, and Noelle. Thanks to all those writers who inspired and encouraged me in my writing. Thank you Franny for your careful editing.

# Chapter One

GLIA Agent Sonja Shankar looked down on Old Earth through the viewing window of a shuttle leaving an interplanetary docking station. Though still poisoned after centuries of being left fallow, the swirling white clouds, turquoise water and green to brown continents looked seductively much as they had in Sonja's school lessons about the twentieth century.

Closer, the idyllic view was spoiled by the ruined and abandoned cities and the deserts of industrial waste. Even the oceans were marred by a too regular pattern of massive solar power panels and the faint gray-green of artificial algae pools that fed the descendants of those unfortunates not able to escape during the colonization of the galaxy—the few millions that were still housed in the vast network of fetid underground shelters built during the last global war.

The poisoned surface and atmosphere might now be almost preferable to those underground warrens, if what she had heard about them was really true. Crowded, filthy, unspeakable—used as a threat by the disciplinarians of her childhood. She had never been there, naturally, even as part of her job. She didn't like to think about how unpleasant it must be. One couldn't really call it living.

But now, so long after the wars, the Earth was beginning to recover and there were a few domed enclaves built in remote, less damaged places for some of the galaxy's governing elite. As an undercover agent, Sonja visited those enclaves frequently, sometimes as a favored lover, always as a shadow on the wall for the Galactic League's Intelligence Agency, the GLIA.

She was pleased that for the first time her current assignment wouldn't be undercover. She would be an official Galactic League Investigator—able to collect information openly and question directly, an opportunity gratifyingly early in her career. She would soon be on her way to the planet where a profitable and popular intoxicant was mined. Pearl was a luxury item bought chiefly by the Galactic elite, though a dilute version was sold through public houses. The official line was that it was non-addictive and was sold in such minute quantities that it could have no effect on the user's health. Unofficially she knew that individuals who could afford to, cultivated the opalescent lavender skin tone and lean hungry look of addiction, a look that had become a fashion statement in some circles. She herself had never been tempted; being always in control in any situation was her preferred intoxicant.

It was hard to imagine how anyone had discovered pearl's psychoactive effect on humans. The story was that some explorers were lost and ran out of water in the caves on the remote planet, xj-21, where it was mined. They discovered a liquid inside opalescent spheres found in volcanic vents and out of desperate dehydration tasted it. It did nothing for their thirst, but they were no longer concerned about that. They would never have been rescued if they hadn't left an automatic interplanetary distress beacon running.

Recently there were problems in the pearl trade. A shortage had caused unrest in some of the colonized planets. There was a rumor that the shortage had been caused by the producer, the Consortium—an organization representing the galaxy's main economic enterprises—to keep the price high. The League was being pressured by the public to investigate.

The Consortium's pearl planet was not directly under the League's authority like colonized planets. The League had allowed mining of pearl on xj-21 because the Consortium had declared the planet not habitable and without indigenous life-forms warranting League protection. Because the planet did not have colonization status, only one facility, the pearl mine itself and essential Consortium employees were permitted onplanet.

But there had always been an undercurrent of suspicion about xj-21. Recently League officials had learned that there were settlements on the planet beyond that for necessary staff, and that the Consortium was even encouraging farming of earthplants. Sonja's job was to collect information so her bosses could determine if there was justification for League intervention.

Her shuttle turned toward the solar-paneled satellite that was her immediate destination. It was the headquarters of the interplanetary Consortium. They were cooperating with the investigation and had agreed to allow her to interview a Consortium official about xj-21.

Though the Consortium satellite retained an antique angular and imposing shape, she knew it was constantly being modified and retrofitted with the most sophisticated technology. The Consortium, always careful about appearance, had kept the formal antiquity of this facility a part of its mystique.

Once inside the satellite, after enduring the protocol routines that allowed her into the Consortium's inner sanctum, Sonja hurried to one of the more private reception halls. She stopped just short of a rococo mirror-scanner, savoring the heartbeat of precious alone-time before the scanner could announce her—a trick she had learned early. That brief moment always gave her the composure necessary for top performance no matter what was asked of her.

She let herself feel a moment of doubt. Sometimes it was hard not to really belong…somewhere. Even the least human sewer rat beneath the Earth's surface knew what it was, where it belonged. She was a changeling, one of those born not to belong but trained to fit anywhere.

She took a deep breath, closing her eyes for a microsecond to release anxiety and slow her heartbeat and bury those negative thoughts. She pushed her short, straight dark hair into a more flattering contour and straightened her back. Her uniqueness was not something to fret about; it was, as it should be, a source of pride.

Then she stepped forward for the scanner to recognize her. Her reflection, of a slim, handsome woman with tastefully understated makeup, dress and demeanor accentuating her Asian and African ancestry, looked back from the opalescent surface. Except for the bit of tightness around the almond eyes and full mouth, she was pleased with the image.

Massively carved mahogany doors opened into a large well-lit room decorated in eighteenth-century French country antiques, complete with cherubs on the ceiling and a parquet floor. The room was much too ornate and fluffy for her taste, although she was sure it served its purpose. The faux windows were set for spring in Versailles. She recognized the faint flower-scented mist from the mouths of cherubs in the ceiling as a disinfectant spray.

A rather convincing android entered the room through a sliding panel and stood nearby at attention. Robots that so closely resembled people, that used so much living human tissue, were generally illegal and certainly too expensive for even most of the elite, earthdweller or colonist. She was flattered. She was to see Consortium elite. She sat on a red velvet chair for the obligatory debriefing scan.

After a few minutes the wall panel slid open again. A medical cart entered quickly and silently, followed by more robots. Inside the cart's shadowy bubble cover was a fragile, bony person with paper-thin, lavender-pale skin. On one shoulder fastening a simple tunic was a purple Tassian sapphire.

Sonja stood up quickly, recognizing an Eminence of the Consortium. She had met highly placed Consortium officials before, but an Eminence? She had never been so honored and was momentarily flustered. She had seen Eminences on coms, of course, but never had been within touching distance. But her presence of mind returned quickly and she stepped to the correct distance to be probed.

An eyestalk antenna emerged from the side of the cart and a voice boomed at her to stand still. The android attendant said in a surprisingly authentic voice, "We are seeking information. Stand very still." Several wiry probes touched her and the eyestalk scanned.

Sonja felt extremely honored as the cool, smooth, silver-tipped probes slid down her torso. One probe rested on the back of her neck, another on her cheek, and the third against her breast. The probes stroked her. The eyestalk slowly moved from one of her eyes to the other.

A surge of what she could only call reverence and love made her feel faint. This was one of the people who had founded the Consortium, the organization that had engineered the survival of human life on Earth and the settlement of habitable planets. That so intelligent and wise a mind was requesting something of her was overwhelming. Her whole life had been an attempt to win this kind of honor and recognition. She wanted to do whatever they were going to ask of her—or die.

As if in answer to her thoughts, the Eminence said, "We know you love us…daughter. What I ask of you now calls upon that love."

Had she really heard the whispered word, daughter? It was all she had ever hoped for. All her life she had secretly believed that she, like other Agency trainees raised and trained in the GLIA institute, was a genetic descendant of an Eminence—a rumor stridently denied by her teachers. Now this! She wanted to cry—to reach out.

Her rational mind recognized the childhood programming and scoffed at her overreaction, her loss of control, but could not change the feeling.

A hollow voice from the cart whispered intimately, "We have a request for your present assignment. We know we can depend on you and your loyalty. We know we can trust you not to act in your role as Investigator for the League, laudable as that organization might be, in any way which compromises us. We know you will aid us in finding the pearl thieves and restoring pearl for us and for the galaxy."

The probes pressed into her until she managed a faltering nod. The shadowy Eminence waved a fragile finger and the probes and eyestalk withdrew. She was overcome by what she barely recognized as an electronically-induced, sudden and terrible sense of loss as the Eminence wheeled away with the words to the robots, "Give the instructions," and disappeared behind the panel.

The android held out a com and said in a rapid, squeaky voice, "It is known you have photo-recall. You will commit the code to memory. It will be decoded for you when it is necessary."

She felt a moment of doubt. What was it really that she was being asked to do? And why were they withholding information now? After all, she was a Galactic League employee on an Agency assignment.

But some of the euphoria at confirmation of her possible connection to the Eminence returned. She *was* a direct descendent of an Eminence. She belonged among the elite.

There would be conflicts with her role as League Agent. She would have to sort those out. That shouldn't be too hard. After all, the Eminences and the Consortium with its vast interplanetary economic network supported the League's authority in most cases.

If a machine could sound impatient at her hesitation the android did. "The code will be erased in exactly ten minutes."

Sonja placed the com over one eye and scanned. Most people would have difficulty appreciating the speed with which her mind worked. In the blink of an eye she could review and understand more information that any ordinary human could learn in a day.

As she handed the com back to the android she mentally folded the code and placed it in her mind like an old-fashioned piece of paper put into a pocket. To recall it for decoding she would reverse the process, exactly imagining all the details of her pocket in the gray plasticine uniform of her school days. Then she would be able to visualize the message and read it back to herself.

The android said, "You will be given the decoding key at the proper time." If she had not known better she would have guessed at a note of disdain in its voice. She suppressed her annoyance at the implication. She was human. The enhancement of mind and body that her job required didn't make her a robot, as the android's bits of human tissue didn't make it human.

"It is only for you to know the details," it continued condescendingly. Then it began repeating the statement very quickly, "This information is to be guarded with your life," as if she were a robot too stupid to understand simple instructions.

She returned to her shuttle wondering why her bosses at GLIA hadn't told her the seriousness of the situation. Was it possible they didn't know? Disturbed by her encounter with the Eminence she decided to use what time she had left in the environs of Old Earth doing some research, starting with one of her best sources, Lydia. Plenty of time for sleep and analysis once she was on her way.

Her shuttle entered a large domed habitation, built recently in one of the less damaged areas in what had once been called Siberia for some of the Consortium middle-management elite. Once inside the dome she took hovitrack transport. The living unit she finally entered was the white faux-stucco and wood construction typical of this Siberian dome. But Lydia, the person who ran a 'consulting' business housed in this unit was anything but typical. Sonja never quite knew what to expect next of the woman. Behind her rather simple but tasteful doorway was a business that supplied all the experiences, 'counseling' and information that answered the need of any who could afford to pay. Nothing overtly illegal of course, but somehow one usually managed to find what one needed. Information was one of those things Lydia had a way of collecting for the right price. If there was anything useful being said among Earth's elite about the pearl trade, Lydia would likely have heard about it.

After the door accepted her ident, it slid open and a robot greeted her rather formally and went to announce her. Sonja looked around the reception area to see if she could guess what mood Lydia would be in. The decor was dark blue to purple with a touch of silver and gray for emphasis. A replica of a classic Greek statue of a graceful boy knelt in a fountain of flowery scented water. Sonja was not surprised when Lydia appeared in a purple-edged tunic with her hair in black ringlets. In the dim light one could almost imagine her as a young and beautiful girl, sweet and innocent. It was only on very close inspection could one see the minute scars that showed Lydia to be an addict of cosmetic surgery. Lydia saw it as an art form. It was what she spent much of her considerable earnings on. Sonja had often wondered how old Lydia really was. Not something one could ask. The only elite who showed the classic signs of age were Consortium elders and Eminences whose power was expressed in the signs of their venerable age. Some people said that they had to put up with those defects because they had been born before anti-aging science was fully developed and hadn't been able to take full advantage.

Lydia thought Sonja to be one of the bored members of the elite caste who occasionally used her services. She saw Sonja's indulgence in gossip and information as her weakness. It was a very useful ploy for Sonja, but she had to be careful what she said or did. Lydia was one of the smarter people she dealt with regularly. Almost too smart. It was why she was so successful. Lydia was very good at getting information.

Lydia came up to her and put a delicate finger on her cheek. "You're looking tired, darling. Time to take a few tucks around those eyes, don't you think?"

"Been partying. Couldn't sleep."

Lydia smiled. "No trouble fixing that."

Sonja pressed a finger into the cred slot on the wall and Lydia led her inside one of the cubicles and sat down next to her. It was rather unusual to get this degree of personal attention from Lydia. Lydia keyed a drink dispenser. She handed Sonja a crystal glass with an pink bubbly liquid that

Sonja recognized as a relaxant.

Sonja leaned back and closed her eyes. She was feeling weak after her long interplanetary journey from GLIA headquarters on the planet Calsor. Finally she said, "Heard a rumor about the pearl shortage. Some interesting gossip—trouble in the trade?"

"You thinking of taking up the pearl habit, sweets?" Lydia asked, smoothing the satin cover on the couch. "Bored with your usual…indulgences?"

Sonja shook her head. "I take my lead from you."

Lydia nodded. "Ruins the complexion. And I never liked that lean stringy look." She smiled. "When my customers use pearl they lose interest in my other more adventuresome entertainments. Boring for me."

"It's the fashion."

Lydia shook her head. "Fashions change."

"So you think pearl won't stay in fashion?"

"Pearl's not just a fashion."

Sonja nodded. "So I've heard. Makes it a good long-term investment. Can one assume the shortage is temporary? I'm looking for a good place to invest my extra cred."

Lydia began gently rubbing Sonja's forehead. Sonja closed her eyes and enjoyed the special attention, her mind still on guard. Lydia said, "You won't be sorry you never imbibed. More and more of my customers are asking for help, but only because they can't get enough pearl. No one is talking about giving it up, but the shortage is working its way from the bottom up." She laughed lightly. "If I had spare creds, I'd invest in a method to shake the habit."

"Anybody working on that?"

"Word is that the Consortium is researching, but to synthesize the stuff, not to help people give it up."

The soft fingers moved down her neck and shoulders. Sonja was glad she hadn't started to review infocoms for her investigation yet. Nothing to tell Lydia. She put on her let's-share-the-gossip voice. "Come on what's going on? You got some inside info on the stuff? Somebody tip you off? One of your Consortium clients in on a deal and willing to share? My cred's good."

Lydia shook her head. "Nothing to tell. Everybody's hungry and there's no yeastcakes, or not enough to go around."

Sonja felt that Lydia was holding back. She was intrigued. But what to use as leverage? Sonja had done some research a while back and believed Lydia was in fact from sector fifteen, one of the declassed areas in the warrens. Lydia had somehow escaped from her undersurface caste. Now it might be time to risk using that information.

Sonja laid out her bargaining chip. "Did you hear? There were complaints in the new dome about fires, way down in the warrens, overheating the dome's water source. And to top that my friend says the warren bureaucrats took perfectly good swimming pool water from the dome for fire control in the earthrats sector fifteen and—"

The hands stopped their motion and lifted away from Sonja's body. This was the edge she needed; Sonja sat up. "Or was it actually sector thirteen?" She caught the fleeting moment of relief on Lydia's face that told Sonja she had been right. Lydia had somehow escaped the warrens—probably still had family in fifteen.

Sonja could see that Lydia realized she had lost. She would buy Sonja's silence with some real information if she had it.

Lydia turned away to hide her reaction, but she said, "One of my favorite clients went to third sector looking for pearl. Bright mind—incredible fantasies. I miss him."

Lydia switched on the visualizer and selected the niche she wanted. Sonja sat up to watch.

Soon there was the face of a midlevel Consortium bureaucrat. Lydia had been very economical in her editing; there was no preliminary superficial background material. The man was weeping and complaining to whomever was wearing the nano-recorder, presumably Lydia herself, that he had been demoted for excessive pearl use, though no one had ever indicated previously that pearl was disapproved of or dangerous, let alone addictive. It was unfair and, even worse, on pain of confinement, he was forbidden the level of pearl he had become accustomed to.

This was followed by were similar statements by other of Lydia's clients, one a planet colony governor and one a spaceship captain. They each thought they were the only one that had suffered the indignity of pearl being withheld. They mourned the loss of pearl as if it were a treasured lover that had been killed, not just an entertaining substance.

Then, to document the numbers of clients involved, Lydia showed her a lot of quick clips of lavender-tinted people weeping, angry, deeply depressed or resigned but sad.

Was the Consortium finally realizing that its own product was unhealthy and instituting a policy of pearl withdrawal? Or were they beginning to control pearl because it was in short supply and they wanted not to cause a panic? The Consortium would save what reserve it still had for the elite.

Sonja said impatiently, so that Lydia would think the information was not important to her, "I already know there's a problem."

Lydia said, "But you didn't know the shortage affected—"

"There is no evidence here that your clients, however important they think they are, aren't simply incompetent, or made so by pearl."

Lydia eyes narrowed as she chose another niche. Sonja watched a blurry clip of a woman picking at the skin of her arm which was covered with bloody lesions. "It went away. I bleed and bleed and it's not there—" Her eyes widened. She whispered, leaning closer, "—It always talked to me. We—" The woman shuddered and tears filled her eyes. "It's still there, but alone. I miss— I—I can't get more pearl. It…we are so alone. It's so quiet." She covered her ears and began to sway back and forth rhythmically then she began to scream.

Lydia turned it off. "Pearl is a bad investment, sweets. It will continue to sell, but no one knows the long-term effects and what that will cost. I expect lawsuits—"

Sonja closed her eyes again and said dismissively, "You haven't convinced me. But I didn't come here to watch psychopaths suffer their delusions."

Sonja opened her eyes. Lydia was standing by the door not looking at her. She must be anxious check on her family in the warrens—if they were victims of a fire. Lydia asked neutrally, "Who do you want?"

Sonja shrugged. "Annie will do."

Lydia looked away and said quietly, "Sometimes what you really need to know is hidden in strange places."

Was Lydia simply trying to discourage Sonja from speculating in the pearl trade, or—?

That last woman on the visualizer had been insane, but was pearl or the lack of it the cause? The real question was still why was the Consortium withholding it, even from these privileged people. What she'd seen certainly explained the urgency of her assignment.

But now she wondered if the problem was this urgent why she had been picked? Was it because of her relationship with the Eminence?

Maybe she had been foolish coming to Lydia, who now might suspect her of being more than a self-indulgent citizen. Sonja tried to reassure herself that Lydia would keep her suspicions to herself for now.

Sonja said dismissively, "Well you certainly have convinced me it's much too risky to invest in the pearl trade." She sighed and leaned back, letting the pink liquid do it's work. Lydia left quietly. She would be replaced by one of Sonja's favorite attendants. Annie understood her tastes.

There was one last visit to make before her transport was ready to take her to the pearl planet. She was expected at a gathering this evening at

Viol's, notorious gadabout and Galaxy traveler. Viol occupied a section of one of the newer domes built in the Arctic. When Viol was at home on Earth there was some sort of gathering almost every evening—always a good base for information-gathering.

After keying in with her ident, Sonja let the greeting robot help her with her wrap and stood in Viol's lavish entry where windows showed the surrounding mountains and snowfields. It was always a little disconcerting to enter a world where clothing was considered an affectation, and formal wear was defined by the quality of one's jewelry. The latest fad was inset stones. She had settled for one single blue stone—carved lapis, a present from Viol, in her navel setting, matched by old-fashioned earlobe inserts, and a delicately carved lapis necklace and bracelet. This simplicity accented the perfect lean line of her body. It would have to do. In any case she did not want to draw attention to herself by too formal or elaborate an outfit.

She went through a bead curtain of Martian jade into the main hall. There was a good-sized crowd this evening. She recognized a few of the people lounging and chatting. There were the usual elaborate jeweled penis covers. Some of the women had lace and draped fabric that accentuated rather than hid their lean curves. One woman had diamonds imbedded to match the curve of her vertebrae. Almost all had the lavender tinge to their skin that indicted pearl addiction. Perhaps she should have worn makeup to hide her color.

Here everyone had intiception implants, some more sophisticated than others. They were useful in intimate settings but their range was limited. Ambiance was generally set on casual which made her job easier. With her state-of-the-art implants the mild privacy shields were irrelevant and she could read much of the interaction without being detected. It was useful and interesting to check the dissonance between inticeptor signals and what she picked up from nonverbal body gestures and expressions. The later were often more useful. Inti communication was always interesting to monitor in a group—who was flirting with whom—who was trying to seem casual, but conducting more serious business.

She set her inticeptor to scan, leaving off send function for the moment. When she went into this information-gathering mode she felt like a swimmer in deep water watching everyone as if in slow motion. Humans were so transparent really; everything about them was written on their surfaces, in their gestures, their expressions, even here among the sophisticated. There was the usual array of primitive emotions—attempts at flirtation, defensive jealousy, anger veiled as sarcasm. It was all so easy and so boring.

There were always the netception sites people could access with the right equipment, but most elite did not want to mar their perfect exteriors and ambiance with such devices, so not many were wearing the larger, more metal-rich devices that allowed net communication outside the apartment. In any case, it was considered rude to surf while in the presence of one's peers, even during lulls in the conversation or to make oneself seem important by the number of call-ups. But someone who was clearly a Consortium official was networking a meeting surrounded by a serious privacy block and thus interfering with other communications in the room and annoying those who wished to carry on several flirtations at once.

But now that she was paying attention to pearl, she noted that pearl addiction here seemed to cause a flatness of emotion in interactions with other people, quite unlike the people she had seen at Lydia's

Viol walked into the room from an alcove, arm around a young man. Viol who preferred at the moment to be referred to as he, was a casual pearl user. Viol prided himself on his self-control, but it was clear he'd changed since the last time Sonja had seen him. Lavender tinted, his graceful tapered figure was almost translucent. Unlike most of his guests he wore a loincloth of a pure white fabric decorated with jewels, a rather gaudy display. Sonja enjoyed the fashionably wispy effect pearl created, though she was contemptuous of the weakness of character that allowed its use. It was a weakness that made Viol less appealing to her. But it suited Sonja's purposes to be seen as the occasional lover of a powerful person. No one questioned her presence at gatherings or was particularly careful about what they said.

Viol ignored her, punishing her for her long absence. The young man with Viol lacked the various shades of lavender of a pearl user. Blond hair, the twist of the well-shaped shoulders—he looked faintly familiar. Had he found some new cosmetic to hide the pearl tint? He too had chosen simplicity for his formal wear—one large creamy rainbow opal imbedded in his buttock with a gold chain draped across his lean hip and attached to the simple, engraved gold penis cover. He turned and she almost did a double-take with her eyes...almost gasped in disbelief. Jason! She hadn't seen that face since her childhood at the institute. Was he to be her replacement because of her new assignment. She had seen it as temporary, expecting to return to her usual job after it was completed.

Jason's eyes held hers for a millisecond, while his fingers moved nimbly and subtly on his glass, tapping in code. A torrent of memories assaulted her—the strongest of the blows that never fell on her small frame because Jason had been there, her unacknowledged champion at the Institute.

Jason's message finally got through her dazed state. It was the code they had used with each other as children, too fast and too subtle for their teachers to recognize as language. Now she didn't acknowledge the communication, but studied his form across the room in her peripheral vision.

"Why are you here?" The squeaky, openly hostile voice emanated from a scrawny figure with arms akimbo, fists on pink flounced hips far below Sonja's normal line of sight.

Sonja looked down. It was Viol's faux-daughter, Arnica, spoiled and annoying. Sonja didn't much like children anyway, not that there were many chances to come across them in her life, but this adult altered to be childlike was much worse than the usual precocious self-conscious offspring of the elite. Even those saw and knew too much. But Arnica operated with the affect of a child, but with the knowledge and skill of an adult.

When Sonja said nothing, Arnica continued. "You might as well go away. That's his new friend. Viol is mad as ginger at you anyway." At the monster's taunting tone Sonja felt her fists want to clench.

The monster child's large eyes squinted, her lips tightened. "I know you hate me. You're not exactly my favorite, either. So just go away."

Sonja took the string of delicately carved gemstones from around her neck and dangled it in front of Arnica, who had asked for them the last time she'd seen Sonja. 'It' studied them for a few moments with nearsighted eyes, then held out a hand, took them and marched away silently.

She looked again toward Jason and Viol. Viol was still deliberately ignoring her. It was obvious that Jason was his new lover. She felt dizzy suddenly. She should leave immediately. Responding to Viol's invitation had been a last minute decision. She should have been more careful.

But she might as well face it head on; if she left it would look suspicious and offend Viol even more. She moved across the room in an agony of slowness. As she reached him, Viol finally turned to her with a false smile and took her hands and squeezed them, saying petulantly. "I'm so glad to see you, dear, finally. How long have you been onplanet?"

Sonja gathered the appropriate persona around herself and put her arms around him and kissed him effusively. "I just got your communication. I've been beauty resting, you know, incommunicado, a sleep cure. I feel so renewed."

He gave her a genuine smile. "I don't believe you. As good as you look I know you never rest. Not your style. But I am delighted…really…to see you. So delighted I'll set aside the whole weekend just for you."

Sonja carefully slowed her reflexes, responding by kissing the lavender tinted cheek. She turned casually. Jason was gone. Viol sighed. "Nothing gets past you does it, dear. That handsome young man is—"

Sonja turned to read the slight flush on Viol's face in the millisecond that he hesitated. Jason certainly hadn't wasted time; Viol was truly enamored.

But why had the GLIA replaced her with Jason? Her heart caught in her throat. Her bosses didn't trust her. Then the message Jason had tapped finally decoded itself and reached her consciousness. He was telling her to find some way to meet him outside in the garden. The roof garden would be set up for privacy. It was one thing for him to be in the territory of another Agent, but to make contact? The coded message had an urgency; some sort of danger—

Viol was saying, "I met him at a health retreat. It was one of the reasons I came home. I haven't been feeling so well. A sleep cure really does help. You were gone such a long time, and…he reminds me so of you." The man was overdoing it with his effort to flatter her. It made his face an unpleasant shade of mauve.

"Is that why he left, just now? You didn't tell him about me?"

"I did, but you see he's so emotional and—"

Sonja squeezed his hand. "Don't worry, sweetheart, I'll talk to him. It will be all right."

Viol kissed her. "Thank you, dear. I knew you would be understanding."

Sonja went toward the roof garden with her heart pounding. She put her hand on the door frame to steady herself and made sure her intiception was set to private.

Jason was in a plant encrusted alcove that would muffle their conversation. Standing close to him in the dimness, looking into his brown eyes, she fell into a vortex of feeling, a waterfall roared in her head, tears about to overflow. The feelings were very different from those she had felt with the Eminence. These were very unwelcome—a vestige of childhood she thought long gone. But still she held out her hand and said, "I don't believe we've met." He reached out as if to catch her. She was so ashamed of showing him her feelings.

He took her hands and led her to a bench making inane chatter for the inevitable recorder that Viol would have hidden. Then, in the light from the artificial moon, in the childhood code his fingers tapped out, "I've come to warn you. The Consortium is allowing you on the pearl planet to appease the League—so they won't interfere. If you go—you won't survive—even if you fix whatever their problems are." His eyes met hers. While he tapped this his smiling lips continued to speak trivialities.

She felt nauseated, confused. Why was he communicating with her in this way? She must not be reading his code right. He was saying the unthinkable. How could she not do her job for the League.

It had to be some sort of test by her League bosses. Did they know about the Eminences attempt to recruit her? Of course they knew about her vulnerabilities—after all the Consortium had a part in her training. The creche where she and Jason had spent their infanthood was a Consortium facility. Did they think she was disloyal? But why send Jason? As far as she knew no one in authority knew about this childish form of communication.

She took a deep breath. The only rule was that one succeeded at any assigned task; that was the only goal, even if death was the consequence. It was her responsibility to succeed. But she was no longer sure what that meant. Not a very comforting thought. Her death in most cases would automatically be called failure.

She was shaking. She could not even continue the flow of inane conversation. She was overcome by childhood memories. Damn Jason; his break in protocol was threatening both their lives.

Had he become a renegade? But that was absurd; he couldn't work for anyone other than the League. It was impossible; his very genetic coding—

He tapped out, "You don't have to work for the League or the Eminences. I came to help you. Come away. There are others like us. A good life."

This was some sort of trick, a trap. She hesitantly moved her fingers, slowly remembering the code. "What you are telling me is treason. You know very well the penalty."

He did not hesitate, though she could see disappointment at her response on his face. He spoke again with his fingers, "There are places that are not under League or even Consortium jurisdiction. Come with me. You can save yourself."

She began to repeat the Institute credo mechanically with her fingers, "I live for my work. Success in my League assignment is all I desire—"

Again his fingers moved quickly. "You've been trained to be like that. You can change."

Sonja could feel herself losing control. Of course he was right. She was going to die—no matter what she did. She was expendable. Again the roaring filled her mind. She was going to fall, crash. She felt her fingers tap out as in a dream, slowly, "Which League enemy are you trying to recruit me for?"

She watched his fingers, pale in the artificial moonlight. Her mind could no longer translate the code. She sat frozen, though her mind recorded the message. Then she drew herself together with a deep breath and laughed. The sound echoed hollowly.

Jason had stopped speaking with his hands and his voice. She couldn't look at him now. Yes, the man must have lost his mind.

In control again, she said out loud so that anyone eavesdropping would hear the casualness in her voice, "The night air is making me giddy. What new perfume have they put into it to make me feel so strange? Excuse me, please." She stood up and went inside, indeed feeling light-headed. She would contact the League. They would deal with this madman.

She continued her research at the party almost as if nothing had happened, putting Jason and his messages away deep in her mind. Many of those she spoke to were recently arrived back on Earth, attracted by the novelty. There was an undercurrent in conversations and on the inti about trouble over the shortage and the dilution of pearl—a few cases of prosecution of the pearl establishments for hoarding—hints about the cred to be made investing in the pearl trade. But with passion not present in their other communications they assured each other their pearl supplies were safe—that the Consortium would take care of its own.

When Sonja left the party she didn't say good-bye to Viol, leaving it to Jason to invent a reason for her sudden departure—jealously would do.

She couldn't believe Jason would really let himself be so vulnerable. He knew she might report him—just send a message to her mentor at the GLIA institute indicating the need for a personal holo conference so she could discuss Jason. Had they sent him as her replacement with Viol?—the finger code just a little personal joke at her expense? If that was so, her bosses would be annoyed that she risked a communication with them reporting him. And, after all, if Jason was renegade or mad he would soon enough expose himself. She needn't risk the security of her present assignment.

# Chapter Two

The Consortium's pearl mine and refinery on planet xj-21 were in a dry, cool desert. Not far away was a deep rift valley that had water and native oxygen producing, algae-like life-forms in its depths. On the edge of that valley a large Earthdome had been built for Consortium employees and elite who could not be expected to tolerate conditions in the open or in the mine and refinery complexes.

The floor of the rift valley was constantly bathed in warm mist. Few humans could tolerate the damp, spore-laden air for long without filtering apparatus or a protective suit. Human skin and lungs were an excellent food source for the local life-forms in an otherwise protein-poor environment. In a few short hours spore soon developed into multicolored growth, quickly coating the warm moist surfaces of unprotected human lungs and skin. Even with the protection of filters and protective suits, humans often developed serious allergies both to the resident life-forms of the valley and to the chemical cleaners used to remove them. No one who had been in the valley was allowed to re-enter a ship or dome without scrubbing down with those harsh chemicals.

In that valley Nombei O'Brien put one unprotected arm gently on a damp, life-encrusted rock and waited. She had only a light protective suit to cover all but her one exposed arm and a small mask-filter to protect her lungs and provide a little extra oxygen.

After a while the red-orange 'leaf' she had spotted as mature but still young enough to train—about the size of her hand—slowly moved toward her. She loved watching the soft undulating motion, a continuous rippling along its soft surface, tentacles reaching out and waving almost imperceptibly each time it moved a little closer. Because leaves did not have a nervous system resembling that of living creatures on Earth, they were regarded as little more than plants. But Nombei knew from experience that wild leaves were cautious and sensitive to any strange scent or taste. She wasn't sure how they perceived the world, but they could taste nervousness or any strong human emotion for that matter. They would disappear down a crack in the rock, responding to any negative emotions. She preferred their company to that of most humans who judged one by appearance.

Suddenly Nombei was caught off guard by the memory of taunts—

"Earth roach, pit snipe" —and worse, when she had first arrived onplanet. The thoughts were an unfortunate emotional slip—the leaf hesitated, its tentacle-like feet quivering. She took a breath to calm herself. Fortunately, she was no longer confined in the warrens of Earth or onplanet as a mine or refinery worker, but was a settler here in the valley where people were judged by what they could do, not by the pasts they wanted to forget.

She even had a few elite customers from the Earthdomes. In response to her slight surge of emotion, the feeling of pride at her accomplishments, the leaf turned an almost imperceptible shade darker and froze.

She filled her mind and feelings with thoughts of her other leaves snuggled into the cozy nests she had built for them in her private dome. They were her friends. The leaf uncurled slowly, again approaching the meal growing on the arm she offered.

Nombei contemplated her unprotected arm with its bloom of symbiont life cultivated to tempt the leaf. She was used to the feel of growth on her skin—the appearance was intimidating, but for the time it would be there it would do no real harm.

Really she was proud to be part of the valley's community. There she was no longer stigmatized by her earthwarren label, 325,063004 O'Brien, but was simple known as Nombei.

She fought a wave of nostalgia for her family and friends back on Earth. She cared about them, but the narrow, dark and infinite tunnels of the earthwarrens where they were still confined were not a place to call home. There one counted status by the number of square inches one was allowed to occupy. Ironic that her childhood in the sewer atmosphere in the warrens of Old Earth was what made her tough enough to tolerate the environment of this new and underpopulated settlement. The deformities that had defined her caste on Earth were the source of her strength here. She was respected as one of those who knew ways to survive. She was proud of her toughness and genetic resistance to poisons.

She didn't want to remember. Earth was darkness and shadow, overwhelming smells, too many people and the pale worn face of her mother dying of the inevitable cancers.

She loved this overgrown valley of perpetual mists. Its closeness comforted her. On the dry plain where she had been brought to slave in the pearl mine, she had been terrified by the open cloudless sky and brilliant red-orange sun.

After she left the refinery and had been allowed to settle in the valley, she had been one of the first to discover that leaves were a gentler way to remove the endemic symbiont life called pelt which quickly covered unprotected human skin. After all, pelt was the leaves' normal diet. Now she made a good living. Customers regularly visited her establishment, or even purchased her leaves to keep at home—those who could afford it.

To prepare for collecting this particular leaf she had scrubbed her skin thoroughly, placed a seeding of the leaf's favorite growth on her hand and arm, taken in only liquids for twelve earth hours and let the growth develop. Now she might have to wait hours before it decided whether she was a suitable host. A quick motion, even a quiver of her hand, and the creature would curl up into a hard-shelled rock look-alike.

She studied the animal as she waited. It was in excellent health and at least a dozen seasons old. Mature animals of this quality were harder and harder to find. The training of a leaf was a long and risky venture if it was to survive the rigors of a human household. Trained to accept a human host and tolerate its emotional ups and downs, the leaf would bring a handsome price.

The leaf finally tested the blue coating on her fingers, but kept most of its body firmly anchored to the rock. She would wait, perhaps even come back another time, while another hunter might pull it by force from the rock, making it difficult to develop a trusting symbiosis. The damage to its tender foot tentacles alone might destroy it. Most hunters counted on a leaf's ability to regenerate body parts and adapt to hostile environments. Some leaves did survive such treatment.

The leaf began to curl around her fingers, tickling her palm with its thousands of tiny sensors. She steeled herself not to react while still enjoying the sensation. One uncontrolled motion would spoil everything. The leaf finally settled on her arm and began to eat with what she interpreted as satisfaction. She eased her arm off the rock and pushed her way slowly through heavy, damp, entangling growth. Even at best visibility was only a few feet in the murky air.

She wiped away the scum accumulating on her direction finder. There were no paths that could be depended on in the valley; in about twenty-four Earth hours the environment could change—a whole new cycle of growth. She made her way back toward the settlement, a cluster of encrusted house-domes and a few larger business domes, hardly even a town.

She came upon a newly cleared path. Her dome was not far now. Dark shapes emerged from the mist—beggars, their bodies completely covered with a multicolored pelt of symbionts. An irreversible situation—beggars were dependent on both pearl and the pelt for their survival, but it made them outcasts, less than human. They claimed to prefer their condition, but what else could they say? They knew they couldn't return to the community. It wasn't just that they couldn't afford the usual chemical cleaning most people used—they didn't have enough healthy skin to survive it.

As usual the beggars began the slow dance that flaunted their pelts of blue-gray and purple growth like armor. They were begging for pearl or the means to buy it. Usually all they had to do was get too close and they would be thrown a bribe of a few creds or a token amount of pearl.

Nombei kept to her path to show that she was not to be intimidated. Once they recognized her, they kept their distance, knowing she was not afraid of them. But one of the beggars laughed, an ugly screeching sound. What must have once been a woman's voice echoed through the mist, an almost familiar sound. The leaf reacted to a surge of emotion it felt from her and almost fell off her arm. Again she tried to calm herself, as she felt the tears flow. Why did it still hurt so after all this time? Pella, her lover, had succumbed to the lure of the intoxicant pearl after years of working in the mine and refinery—she could be one of the beggars.

She thought bitterly that even now pearl was still legal. The Consortium still denied that the substance was harmful and claimed that the number of addicts was "acceptably low." That just meant that the profits were too high for them to be concerned about addicted workers.

The official line on Pella had been that having worked her allotted years, she had left the planet for a colony. Rumor was she had gone with another lover. Nombei hadn't believed any of it, though the traces of Pella she had followed hadn't located her onplanet.

Nombei did not look back as she headed toward her dome trying not to imagine the Pella she knew—tall and lean with glossy dark skin—under all that growth. The leaf was still quivering. Again she cleared her mind, thinking of water flowing over rock. Water here was always milky and slow-moving—soothing and cooling, thick even when it came down as rain.

Today there were suited workers out clearing away the new growth near her dome. Everything outside the domes had to be done by human labor. Any type of robots they could afford had metal components that disintegrated quickly in the wet, corrosive atmosphere of the valley. The beggars would clear, but only if they were paid in pearl.

She hurried through her back entrance into the walled-in area with its carefully placed stone shelves where she kept the leaves, just a fine mesh of tough silicone netting to keep the whole area enclosed. The leaves themselves kept their nests clean of unwanted growth.

It always pleased her to see the neat, orderly rows of nests. On one side were the worker leaves. They were tough and well-trained enough for the customers who came to her for cleaning. On the other side were the nests of those who were being trained for sale.

She was very particular about her customers. Owners who never went outside their compounds into the wild or used chemical washes too frequently could starve a mature leaf. She insisted on observing her customers' personal habits and meditative techniques and often visited their dwellings. Very rarely the orange bubble appeared that indicated reproduction time, but if it happened, she insisted that the leaf be returned to the wild as she did with her own worker leaves. Not only did leaves not reproduce successfully in captivity, they inevitably died if not released.

Carefully she encouraged the new leaf to occupy the nest she had prepared, then finally went to clean up—time to emerge from the dampness. She could feel her lungs getting clogged in spite of her breathing filter.

After the cleanup she went through the environmental seal into her dome. Her assistant, Marla, came up to her when she entered her office. "There is some sort of official out front demanding to talk to you," Marla whispered. "Got a major protective suit on. Must be from off-world. Couldn't get him to clean up." Marla looked nervous, unusual for her. Nombei had picked her for her unflappability. Was there trouble? Inevitably there was a criminal element, and she couldn't afford to be that choosy about her customers yet.

Nombei was annoyed. No telling what off-world bugs the man might have brought in. Leaf groomers were sensitive, vulnerable to strange microbes.

She watched him for a minute through her viewer as he paced nervously in her reception area, careful not to touch anything. His elaborate protective suit, with the insignia of the Consortium boldly displayed on its sleeve, had the crispness of the newly arrived in spite of the growth that had begun to cling. Nombei wasn't impressed. She spoke to him through the com asking him what he wanted. She could see his face flush even through the tinted glass of his mask. Clearly he felt insulted at not being invited inside, but she wasn't going to risk contaminating her creatures with some off-world disease.

"You can come inside if you take your suit off or go through my cleaning spray." She did not bother to explain.

He said angrily, "This is ridiculous. I must speak with you privately. Official business."

Nombei sighed. She would have to cooperate. The man could make her life difficult. But she had to get him away from her dome if he wouldn't go through her cleaning procedures. "Where do you want to meet me?"

"Come to the main Earthdome at five o'clock—earthtime. Consortium office, number thirty-seven." Then he left before she could protest.

It had been years since she had been to an Earthdome. Going inside meant submitting her skin to a chemical scrub when her whole business was designed to avoid that poisoning. She sighed. If they let her in at all. Valley settlers were barely tolerated in that elitist enclave, even if their services were required. Well, what choice did she have? They could put her in prison if she ignored such a summons.

# Chapter Three

While Nombei debated the risks of non-cooperation with the authorities and Investigator Shankar began to travel the long distance from Earth to xj-21, several shapes huddled in the warm, murky mists of early morning in the rift valley. They had the outline of humans, but, like all beggars in the valley, were entirely covered with a colorful pelt. If one were to look more closely—if one could bear to stand within touching distance of the malodorous humps—one would see that the pelt was made up of the symbiont life-forms of this damp valley.

One of the beggars, the tallest, stirred and shivered and a clawlike hand reached out to pull away the tendrils that attached it to the surrounding growth. Once freed, it poked at the others and they stirred. Slowly, they began clearing away the invading growth. After a few minutes they all moved away from a wall and began to uncover a doorway, stone stairs, a walkway, a wall and finally a window. More and more frantically they scrubbed at the glass, removing the thick purplish scum that obscured it.

Finally, at a sound from within, they expectantly hunkered down a few feet away. Only their green tinted eyes staring at the window seemed human.

After a time the window opened outward a crack and a gloved hand reached out to place several tiny capsules on the narrow, newly-cleared sill. Then the window closed abruptly. The beggars snatched at the capsules greedily, stuffing them into plant-draped mouths. Then they sank down hunkering again, quivering as the substance took hold. After a moment the window opened and the gloved hand appeared again through the narrow crack, waving them away imperiously. The window slammed shut and the shapes moved off a short distance to crouch against an uncleared mass of plants. They were still close enough to see the cleared window through the swirling morning mist.

Behind the closed window, in the cooler, dryer environment of his well-maintained public rooms, the owner, a Mr. James Huniman, yawned and peeled off the glove. He dropped it in a slot next to the decontamination showers that all customers must pass through to enter his establishment. He prided himself on providing a clean safe refuge for the motley denizens of this valley community as well as clients from the Earthdomes and the farms.

He peered out the newly-cleaned window to make sure the beggars had settled a sufficient distance from the doorway—just far enough not to intimidate his clientele but close enough to keep away other unfortunate creatures of their ilk. He could not quite bring himself to call them beggars as did the rest of the valley. That name reminded him too well of their human origin, that not long ago they might have been his own customers, that he was a supplier of that substance, pearl, that was very likely responsible for their surrender to the environment. He might even have known them by name.

Recently, the authorities had come inquiring about a few of his customers. He reluctantly had to admit that as far as he knew they had become beggars. The officials hadn't even seemed surprised. People who used up their creds paying for the pearl could not afford the cleaning necessary to be allowed inside a growth-free dome. After that there was no choice but to join the beggars. If they could continue to get pearl they didn't seem to be harmed by the growth, or even mind it much.

He reassured himself that he was the only one who really cared about these five outside; he was helping them, protecting them, making them feel useful. Pearl was what they wanted, what they would work to get. He tried not to think about what kept them alive day to day, whether they had any thoughts or pain.

He hurried his other workers in their preparation for his day's clientele. Everything had to be quality—the glittering luxury of the opalescent and velvet surfaces, the flawless mirrors, the pure and tasteful substances to be served. And especially the exotic entertainments, his specialty, those from that time of excesses—the twentieth century.

His pride was that his customers could forget the hardships of this place. He was a legitimate businessman with the cleanest, best run establishment in the valley. Customers would pay a month's cred for such an illusion, making him a rich man. That and pearl. He had invested his profits in an ample supply of pearl in the days when stockpiling hadn't seemed necessary. He wasn't worried about the rumors that there were problems at the pearl mine.

The sound of a hovi outside the newly cleared window did not intrude on his satisfied thoughts. He assumed a customer was landing at his hovidome—perhaps some farmers from the plains. His staff would take care of them.

Outside, the heat and motion of the hovi had temporarily cleared away the mist. It landed on top of the mass of growth beyond the doorway and silicone nets scooped up Huniman's pearl-dazed helpers before they could disappear into the maze of growth. They were carried away struggling and squirming, pelt-covered arms and legs sticking through the net.

Huniman was not aware of the absence of his helpers until that afternoon when his valley customers complained that they had been bothered by beggars outside. He planned to punish them for not protecting his customers from other beggars by cutting their dose.

Huniman did not really wonder about them until the next morning when the glass was not cleared and the door would not open because it was wrapped in soggy growth. He called the street crew, cursing because the cleaning would cost ten times the value of the small capsules of pearl. Then one of his employees remembered seeing the hovi and the struggling figures in the net.

When he called on the authorities, the official denied any people had been arrested the day before in his district and asked for identification of the missing. "Names, place of residence, social benefit numbers, work permit numbers?"

Huniman patiently explained that they were beggars.

She smiled. "Without identification individuals don't exist."

Huniman quoted the planetary law: "Civil statute 3a7P49—individual civil rights cannot be interfered with without evidence of a crime."

She chuckled tolerantly. "Beggars disappear all the time here. Without specific identification, how'll we know we have found the beggars you describe? You see our problem."

Finally, the official gave Huniman permission to go into the detention center to look for his helpers. He donned an environmental suit and slogged through the detention center. He almost believed that the beggars that volunteered themselves and followed him out were the same ones that had disappeared. He called the cleaning establishment and canceled his order. The next morning the entrance and the window were cleared as usual.

# Chapter Four

Nombei made her way up through the haze of incessant dampness on a steep path that zig-zagged out of the valley. When she finally emerged from the mist into clear, dry thin air, the semi-opaque surface of the massive main Earthdome loomed above her. She was not looking forward to going through the chemical bath that would be required to enter its artificial, earthbased environment and gravity simulator.

The first thing she noted as she stepped out of the chemical cleaner into the Earthdome was the distinctness of objects in the bright yellow light and the heaviness of the air. Too much oxygen made her giddy. The stiff white outfit provided by the security robots after the bath chafed her skin. What a peculiar dusty odor. She immediately started to sneeze. She put on dark glasses and took the pills they had given her.

After she had recovered from the sneezing attack, she hurried down the neat spotless lane lined with palms and flowering bushes, each plant with its own light system simulating Earth's sun, season, and latitude. Everything that grew inside this Earthdome was from Old Earth as it once was, carefully preserved in the archives and recreated here. Most of the light in the dome came from artificial sources imitating the Earth-sun cycle.

Every inch of the public space inside the Earthdome was planned for efficiency. Offices, dwellings, stores, and walkways were hidden and separated by carefully placed living dividers and gardens with decorative as well as useful plants.

She had been told to go underground where there were actual enclosed rooms to ensure privacy. It took two tries before she could control her distaste at the thought of going underground and enter the elevator. As it moved smoothly down the elevator still reminded her of the first eighteen years of her life in stink and darkness in spite of its bright light and wall paintings. She had been away from the Earth for almost as many years, but she still felt again the horror of being trapped in an unforgiving, oppressive habitation and caste system.

She went down several levels, but when the door opened, instead of dim corridors and tiny rooms, the wide hallways were well lit and sweet smelling with more plant beds and artificial breezes. She laughed at herself. With all the wealth that this Earthdome represented there was no reason why the lower levels should be any less pleasant than the surface. After all, everything under the Earthdome was artificial. No doubt there were places on Earth as pleasant for those who could afford it.

In a narrow room an official was waiting impatiently behind a wide empty desk. Though his dress was carefully casual in keeping with the Earthdome styles, his bearing was that of a middle level official not so secure in his caste privilege that he did not need to exploit his bit of power.

She didn't apologize deferentially as she knew he expected her to do in keeping with her caste on Earth, but sat down on the chair placed for her and waited.

He condescendingly offered her a drink. An expensive bottle of blue-fruit brandy sat ostentatiously on the sideboard. It was a flattering gesture intended to disarm her. She would have loved to try it, but feared its effects on her judgment so she declined.

She watched him control his annoyance. He had seen her refusal as rudeness. He poured himself a drink. "I won't waste my time with protocol and ceremony since you so clearly disdain it, but will get right to the point. The Consortium has picked you as the best candidate for a task we need done. Needless to say, I don't necessarily agree, but it is their decision and my assignment to implement that decision and ensure the success of the project. Before I can detail that job, however, I must have your pledge to keep secrecy about the matter."

Now he was watching her, his eyes slightly out of focus. What was he thinking? She almost felt sorry for him in spite of his caste privilege, having to do work that he might not agree with—other people's work, the Consortium's work. It was a blessing having one's own business. She was pleased to have that much power over her own life. She said, "I have no reason to repeat what you tell me. In any case I am aware that you have the power to delete my memory."

He nodded. "As you know, so far all attempts to remove the pelt-forming parasite from human skin once a person is completely enveloped have failed."

"I wasn't aware that any attempt had been made by our venerable science establishment to rescue the beggars."

He frowned disapprovingly. "In spite of your opinion of the Consortium, we are concerned about the welfare of even the least of the human population, here and elsewhere." He paused and tried on a brief smile. "It's because of your knowledge of one of this planet's more benign life-forms—leaves you call them—that we want you to participate in a project to clean up some of the…poor unfortunates—"

Poor unfortunates—the beggars were certainly that. But what was the real reason the Consortium wanted them cleaned up? "I don't see the value of depleting them while they're still addicted to pearl."

He smiled. "This will be an opportunity to do both—help the beggars return to human form and research the possibility of a controlled withdrawal of pearl."

Nombei put her hands in her lap and locked her fingers together. The man was lying. The Consortium had no interest in rescue missions. Pearl was the source of profit from this planet.

His voice droned on. "Of course our best possible outcome will be individuals found and saved. The purpose of our research is to isolate and eliminate those factors that will—"

She hated his pomposity and finally dared to interrupt. "I'm no scientist. I'm sure the Consortium has adequate research facilities."

He controlled his annoyance at her rudeness with another sip of brandy. "This isn't a matter of simple research. All we are requesting is help in cleaning them up safely so that they can be restored to useful citizenship. Then there will be hope for others."

In spite of her fear of the man's potential power over her life, she couldn't help saying, "I don't believe that you or the Consortium are the least interested in the recovery of beggars."

The man was almost sputtering. "You dare criticize the Consortium?"

It was always the same; the truth was unspeakable. Living in the valley she had almost forgotten about that. Nombei sighed. What was he asking of her? "Pelt is the least of their problem. Pearl—"

"The wretched condition that those misfits have brought upon themselves was not caused by pearl use. In fact, there is evidence it is pearl that keeps them alive in spite of their wretched life-style. None of our scientists have found any chemical reason that pearl should be banned." There was a threat in his narrowed eyes now. "We are aware that you are one of those that question the use of the intoxicant pearl."

How did they know that? She had never openly taken a stand or joined the group petitioning for the restriction of pearl use. She was always too vulnerable as a low caste refugee from Earth, always in danger of losing her business or even being imprisoned. She had her business and residency papers with the Consortium. She said, "It's true. I do see what pearl does to people. I understood that even when I still worked in the mine."

The man smiled, sensing he was winning. "You don't need to be a scientist; we have those. And you won't be involved with pearl. You will be helping beggars." He looked at her slyly for a moment. "And there is one who was special—a friend."

He knew about Pella. She remembered that beggar on her street whose voice reminded her of Pella. Did her anguish show on her face?

Nombei saw Pella's defiant face again—the last time Nombei saw her. They had both earned their right to leave the mine. But Pella had to go back to the refinery, to earn more creds she said. When Nombei asked if it was because of pearl, Pella had shouted that she was not an addict, that it was because she was tired of Nombei's cloying, boring dependence on her. That last moment had hurt so much that Nombei had tried to shut out any thoughts about it ever since. She had concentrated on her work, and put all her love into her leaves.

But by now, Pella could well have joined the ranks of the beggars. Pella the beautiful. Pella, her ebony skin glistening in the hot sun outside the mine the first time Nombei had seen her. Those long strong muscles and bones, long lean body, a smile like sunshine on a stormy day. Nombei had fallen instantly in love. Now she was sure that beautiful Pella was one of the rotting beggars that haunted the fringes of the settlement. It was too much to contemplate. She had to know. "Do you know where?—"

He interrupted her. "One of the reasons you came to our attention is because one of the subjects we found for our project is an old friend of yours."

"What do you mean 'found?'"

"Beggars brought into the valley detention center volunteered. Of course, we selected the healthiest, the most genetically fit. Your friend, Pella Allison, happens to be one of those." He waited a moment to study her reaction. She tried to kept her face impassive, but she was sure her feelings were written there.

He went on. "You and your…charges…will be moved immediately to a facility at the mine where an isolation facility has been set up for this project."

She wondered angrily why he bothered to act as if she had a choice. "I have to go back to my dome to get organized. I'll need to bring my own equipment—"

"You will give me a list of what you need. Your assistant will be informed that you are to be away on a mission for the Consortium—to treat people in another area of the planet. It will be described as a great honor for you. She will be left in charge. I am sure she can handle your business while you are gone, especially if we take much of your 'stock' with us."

What would they do if she refused to work for them? Destroy her leaves? Put her in prison? Kill her? All her newfound sense of independence, her pride in her achievement, had been an illusion. She was as much a prisoner here as she had been on Earth or in the mine.

# Chapter Five

Awakening from the hypnotic drug required to endure the trauma of takeoff and warp, Sonja opened her eyes. The deep nausea she felt told her it was a rough trip. She unbuckled and sat up, remembering she was the only passenger on an interplanetary cargo vessel not programmed for human transport. Unmanned cargo ships did not normally have to go through the takeoff and landing procedures required by the presence of human passengers. But in spite of the nausea and the wear and tear on her body, she was relieved not to be on a typical tourist ship with its giddy and enthusiastic or hysterical and deeply annoying passengers. She leaned back in the uncomfortable lounge chair and waited for the symptoms to pass. Once she recovered and before the ship entered the next warp, she would take advantage of her awake-time to study infocoms.

As a representative of the Galactic League she would have to take a cautious approach once she was on xj-21. The League was ultimately responsible for the welfare of whatever human population had settled on the planet, League sanctioned or not. If the pearl supply was threatened, the Consortium would leave and the settlers would be left stranded. Or if the League were to close the pearl mine because of infractions of the mandate, forcing the Consortium to move offplanet, any human settlers would have to be moved to a legitimate colony. Moving the abandoned humans or allowing them to stay and colonize a resource-poor planet without the support of a Consortium infrastructure were both prohibitively expensive. And the League would have to force the Consortium to clean up their leavings or do it themselves.

Sonja wondered what information was hidden by the code given to her at the last minute by the Eminence. But that message wouldn't decode until the Eminences were ready. Had they withheld the code because its instructions conflicted with her League assignment?

When Sonja began the last leg of her journey, Nombei had already arrived at the mine with her charges. She and the 'volunteers' were sealed off in the infirmary with a few medical robots to protect the rest of the facility from pelt growth.

She was impressed with the thoroughness of the preparations. The

Consortium techs had even brought the leaves' own nests to make the transition easier. After making sure her leaves were comfortably installed in their new moisture controlled space, she went to contemplate her charges.

The beggars were unconscious, each inside a transparent capsule. They lay in awkward poses like grotesque statues, rigid with pearl and symbiont pelts of gray-blue life. The long body and slim limbs were the only clue that the figure lying in one capsule might actually be Pella.

If Pella were finally restored to human proportions she might well be a scarred, shrunken hulk. Certainly Nombei would not be thanked for the rescue. Maybe, mercifully, Pella wouldn't remember Nombei. Tears came to her eyes. It amazed her that she couldn't stop loving this woman. If Pella lived, Nombei would take care of her—the price for wanting her alive—the price of loving. Now she knew she would do as she had been told. What was the alternative for Pella? It was said that on pearl a human could live a long time just slowly wasting away. Perhaps the rumors were true that those taking pearl never really died, just became rigid and motionless.

The first thing she needed to do was evaluate the state of their skin to see if there was enough healthy tissue left for the leaves to restore them. She opened the capsules one at a time. As they warmed, the air in the room became fetid with the gasses given off by the lush blue-gray growth.

Nombei tentatively held her hand near blue tinted lips. Yes, a faint breath. She persuaded a leaf to attach itself to each pelt. Pearl was a poison to leaves, but the living pelt coating these poor souls fortunately did not contain pearl so her leaves could safely consume it. When they all began eating she was relieved. She had asked for only the most hardy and seasoned of her collection because the only food source for them here would be these pelts. Now at least these leaves wouldn't starve.

Five beggars had enough healthy skin left so that in time she felt they could be restored. And one of those was the beggar she assumed was Pella. With the others she would have to take a very cautious approach; their symbiont coating and pearl were all that was keeping them alive. The flesh the leaves exposed had too much raw muscle, not even a protective fat layer left. She could try some artificial skin along with gradual grafting, but growing skin for them from their own tissue was a slow and expensive process. She doubted the Consortium would agree to the time and expense, but would ask. If they wouldn't agree, those she couldn't help would have to returned to the valley. For now she must concentrate on helping those she could restore. Even for them it would take weeks for the skin to begin restoring itself.

But after a few days they began to take on more human shape.

By the time Nombei felt it might be safe enough for her charges to regain consciousness, Sonja Shankar had arrived on the moonbase. The messages awaiting her from the League told her that the situation surrounding the pearl shortage had worsened in the time it had taken her to travel. The reports of pearl shortage had gotten into the general news and there had even been a few riots in some of the more populous colonies. She was instructed to give pearl theft her full attention.

Since she had been traveling on an unmanned cargo ship not fitted with windows or viewers for passengers or crew, there was no way for her to see the planet until she was on the shuttle that would take her to the surface from moonbase. The shuttle orbited the planet once on its descent. She noted that there were several Earthdomes tucked away on other parts of the planet as well as a few small and primitive settlements with agriculture, which meant permanent colonization was being attempted. Neither the new Earthdomes nor the settlements had been reported to the League.

Then below her the hills opened into a broad plain with scattered farms and their small domestic domes between outcroppings of rock. This farming community, connected by a network of rails for transportation, was clearly too prosperous not to have been initiated and supported by the Consortium—clearly a violation of their mandate. The farming plain ended abruptly at what appeared to be a sea of purple and orange clouds that must be the edge of the huge rift valley. She could see the top of the massive main Earthdome built into the side of the chasm rising above the cloud sea. Across the chasm, far in the distance, there appeared to be a shore of red tinted mountains.

When she emerge from the shuttle on the ground near the mine, the first thing she noticed was the redness of the light, like a permanent late afternoon glow at its brightest on Earth. The sky was a cloudless blue lavender, two small moons appeared faint white above opposite horizons.

She wore the environmental suit with oxygen mask she had been told was required by the planet's atmosphere. According to the Consortium the atmosphere was toxic to humans and lacked oxygen. But she could see that a few humans on the loading dock were working with the robots in the open atmosphere. They had thermal suits for the cold, but were without even a rudimentary oxygen mask.

As she climbed down from the shuttle she felt the lightness of gravity—that would make for a thin atmosphere, but apparently not too thin for human survival. The mine was in a low range of desert hills. Near it was the dome over low buildings of the pearl mine, and, in the distance, about a mile away, was the larger dome over the more complex buildings of the refinery. Several people were rushing past the mechanical loaders to meet her. She waived away the apologies offered by a flustered official. Though she might have relished the formalities of an official arrival in keeping with her new role, information gathering, not protocol, was her priority here. She refused an official apartment in an Earthdome and insisted on being housed at the mine.

The apartment they provided for her was orderly and comfortable, though it looked as if its previous occupants had just left for the afternoon. Personal effects were still present, a scarf draped over a couch, clothes still in the storage areas, but the robot servant had been reprogrammed. She would need to locate the previous occupant for questioning, along with the rest of the staff, especially those that had been removed from their jobs.

But first she made a preliminary check of the mine. She noted the scarcity of personnel and how ignorant of the mining processes the current staff seemed to be. Yet all the information she had been given before arriving indicated that limited production was still being maintained. When she asked to see the current production schedule, the official in charge looked at her, flustered. "I am not authorized—"

"Not authorized by whom? Who do you think I am?"

"You are the League's Investigator Shankar," the official said meekly.

Sonja waited.

The woman admitted, "Currently there is no raw pearl available here or at the refinery."

"So pearl is currently not being refined—or mined?" Sonja asked.

The woman nodded.

She questioned the rest of the current human staff, but they knew little. They had arrived recently at a facility staffed by reprogrammed robots where mining was at a standstill. What was left of the mine and refinery workers had been confined to their dormitories. The officials had instructions to maintain the status quo until they were given further instructions.

Nothing about this had been in any of the reports given to her. She had been told about a slowdown. Did the League and the Eminences know that production had stopped? But how could they not? There was no reason to think that her bosses at the League would withhold that information from her. Interesting.

The person in charge of the planet, a Dr. Dubois Chalmers, had the title of governor, although he was actually a Consortium employee and not elected as he would be in an official colony. She had researched him—not a lot of information. Elite but middling caste. He had had the Consortium managerial career one might expect. She had a lot of interviewing to do, but first she would talk to Chalmers.

He was not in residence at the mine, of course; only the main

Earthdome would have the kind of earth-based habitation required by his status. Like everything else at the understaffed mine, the personal hovi she took was specially designed for the planet with its slightly lower gravity and very easy to use.

Chalmers' family quarters and lab took up one whole sector of the top story of the massive main Earthdome. As she entered his domain she noted its resemblance to Earth's domes for the elite. This Earthdome as well as the newer Earthdomes she had seen circling the planet had been built for more than a few necessary Consortium employees. No doubt some of the elite pearl addicts wanted to be closer to their favorite substance. The Consortium was turning this planet into a new destination for the elite in their search for distraction, especially those who had a passion for pearl. Another lucrative project of the Consortium. This planet was not as inaccessible as she had been told.

She was finally ushered by a robot into a large, low-ceilinged room with scurrying technicians and state-of-the-art research equipment. She had no trouble identifying which person was Chalmers; he was the only one not in tech uniform.

To her relief, Sonja noted he had none of the signs of a habitual pearl user. He dressed simply in a tunic of quality fabric and looked young and lean, but it was impossible to tell the age of someone with his caste resources. Age retardation was illegal by Galactic code, but members of the elite practiced it regularly. He was a bit too pale and muscular to be considered classically handsome, and he had opted for the hairless look rather than be bothered with artificial hair restoration—something in his favor.

He ushered her into a private office, waving her to a seat farthest from the door while he stood leaning against the pristine realwood desk. He was deliberately trapping her in the chair by standing between her and the door, clearly to make her feel vulnerable. This man's drug of choice was power. She took the seat anyway; sometimes it was useful to seem vulnerable.

After looking her over in an unapologetically sexual way, he said, "I can't think why they sent you here; we shall shortly have the situation in hand. A few more tests and the problem will be solved and the supply resumed."

Sonja was puzzled. "You've found thieves, then? Recovered the missing pearl?"

He shook his head. "But there is still a good supply deeper in the mine. Our problem is getting access to it. You can learn the details from the records at the mine." He smiled, moving nearer to touch her arm. "We're always glad for visitors to our poor planet, especially representatives of the

League. You'll be a welcome addition to our dinner table. There are few enough amusing and educated people here."

His presumption astonished Sonja. She expected more respect given her position as representative of the League. "Governor Chalmers, I am not here only about the failure of an economic enterprise—the extraction of the mineral pearl, which justifies Consortium occupation of the planet. There are obviously other serious breaches of your contract with the League. Even in the short time I've been onplanet, I've noted human colonization is already taking place. You didn't even inform the League that there is a human workforce in the mine as well as the refinery."

Chalmers turned away studying a map engraved on a wall behind him. "There will be discussions about colonization once we can afford more terraforming—"

"But why haven't you informed the League that terraforming was not necessary for colonization?"

"One cannot manage a facility without some personnel. We are not responsible if some human sewage spilled out and polluted the place with squalid settlements. The planet *is* essentially not habitable as is. I wouldn't call what they do out there living."

"Nevertheless, there is organized settlement outside the Earthdomes. It's clear you haven't fulfilled your responsibilities. Have you even informed the Consortium authority that mining and refining of pearl has stopped altogether? Since I left Earth the situation in the pearl trade, especially in the colonies, has become much worse. The League cannot maintain peace in the galaxy if it is not kept informed."

"To what purpose? Knowing the seriousness of the situation would just increase the pressure and panic. There is nothing to worry about long-term. I am approaching the problem on several fronts. We are developing a method to remove the chemical vapors that interfere with deeper penetration at the mine."

"There is no mention of vapors preventing mining in the information we have. Again you haven't—"

He interrupted her with a too familiar hand on her arm. "You can understand how we didn't want to burden people with useless information when we have the solution. We will report to the authorities when our program is completed and we are again in production." He smiled reassuringly, "You will get the necessary details for your report in due time—about my solution for the pearl crisis—how limited settlement on this planet is necessary. So you see there is nothing of importance for you to do except, of course, entertain us at our table." He leaned toward her in a manner that he seemed to think was seductive, "…and elsewhere."

The man didn't seem to be worried about what she might report. She in turn smiled confidently and stepped away from him. "But what about the Consortium's profit margins? Why would you tolerate pearl being stolen. Even a small amount in the long run—"

The false geniality faded from his face to be replaced by a fleeting tic of annoyance. "As you will see when you review the records, we have investigated. It seems unlikely Pearl could have been taken offplanet. I personally think that no pearl was taken out of the caves—the thieves just moved it deeper. Reports by miners are unreliable. The chemical vapors that seep into the mine preventing us from going deeper, affected their judgement about what they saw."

"The reports by mine officials sent to the League—"

"Those officials were removed for incompetence. They could well have been responsible for the theft. That makes pearl unavailable at the moment. I'm confident that once we have cleared out the poisons we will find the stolen pearl."

"Have you been down in the mines yourself?"

He actually flushed. "That wasn't necessary."

"Your techs went down deeper themselves and found pearl still there?"

"Our technical readings from off-site indicate there is sufficient still there, but miners have not been able to go down into the lower passages without losing consciousness. That's why we have put total priority on removing the toxins in the passageways—neutralizing them. We are close to a solution that won't harm pearl. Once my plan is implemented, it may be possible to replace the human worker with a robot for the first time."

"Have you successfully sent down nonmetal robots after pearl?"

"Not yet—there seems to be some electronic interference even with them, but medical robots were able to retrieve injured miners so we believe eventually—"

"I'll have to inform the League as well as the Eminences that mining has stopped and I'll need to interview those people in charge during the theft, as well as the workers still onplanet."

There was just a flash of panic in his eyes before the confident smile returned. "Informing the Eminences of how bad it is here before you have any results of your investigation will make your job as well as mine nearly impossible. I would strongly suggest waiting a few days until you have had a chance to evaluate the situation for yourself. As for the staff, few original officials are onplanet. You will have to contact Consortium officials off-planet for that information. You will find a small crew of functional workers at the mine awaiting resumption of operations."

His voice was low and confidential, to make her think she was being recruited for some inner circle. "Meanwhile, we are making progress on both a synthesized and a recycled version of pearl. So you really don't want to waste too much time on futile pursuits." He placed a hand on her chair and leaned closer. "A handsome, intelligent young woman like you—"

She got up and pushed her way past him and stood by the door—a gesture that was meant to make him feel dismissed. "I am aware of the long and arduous and completely unsuccessful attempt at a manufactured product. Nothing I have read in my research would indicate you could come up with anything better. I'll certainly need to evaluate any recent research, especially for removing the chemicals, or whatever it is that prevents collection of pearl. That matter was not mentioned in my briefing package. I can only conclude you have not kept the League or even the Consortium up to date on your research. And I'll need to know everything you have done to locate and apprehend possible thieves."

The man's color heightened, but, to his credit, he went on smoothly while opening the door for her. "Theft is ultimately not a problem. There is no way pearl could have been taken offplanet or refined here without us knowing. The thieves' only hope of profit would be in negotiating a deal with the Consortium for returning raw pearl for refining. If you want to play the game of locating stolen pearl and catching a few inept renegades who haven't a chance of ever making a microcred off the booty—"

"Nevertheless, I intend that, along with my thorough investigation of the situation. I expect your full cooperation." She turned to leave.

He put a hand on her arm, forcing her to stop. "Go ahead—do what you must—but first things first. The bulk of the pearl is still in the caves to be collected." His manner changed from a confident superior to that of a co-conspirator. "Since you'll be in residence at the mine and nominally in charge there for the time being, you could be of help to our research."

She looked at him in as noncommittal way as she could muster. Important not to offend him too badly this early on.

Satisfied, he went on. "We have a few recruits we think will be resistant to the poisons in the mine. You will be in charge of their training. I'm sure you will keep me informed of their progress.

He was expecting her to defer her investigation in order to work for him. "I'm sure your techs can do an adequate job." She left without saying anything else.

But on the way back to the mine she was annoyed at herself for not appearing more agreeable. She needed to gain his confidence; he could make her job difficult if he chose. Once back at the mine she sent a polite message promising to keep him informed on progress of the miners.

# Chapter Six

Nombei did not wake Pella up first. She wasn't eager to face those judging eyes. Each of her charges awoke without incident, sleepy and confused but sane. They would all survive their adjustment to normal human condition. Even the scarring might not be too bad. They were confused and disoriented but that would pass in time.

Then she went into Pella's cubicle. Until this moment she had been able to keep her feelings in check. Pella had remained just another damaged human being for her to heal. Now, as she looked down at the ruined skin on the barely recognizable face of this woman that she had loved, the pain of their relationship and its end came back with an intensity that nearly made her faint. She knew that she would never be forgiven for this rescue, just as she had never been forgiven for anything else, even her own adoration of the woman.

Nombei remembered the first moment that she had seen Pella, one of the floor managers at the refinery. It was the long, tight-muscled line of her graceful body that had first caught Nombei's attention. The woman was taller than anyone else in the mine including the Consortium supervisors. Even in the simple gray uniform of the mine worker she was strikingly beautiful as well as exotic. Nombei had found it hard not to stare at that satiny brown skin and large luminescent black eyes.

Pella had laughed and been silent for a moment when Nombei had asked why she was so tall. Then she told Nombei about her childhood in a family that had tried to settle and farm in the desert. In spite of a sparse near-starvation diet and with the help of the lower gravity, she had shot up like a weed.

Nombei sighed. It had always been an unequal relationship. Though Pella had recognized Nombei's intelligence and humor, and had taken Nombei under her wing when the others had treated her badly for being a low caste earthrat, in the end Pella had done little more than tolerate Nombei's adoration.

Pella tried to open her eyes. The lashless eyelids fluttered lightly but did not fully open. There was no stinging blue-gray film across her eyeballs—no dust of spores to be brushed away. Just pure light on her unfocused eyes. She took a breath of dry sweet air and there was no fit of coughing. Another breath. Her lungs were clean but weak and she was afraid. Something terrible…something wonderful was missing. Where was she? Where was mother? Where were Juju and the baby? What was this terror of knowing? Why didn't she want to remember?

Re…membering A long way—away…feeling…what?…a toe; what was that was not there?…a leg, a hip…the toe moved but nothing else…two toes…and in between a re…membered warmth.

She squeezed her eyes shut. Still she saw…a red light through the lids. Her arms flailed up to touch her face…out of control. The dry, raspy palms of her hands scratched against her face as she covered her eyes. But even then the dark was not complete.

She lay there for a long moment, her body shuddering. What was missing? She wanted…not to remember. She unconsciously reached out for a tab of pearl to help the forgetting—to take her away—to be with them. She suddenly realized she hadn't tasted pearl for a long time and touched her arm with a dry raspy palm—and felt a moment of terror. It was also gone, the soothing fur of Friend—her comforting coat of blue-gray life.

It came—a white streak of pain through her re-membered body and a sound built past her cracked lips—from a low rumble of breath to a high pitched scream at the pain in her now naked, peltless body and the agony of knowing she was alive and once more that tiny human slug of flesh born with the name Pella.

When she heard the muffled scream of pain, Nombei sighed and turned up the sedative. She would wait a while longer before letting Pella wake up.

Pella lost consciousness, only to wake again to more memories, remembering the massive transport that had taken them away from Old Earth to their new home on this planet. Her father had loaded them into an insulated cargo box he had fitted out for them. She recalled his worried face, as he hurried them in the dark. He worked for the Consortium so he could bring them onto the transport. He had promised that once they were onplanet, they would be allowed to be colonists. Others had done it. They would be given a piece of land to grow their own food. They would build a real house, not the twenty square feet in a dark and stinking hallway in a vast, enormous labyrinth of hallways where she had been born on Earth. The thought of a real house, a place to grow plants and run in the light of a new sun, had made the weeks in the stifling stench of the cramped box without enough water and an inadequate portatoilette almost tolerable. Her father hadn't dared visit them more than to bring more oxygen and food. Had he known there was little chance of their survival as he was smiling and promising them a new and wonderful life away from the garbage pit they called home?

At the end she had wished them back on Earth, her mother weeping softly next to her in the dark. She remembered wondering why the baby had stopped crying.

When they knew they would soon land she had taken the pill her father had given them and had gone unconscious…but hadn't died. She had awakened, soaked in her own urine, the planet's bright red light in her eyes as her father dragged her out of the box.

Now Pella opened her eyes slowly. There was no one there, just a gray emptiness. Her eyes would not focus. Where was her father? Why was she angry? Yes, he had pulled them out, but the baby was barely alive. Only she and her little sister, JuJu recovered quickly.

Where was Juju? Yes, now she remembered. Her father taken them along with the crate from the cargo ship to a bit of land beyond the mine and Earthdomes—desolate desert with strange plants, craggy rocks. The cargo crate had been their first home.

At first, after she recovered from the trip, it had been wonderful. So much space. She remembered the joyfulness of being in lighter gravity, running and jumping, climbing rocks. That was when they still had enough fresh rations, before her father had to leave again on the transport and the baby got sick from the less than Earth-normal gravity with low oxygen and not enough water.

In the end it had been she who had buried the baby in the hard gravelly soil. Then the sun had been warm. How long had it taken to get used to the planet's different length of night and day?

It had taken them so long to get anything to grow from what seeds her father had gotten them. At least there had been a few plants growing wild that had escaped the Consortium's official plantation. How many buckets of water stolen from the Consortium's aqueduct had she carried to scrawny plants?

At first they didn't believe that the short winter would be so cold and dark. There had been little to burn in those early days. There was only the tiny solar-powered heater. Barely enough heat to warm their hands and keep them alive. And so little to eat in the winter that was not old discarded ship stores.

And her father had to keep working for the Consortium, he said, to protect them. He'd stay with us when he retired…when the "farm" started to produce…. She remembered his sadness then his smile, the lips curling up too far as he made promises. There would be a new atomic stove so they wouldn't have to work so hard. There would be more provisions. More colonists were coming soon. There were new crops which would grow better in the harsh soil. Each time he came back with something new for them to care for. She had loved the nannygoat that had survived through one whole winter only to succumb in the spring to the poisonous growth native to the planet.

Her little sister Juju was sick even then. Her body hadn't taken well to the place. She had been so little when they came that she never grew right. Her bones pained her often and she didn't thrive on the ship stores her father managed to get for them. Somehow Pella grew taller and stronger in spite of it all, perhaps because there was no choice. Her mother worked, but did not thrive. Then the birth killed her

The screams of her mother invaded her brain now; she could not shut them out. She had to hear her mother dying with the birth of the baby brother who was to replace the child who had died. Now there was no comfort of pearl to make the screams go away with a swirl of joy and colored light. Her father had not been there when her mother died. The baby had been early. There was no way to get him to come, no one to call to for help.

Alone in the dark, Pella buried her mother and cared for the weak screaming boy. The nannygoat was still alive then. And Juju had been strong enough to care for the little thing while Pella worked in the gardens or collected the hard cones of the planet's desert plants which were the only thing there was to burn for cooking and heat through the dark cold winter when the solar stove did not work well.

Her father did not come back after her mother died. When the few stores he had brought and the last of the tubers were gone and the nannygoat was poisoned, she lay one long night in the dark listening to the baby whimper. In the morning, terrified and desperate at what might happen to them, she tied the baby under her coat, put Juju on the sled under all the bedding she could find, and crossed the frozen desert to the main Earthdome.

After the solemn white-coated guards took them in she had never seen Juju or the baby again. She had been sent to the refinery to work, then trained as supervisor for the pearl mine. They told her Juju and the baby were adopted. They said her father hadn't returned because he had died at the asteroid transport station when a rocket misfired.

Nombei sat down next to Pella again, waiting for her to awaken. The days of rest in this sedated state had made her look more human, more herself. No longer was she so skeletal. The flesh of her cheeks had a healthier glow. She had filled out, making the lines of her face softer, and the hideous mottled scaliness was fading. She could almost imagine her Pella back again.

Pella opened her eyes. A dark shape cut out some of the light. Pella blinked and tried to focus. For so long her vision had been blurred by a greasy coating of symbiont. It was a shock when the shape sharpened into a familiar face. Her mother? Her eyes snapped closed and she shook her head to remember. Her mother had been dead for…how long? The memory would not come. She looked again cautiously. Nombei? No, she would never see Nombei again. But why did she think that? She loved Nombei, didn't she? Nombei wasn't dead. Then the shame came back. Those last taunting words she had thrown out about how Nombei wanted to own her, keep her prisoner. Words that had come from her need for pearl and her shame at that.

When the brown eyes blinked open, Nombei sat still. Pella stared at her for a moment as if puzzled, then quickly glanced around the blank gray-green walls of the room. Her gaze bounced back to Nombei's face.

As if to answer her unspoken question, Nombei's voice said, "Pella, can you hear me?"

She closed her eyes and opened them again to check—to make sure. The blurry face too wide, the streak of gray in the thick hair not right.

Nombei touched her hand gently, hoping to reassure her, to soothe her, but Pella jerked back as if the touch had burned and whispered, "Where is this? Why are you still here? I told you—" Then, as if she remembered something, she smiled nervously. "That was a long time ago." The hand Nombei had touched moved, the fingers grasping as if learning to move again. Then Pella lifted her fingers to a few inches from her eyes. She frowned at the scarred, mottled skin and let the hand drop to cover her eyes. Nombei heard a choking sound. Then Pella took a deep breath. She whispered, "I didn't want to be rescued. Why am I still alive?"

Nombei looked down at her own hands. She didn't want to admit her suspicion that Pella had been included to get Nombei to cooperate—because of her wish to see Pella again. She tried to hide the emotion in her voice. "You were cleaned up because the Consortium wants something from you." She looked directly at Pella then. "Anyway, people don't die, no matter how much pearl they take. The worst pearl does is put you into a kind of coma. Even the pelt couldn't kill you. Pearl kept the pelt from consuming you. The authorities—"

"How did you find me?"

Nombei's heart nearly stopped at those hissed words. She answered hesitatingly, "I didn't. They found you in the detention center. They said you volunteered. It was my job to get you free of the pelt. I—" She rushed on breathlessly, not wanting to give Pella a chance to speak. "I have a business now in the valley. I developed a method for removing pelt. After you…went back, I went to the valley settlement. Now I'm independent, a businesswoman." She couldn't help showing her pride in her voice. Not many from the mines or the refinery ever achieved as much.

"You think I don't know what you've been doing? Where do you think I've been all this time?"

Nombei shook her head. "Not in this valley. I looked for you."

Pella gave a pained cough of a laugh. "Where do you think I got the fur coat, then?"

"You haven't had it that long. Most of your skin is still intact," Nombei said matter-of-factly.

Pella tried to sit up. Nombei held her lean shoulders gently. "But your skin is still very fragile. Best you stay still."

Pella relaxed, her face impassive, her eyes closed. "Remind me what I 'volunteered' for."

"I'm not sure. They said it is an experimental program to help some of the…unfortunates who couldn't resist the pelt disease."

Pella laughed. "I remember now; they promised to supply us with pearl if we volunteered for a research project. We all thought we were incredibly lucky. Nothing about getting rid of our pelts, though. I'm not so sure I'm happy about that. We are working on considering ourselves a new species. Pelt pride we call it. Besides, scaring people with our nastiness is a living. We figure if we could get pregnant it would come out hairy."

Nombei wanted to laugh, too, with relief. It was the old Pella covering her pain with bitter humor.

But now Pella's voice was hard, her bitterness undisguised. "Just tell me what they really want from me."

Nombei looked away out the one window at the expanse of dry, rocky and hostile desert. "They haven't told me. There were rumors in the valley before I left that the Consortium created a pearl shortage to raise prices. It has something to do with pearl. That's where we are—at the mines."

The eyelids popped open again. The dark eyes stared at her, out of focus for a long moment, but Nombei could still hear her fear as Pella said, "What do you mean? And why would you, the anti-pearl purist, want to help them?"

Nombei could not look into those eyes any longer and turned away.

Pella spoke, her voice full of anger now. "It's me again, isn't it. They offered you me. Another chance to save me. But you know I don't want saving. I never did. Why?"

Nombei let her feeling of hopelessness turn into anger. "I don't know. I guess it was the challenge. I never tried to clean up anyone so far gone to the pelt. It certainly wasn't easy, saving you. Can't imagine why I bothered. But you're stuck; you're alive and on the mend, your pearl habit stabilized. I'm sure you can manage to mess yourself up again, though. That's the easy part."

Pella laughed—a genuine easy sound, the bitterness gone. "It really is you. But I still won't say thank you, although I suppose I should."

Nombei couldn't help but turn back at the welcome change in Pella's voice. The old Pella was really back, her mind intact, although more tests would be necessary to check for damage.

Pella was studying the scaly new skin on the back of her hand. "I'm afraid to ask. What do I look like now?"

Nombei tried to take that hand, but Pella pulled it away. Nombei said, "Like you might recover that glossy brown shine to your skin someday. You're one of the lucky ones—there won't be much scarring. But how does your head feel? Any pelt distortion of your sight now? Are the colors normal? What about—?"

"No hairy hallucinations, but I was used to that gray-green haze. Everything is too bright, not fuzzy enough, and I'm getting a splitting headache, not to mention other parts. Will it ever stop hurting?"

"I'm going to put you back to sleep now. I just needed to—"

"Check and see if I was totally brain damaged. I would say maybe there is still half left and all of that hurts."

Nombei turned up the opiate and Pella's eyes fluttered gratefully. This time she let Nombei take her hand.

Well, at least the woman still has her mind and her sanity with the pelt gone, Nombei thought gratefully.

As Nombei turned to leave the room, she saw that there was a strange man in a Consortium gray uniform in the doorway. He must have overheard their conversation, but had stayed out of their line of sight. She noted the faintly blue-purple tint to his skin.

He stepped back into the hallway, clearly waiting for her to follow. Why was he hesitant to speak to her in front of an unconscious volunteer? She followed him into her office. He closed the door and stood looking at her bookshelf. "Quite the impressive collection."

"For a mere earthrat you mean," she finished for him.

He did not bother to respond but said, still without looking at her, "You are to be commended. Most of your subjects on the mend."

She said warily, "By no means sufficiently mended to be awake for more than a few minutes without heavy opiates for the pain. The damage to skin is not much different from extensive burns, except that there will be less scarring. Those who can recover still have open sores. It will be weeks before they can begin to function normally. And the others, if they have received the treatment I recommended—"

"That's not your concern. Although I believe they've been returned to the general population of beggars as incurable. But you should be quite pleased with this success; These recruits have been restored well enough, due to your methods, to proceed with our project. Even if they are awake for only a few minutes at a time they can begin being prepared. Once they are stronger their training will be taken over by others."

"I will need to meet with those who'll be working on the pearl withdrawal part of their recovery. Then I suppose my job will be done and I can go home."

He shook his head. Why had she ever deluded herself into believing they intended such a program. She said, "At least let me see a follow up report of their withdrawal progress."

He said abruptly, "That isn't your concern. We will need other recruits cleaned up. You will remain with the current group of volunteers only until more arrive."

"You expect me to clean up more beggars?"

"Yes, and you will continue to train our staff in your method. You may be relieved of duty when we have completed analysis of your techniques."

Nombei suddenly felt helpless. "I won't abandon my leaves. You'll have to fly them back to my dome with me."

The man said nothing.

"You got us here. You can take us back."

He stared at her for a moment, obviously put off by her tone. She imagined him calculating her usefulness against his annoyance at her presumption. Then he smiled, not looking at her. "We will take all that into consideration. Leaves are easy enough to obtain."

So she had a few more days until they likely decided they didn't need her anymore. Then probably the best she could hope for was a mind delete and reprogramming. The recycler might be better. She decided not to think about that just yet.

# Chapter Seven

Sonja Shankar finished her interviews of the current mine and refinery officials quickly—As Chalmers had said it seemed a wasted effort because for the most part they were new since the crisis, transferred from other Consortium-run planets and knew little, but she wanted to be thorough. There were edited interviews of those that were replaced, of course. She would try to locate some of them in their new posts if possible.

She watched interviews of miners, especially those who had been sent deeper into the caves. She did not approve of some of the Consortium's interview methods, but she had to admit that it did help eliminate suspects.

It was strange. After the accessible pearl was missing, the miners who tried to go deeper did not complain about poisoned air or even heat—they claimed that something or someone, invaded their minds and kept them from taking pearl. Those who believed that force to be an illusion and tried to ignore it to collect pearl, lost consciousness and had to be rescued. Though they didn't die, those miners never fully recovered. As far as she could tell they were still unconscious.

She couldn't find evidence of anyone at the mine having the freedom of movement or resources to steal pearl. Certainly the mine and refinery staff that remained onplanet now were virtual prisoners, without the means to hide pearl or take it offplanet.

Not that there weren't interplanetary crooks with the means and knowledge of sophisticated technology to steal a valuable commodity even from the Consortium. Pearl was not bulky even when unrefined. But how had they gotten past the Consortium's rather formidable security system? And, more importantly, where was the missing pearl now? None had shown up on the galactic black market, at least according to her sources.

The mine and refinery were well-guarded and the only available transport belonged to the Consortium. The planet was well monitored—difficult for anyone other than someone in authority in the Consortium to have removed pearl from the planet.

Yet the disappearance of easily accessible pearl had happened remarkably quickly and without a trace. The reports said that one day it was there and the next day it was not. Some miners said they believed that the same force that overcame them when going deeper had removed or dissolved that accessible pearl. Unfortunately most of the staff and some miners had been removed from the planet under suspicion. Ironically, it was very likely they then suffered memory deletes, so that if they had taken or hidden pearl they wouldn't remember where it was. If the situation wasn't so desperate one could see it as funny. Certainly some of the Consortium's enemies would be entertained.

Governor Chalmers had seemed so confident that he would solve the problem easily. Had she missed something? She had to suspect him of course. But investigating him would present difficulties, and required a new approach. Where to go next? She needed to do more research on how pearl might have been transported out of the caves and offplanet.

As a League Investigator she needed to report on settlements onplanet as well as the pearl theft. She had found out about a group who called themselves the the Godong only after she arrived onplanet. As far as she could tell they had been kept secret from the League. As part of an early exploratory testing of the planet before pearl was discovered, and in spite of the Galactic League's restrictions on genetic alteration, a race of humans had been tailored by Consortium scientists to fit the harsh reality of the planet's low oxygen atmosphere and desert environment. The Consortium had allowed this community to exist in spite of a League ban on settlement. It was obviously useful to have a pool of workers who could tolerate this planet's harsh environment. They could do jobs an Earthdomer would have to do burdened with heavy awkward environmental equipment. The workers she had seen on arriving, working in the open, were Godong.

The Godong lifestyle was so harsh that most other humans could not survive in their settlements, however desperate they might be to escape the Consortium, though some were still trying. As well, Godong found it difficult to live in earthtype environments. There were no official records of the locations of their settlements. They were semi-migratory and known to stay well hidden. She would need some help.

She made a trip to one of the moons, which supported a transport and holocom station in order to send a preliminary report to the League. For some reason her report did not go through, but her holocom to a man who now called himself Mark Star did. Mark had been a fellow classmate at the GLIA institute who had failed the rigorous exams and been expelled. She knew that currently he was active in this galactic sector as a dealer in black market goods, but was allowed to remain at large because he was occasionally useful to the League. She had played no small part in winning him that role and would make use of that now.

While she understood that his present way of life was an adequate challenge to his intellect and skills, its risks did not appeal to her. He thought her naive in her loyalty to the League and teased her about that. But she was proud of her part in maintaining the stability and security of the galaxy's order through her work for the League.

She sat in the hologram reception cubicle waiting for his appearance, remembering the last time she had been with him in person. She smiled. Along with their professional relationship, there was the on-again off-again sex that was useful and sometimes enjoyable. Holographic sex could be amusing sometimes, although the sensory input was often inadequate, depending on the distance of transmission. But it was certainly safe, which was of concern to her because, unlike most humans, she had to maintain the viability of her ova for her institute's propagators. It was an honor that sometimes became a nuisance. Accidental pregnancy was not, ultimately, a problem of course—just an embarrassment.

Mark appeared lazily, a fuzzy, cuddly squirrel-like morph of himself coming in focus. From his demeanor he obviously assumed sex was in the offing. He certainly was just as likely as she to use sex as a manipulative tool. His lips brushed hers, catching her off guard with his sensuality even before his face came into focus.

She liked this version of him even better than reality as she remembered it. She adjusted her own image, making it cat-like. He laughed, appreciating her joke. He morphed into a more realistic form and she did the same.

"So what is it I can do for you, then, sweetheart?" he asked, adjusting a fold in a silver lamé cape.

She was grateful that the holographic transmission was as unsophisticated as it was. It would be harder for him to read her. "There have been reports of the increase in black market commodities in Sector Three. As you know the Consortium is very fussy about—"

"Let's see what commodity in this sector could possibly be of interest to you. Nashian gold? Red oriion fruit is great but there is not much profit in it." The scent of red oriion flower wafted over her nose and a look of exaggerated surprise passed over his face. "Oh yes, I know! Rumor has it the Consortium has created a shortage of pearl—to justify raising prices. That must be what this is about. But you know I avoid the nasty stuff. Why on Jupiter would I know or be interested in it or in anybody who is?"

Sonja studied his shifting image. Did she know him well enough to believe that he had nothing to do with pearl theft? As he said, he didn't respect users any more than she did. Pearl took the edge off, not something he could risk. And he wasn't likely to take on the Consortium, either. He was too good at making cred other ways. If he was involved, it was for some other reason.

She knew his curiosity would win him over. He would want to know about the pearl situation as badly as she did, if only so he could profit from it. He sold information for the best price but preferred to sell to the GLIA. He wanted badly to make them regret they had thrown him out of training. Maybe someday they would.

The problem was getting any information out of him. But she had her ways. Certainly he would want to show off how clever he was.

Silence. His image faded. Still she waited.

His form sharpened into a peculiarly unpleasant version of himself. He had given up on the sex. He would be after something else—information, certainly.

"Not a lot of free-floating pearl out there. If someone did take it, they are playing it close. Makes me think the Consortium really is looking to drive up prices," he said.

"You think I wouldn't know if that were true?"

His image morphed. He became ancient and twisted, a caricature of an Eminence and cackled. "You're not exactly the big guns in the League and you don't work for the Consortium either, not directly anyway. If the pearl trade were really in jeopardy would they send just one lonely little operative?"

She was offended. "I am an official investigator, not undercover this time. But even the League needs to keep the situation quiet. There's already trouble, even some riots."

"Are you looking to sell pearl at black market prices to keep a bit out there until the Consortium decides to go back into production? Is that what you want?"

She decided to play along. "Maybe."

He took a form closer to his own true one and looked directly into her eyes. "You're lying. If the Consortium wanted to leak pearl into the market they wouldn't have you come to me. They have a lot of less risky ways. You're after something else. Maybe pearl's really used up. Maybe they can't get any more water out of that stone. That's the word among us outs."

She said, "You sound awfully sure. I've seen all the records and there's nothing that tells me there's no more pearl in the mine."

"They're natural caves, not a mine. Excavation was never necessary. They just pick it off the walls. So what's the problem if the supply isn't used up?"

"That's what I'm trying to find out. You're telling me nobody knows about a supply of stolen pearl out there?"

He shook his head. "But I'll do some research for a price."

The statement hung in the air. She let the silence be her comment.

He laughed and morphed into a D-level market tech, tight gray formal suit and all. "I want the right to market pearl when we find the stash."

"You find stolen pearl and you can get whatever level position you want with the Consortium."

He faded again, saying, "You think I wouldn't have found the stuff already if I could? It hasn't shown up in the marketplace and you aren't the first to make an offer for its recovery. There are a few others out there that miss it." He came into focus and laughed. "Seems like there's a lot they haven't told you. But even you can imagine the Consortium trying to raise prices."

Sonja was annoyed. There was no way to tell if he was making it up as he went along. He knew it wouldn't be in Consortium records if offers to the galactic underworld had been made. So she couldn't check up on what he said. It was worrying. There had been a shortage of pearl long enough for anyone to get whatever price they demanded—so why hadn't the missing pearl already appeared on the black market if it wasn't a Consortium plot? Unless the thieves hadn't been able to move it offplanet. So where was it? The Consortium could easily hide it; they controlled the planet. Was her investigation just a coverup, as he suggested? It didn't make sense.

He morphed again into a question mark. He didn't like not knowing things, not having answers.

She said, "Say, theoretically, that there are thieves and they can get into the caves and have the technology to take out all the accessible pearl. Where is it?"

He looked uncomfortable for a moment, not confident and inscrutable. He didn't know where it was.

While he was a little off-balance she said, "You can help me with one thing. There are settlements on this planet I need to check out—the Godong in particular."

"So go. They're no secret to the Consortium."

"Are you surprised I don't trust the info they give me? And why would the Godong be cooperative to an agent of the League. Sources say you have connections. What will it take to get close—what should I offer them to get their cooperation?"

He brushed her lips again. Bored with the conversation.

"What buys me some information from them?"

"Why should I help you? They're harmless. You'll just report them to the League because they're genetically modified and illegal settlers. You going to get them neutralized?"

"They'll be in my report. The League will eventually decide the fate of everyone on the planet. Right now I just need talk to them—find out if they know anything, if they could be hiding stolen pearl. And you owe me."

He laughed. "You mean that last little favor, getting me jobs with the League? I don't know how you did that. I guess I could be recycled algae by now…or astrodust. So…anything your heart desires, sweet orris blossom."

Sonja landed her hovi at the bottom of a valley in the foothills of the range of mountains far to the north of the rift valley and the pearl operation. From above, the place looked as desolate and uninhabitable as the rest of the planet, but as she got closer to the bottom of the valley she spotted the remnants of an agridome and aquatower that Mark had mentioned and then the gray wispy forms of what passed for organic life. The records described the place as one of the earliest settlements, ostensibly long abandoned as a failure. The location had originally been picked because the mountains held a dusting of ice and snow on their tops, an occasional source of water, and there were reputed to be underground lakes which were unfortunately high in mineral content. There had been a desalinization plant which had turned the lakes into caustic mud holes. Then the Consortium had opened the pearl mine and further colonization was ostensibly forbidden.

She climbed out of the hovi near the tower and began unloading the heavy containers of refined water and flour that Mark had suggested.

She was unloading the bucket of amaranth seed when a wispy shadow moved into her peripheral vision. She took out the last of the provisions and passed her hand across the dash of the hovi to lock it so that no else could fly it. Then she stepped away from it and stood in the shadow of a rock, waiting.

Whatever Godong were here were the descendants of the earliest settlers—those few that had survived. She had tried to access records in the science institute about the Godong. Information was hard to get because of the original adjustments to their genetic profile. Genetic alteration of humans had long ago been made illegal.

Yet there had always been rumors of continuing experiments in genetic alteration of humans. It had been whispered that she herself, along with the others in the guild of undercover operatives for the League, were from genetically altered embryos. But it was not something she had thought much about. Certainly she knew of private "alterations" that members of the elite had benefited from.

But there was a certain logic in the idea, an argument that could be made for speeding up the evolutionary process—so a human population could survive on a new planet.

Humans had evolved originally to fit the conditions on Earth—a fact that had made planet colonization difficult at best. Even with one factor, the variations of gravity, there had always been major problems for colonization. Early nonearth colonies—on spaceships, docking stations, asteroid colonies—were small enough to allow for the creation of earthlike conditions such as artificial gravity. But even when planets were picked to resemble Earth as closely as possible, there often were fatal differences—a planet might never be colonized permanently unless humans evolved to fit it.

She didn't really know what to expect of the Godong; there was so little information about them. They were drought and cold tolerant of course. Small size would be necessary since lower gravity caused normal humans who grew up here to be taller and thinner with less muscle structure than in Earth gravity. But without adequate calories, large size was not an asset. Even a non-Earthdome settler here had access to gravity equipment to help maintain their muscle and bone structure, if they chose to and could afford it. The suggested regimen for maintaining muscle tone was a day in Earth gravity for every week onplanet.

A tiny, big-eyed creature wrapped in a thin gray cloak appeared from behind a rock and stood at a distance watching her. Was this Godong an adult or a child? There was no facial hair on its translucent red-brown skin so she assumed it was female. It held out a spindly hand and beckoned to her. She controlled her distaste at its grubbiness and followed it, adjusting her stunner, secured under her jacket. After a few minutes it pulled back a cloth and entered a hole in what appeared to be one of the local rocks. She followed it in and realized it was not a rock at all but a well disguised mud and fiber shelter that admitted ambient light only through its translucent door covering. It was only slightly warmer inside.

When her eyes adjusted to the gloom she saw that there were maybe twenty people inside, all shorter than Sonja was, with sticklike arms and legs like the child. What first appeared to be animal-skin clothing under their cloaks was body hair almost furlike in its thickness. Only their faces were clear of fur—their translucent cheeks darker than those of what she now realized was a child. Some of them had slight goatees, the only evidence of a different sex.

There was an ancient heater in the middle of the shelter with a pot of a steaming, evil-smelling substance. She recognized the stove; she had seen one before but only in a museum collection. It was one of the early survival stoves, a rechargeable solar heater. The smell was making her feel lightheaded so she adjusted her nose filter.

These people didn't seem to need auxiliary oxygen. Was it one of their genetic alterations from the beginning or a survival adaptation?

Most were chanting over an old woman wrapped in ragged blankets lying near the heater. She was breathing heavily, clearly in distress. Sonja judged her to be an ordinary human—surprising in these circumstance. Again Sonja controlled her distaste, stepped forward and offered her auxiliary oxygen mask.

The old woman waved it away, clearly annoyed, as if Sonja should understand that it wouldn't help. She said, "So what is it you want? You're not from our science board persecutors since you brought us illegal resources instead of the usual useless baubles. I see none of the equipment they use to prod and poke us."

At the woman's words the child clutched at a string of glass beads around her neck as if afraid the old woman would tear them off. The old woman might well be on the top of the pecking order here in spite of her frailness.

Sonja squatted down near her and said, "I'm Sonja Shankar, an Investigator for the Galactic League."

"I'm called Mammon here, though in your records you will find me as Mary Maloney, tech third class. The child is called Babe." The woman coughed and sat up. "So has the League finally decided to do something about the Godong menace, as the Consortium people often threaten they will? Are they to be thrown in the recycler or subjected to genetic cleanup and a mindscrub?"

Sonja shook her head. "My job is just evaluation and information collection. You're not Godong."

"The record will probably say I died escaping the mine. That was years ago. These kind people took me in. Babe is my granddaughter."

"The immediate crisis is that there has been some theft of Consortium property, pearl. I, we, are hoping you can help us locate the thieves."

Mammon waved an impatient hand at the chanters. "Does this look like a group of people capable of stealing from the Consortium? Anyway, we have no interest in the trash that the Consortium dumps on our planet. Only Gawaya herself knows the extent of what humans and their Consortium of evil do to cause her rages. Look to those who sent you here for that kind of information."

"Gawaya?" Sonja asked, remembering that these people believed in spirits, although the way Mammon said the name didn't match the information Sonja had. "Your spirit, your rock goddess?"

The Godong present began to sway and bob, mumbling louder.

The old woman coughed again, then said, "You haven't done your homework or you would know better than to speak her name. We believe off-worlders and the trash you bring here are the reason that her anger grows by the day now."

One of the Godong said in a whisper too near her ear, "Gawaya is rumbling. I heard it myself. She is getting very angry. The stagalake is drying and getting hotter. Tell the Consortium to leave the planet before it's too late."

Stagalake? She hadn't seen any surface water; it must be an underground water source. So that was how they survived. Sonja said, impatiently. "There's ongoing volcanic action on this planet; it's not a spirit or some kind of supernatural—"

Babe interrupted proudly. "She is too real. She saved my life in the caves. I saw her, fluttering and flying to me. I was going to drown in the stagalake. Once you start sinking no one can save you. It is too thick; it eats your skin. I was already burned. Gawaya pushed me out. That's why I am allowed to be here with the grownups. I was saved by Gawaya so I am sacred." Babe held out a leg free of fur and deeply scarred.

"I'm sorry you were hurt, but don't think a spirit of some sort had anything to do with—" The chanting drowned out her next words, and even Babe had begun to chant and nod.

Sonja looked at her wrist chronometer. She had no time for this. She leaned nearer the old woman. "You're from offworld—a tech. You must understand that the force you call Gawaya is a natural phenomenon. Volcanic action—"

The old woman shook her head and said, "I thought that way before. Now I know better. I wish Gawaya could drive out the Consortium and its corruption and trash. If we believed it would help force them out we would try to steal their junk. But look at us. Do we look like people with the technology to steal and market pearl?"

"You could be helping the thieves, hiding them. Your people know their way around the desert."

"That would just guarantee our extinction."

"I can always bring in some security people and robots to search if you don't want to cooperate."

"You think they haven't been here several times already looking for your missing pearl?"

"There was no record of such a search."

"We don't officially exist here so why would they need to keep records? Keeping records would expose us as an illegal settlement of mutants, an experiment believed to have ended fifty years ago. We exist because they want to continue to study how we survive and to use us a workers."

"But you know about pearl disappearing from the mine?"

"What else do they care about enough to send the security force to search our huts and then bring in someone like you?"

"What do you and these people know? I can promise you much more of the type of supplies I brought, illegal or not, if I get help with this."

"The one who sent you here knows as much as we do."

Mark again. What was his game? Maybe this was just a way to take the heat off himself. Still this woman knew something. "So Mark brings you pearl and you hide it for him. Or do you collect it and he takes it offplanet for you?"

The old woman laughed, a sound that turned into a fit of coughing. Again Sonja offered her auxiliary oxygen mask almost without thinking. This time the woman accepted, but instead of putting it over her own nose she reached down and picked up a grimy green bottle and fed the oxygen into the corroded valve at the top. She took a tube that protruded from its side into her mouth and the coughing subsided. Then she said, "And where are all the luxury goods we purchase with our wealth? Why haven't I got a doctor to cure me of this disease? Why put up with this?" She waved a feeble arm around the room.

Sonja said, "Help me and I'll see what I can do for you."

Mammon shook her head and chuckled. Then she had another fit of coughing. "Being an ordinary human has its disadvantages here."

"You can go back with me. I'll get you treatment. You could have a lot of good years ahead."

"And betray my family here? I'll die here when I'm ready, thank you. Anyway, if I recovered they would just send me to an asteroid mine. There's no place for me among ordinary humans."

While Mammon suffered another fit of coughing one of the Godong watchers said dismissively, "You'll have to consult Gawaya. Pearl is hers."

Then Mammon took a breath of oxygen and said, "In the beginning when the Consortium first came some of Gawaya's children were experimented on. Too many were poisoned."

Another Godong said, "Gawaya punished them for working for the Consortium. Gawaya has forgiven the rest of us. We will pray that her rage does not destroy you before you learn about her ways."

Sonja persisted, asking, "What is it that we must know?"

The old woman took another gulp of the oxygen. "You'll call what I tell you the superstition of wild people as the scientists do. They study our beliefs as if they're green and red spots on a desert plant."

"Tell me anyway."

"Go to our shrine. Babe can show you. You will either know or you won't." The old woman turned over, her back to Sonja, and closed her eyes.

Sonja took off her chronometer and held it up in front of Babe. "Take me to Gawaya's shrine and you can have it."

Babe lead her outside and started down a well-worn path and Sonja followed. When Babe went down into a crevice in the ground, Sonja hesitated for a moment. Was it a trap? But what had they to gain by harming her? Her disappearance would just bring the security force. She followed into the dark, switching on a small lamp from her pack. Babe was scampering down a steep slope inside the cave as if she knew every rock. Maybe she did.

At the bottom the cave opened up to a cavern that showed yellow in her light and smelled of sulfur and heat. Where there once had been water there was a shallow hollow that extended the length of the cave. At the deepest part there was still some steaming mud bubbling from underneath. Next to that was a rock pile with heaps of what must be offerings. Babe led her past the rock pile into a deeper chamber that was so hot she eventually had to loosen her jacket and wipe her face. A group of adults was there mumbling supplications to Gawaya. Babe reached over and switched off Sonja's flashlight. After a minute she could see by the glow from the hot mud. She went closer and the group reluctantly parted to let her through. In a crevice of the rock was a single opalescent globe, but instead of the cool opalescent purple she would have expected, it was a glowing and pulsing red. Was there a supply of pearl in these caves? There hadn't been anything in the reports about the existence of pearl here, purple or red.

As if answering her thoughts, Babe, who had come up close beside her, whispered, "The color is how we know she is so angry."

"Has this pearl always been here?"

"Not always here. It moves around, but it's always been in this cave—from before I was born. But after the Consortium was on-planet awhile, Mammon says was when it started to get angry red. It's even gotten redder since I can remember; even after I was rescued by Gawaya."

"How old are you now?"

"Seventeen Gawaya years."

"You call the planet Gawaya?"

Babe nodded. "She is Gawaya, too."

"Do the scientists who come here know about this… red pearl?"

"They say it is interesting but not useful. They say it contains no extractable drug. They looked and looked with their instruments, everywhere, but didn't find any. Mammon says they're too stupid to be able to find their own backsides." She smiled with a spiteful satisfaction. "We think you are stupid, too."

"Why do you say that?"

"Too stupid to listen to Gawaya."

Sonja sighed. "What is Gawaya telling me?"

Babe said in a rather pompous voice, "Mammon says if a person is too stupid to hear it for themselves then they're not ready to hear the truth and it's dangerous for them to know." The people around them nodded in agreement. Typical mystical obfuscation, she thought. Make people believe that if they just try hard enough they will be as enlightened as their leaders. And if they don't understand it is because of their defects. Another way to have power. She moved toward pearl, to pick it up and look at it more closely.

There was a gasp and the people moved quickly to grab her and drag her back. She pulled out her stunner, aiming it at them. They let go and disappeared into the dark, Babe with them. Her shouts after them echoed through the cave.

Sonja turned to find the red pearl gone. It must have been knocked by their struggle onto the floor of the cave and rolled away, maybe into the mud. She turned up her light and looked for it but did not find it. She went in the direction the others had run, but found no one. She called out to Babe to come back and lead her out, but babe did not answer or come back. She only heard the reverberating echoes of her own voice.

She climbed back up where she thought the passage should be, trying to find the route they had come down, then tried calling Babe again. But she heard no response, nothing but a faint rumbling along with the echo. She looked carefully and found a place where the rock seemed worn into a path. She was just feeling confident that she would actually find her way out when she heard more rumbling. Had the ground under her moved or was it just her imagination? Then she saw the moving shadow. She ducked behind a large boulder and flattened herself against the cold rock as a stone rolled and bounced down the passage and crashed at the bottom. Had the chanters tried to kill her? She waited, fearing more rocks. Finally, when there was no more sound, she moved away from the rock. She heard a hissing and leaped back into her sanctuary, crouching down, but no stones came down. Then she heard a light footstep from above and drew her stunner. It was only Babe who stuck her face around the rock. Sonja lowered the gun and said, "Was it you that rolled the stone at me?"

Babe shook her head with a puzzled look. "Why would anyone do that? You're not good to eat." She giggled at her own joke, a breathy sound, then sighed. "You are such a dummy. You're not even on the right trail. I had to come back for you. This trail isn't used because of rocks falling. All that shouting must have loosened one. Come on; we have to go back down. Try not to make noise. Gawaya doesn't like it; she will throw more rocks at us."

Sonja returned gratefully to her hovi. These pitiful beings were not likely to have been involved in any sophisticated pearl-stealing plot. They had neither the technical means nor the will. Mark had been having one of his little jokes, an annoying waste of time. She would have a talk with Chalmers about rehabilitating the Godong. Certainly their situation would have to be reported to the League. Theirs was no proper existence for sentient human beings no matter how peculiar their genetic coding. That child needed food, access to medicine, and schooling. She would be perfectly capable of a tech job with a little education. And Sonja would have to follow up on the Godong who were already working for the Consortium.

On her way back to the mine, Sonja landed her hovi in the shadow of an overhanging rock. She had seen enough of the planet to realize that it was marginally habitable. With effort, help and a lot of technology this planet could become a full-fledged, mandated colony even without the pearl industry. That being the case, there might be some on the planet who would want to see the pearl trade fail. The Godong she had just visited, some of the more recently settled squatters in the valley, and in other tiny pockets around the planet, and perhaps even the farming community, might want to sabotage the pearl industry because they wanted get rid of the Consortium and force the League to allow an official colony. Just what the Consortium wanted to avoid if it was to maintain its control of the planet. But she was not convinced that any of the squatters had the means to steal or destroy pearl without making it obvious how it had been done.

The desert Godong she had just visited had no modern technology— not even wheeled vehicles. Even if they could get to the mine, a daunting prospect, how would they go about removing pearl? Were there other points of access to the mine caves? But she had studied the records. All the subterranean passages leading away from the mines shown on the Consortium maps were deep, with temperatures beyond the tolerances of organic life.

Efforts had been made over the years to find pearl elsewhere on the planet but none had ever been located. So the anomalous red pearl-like object in the Godong cave was intriguing. She had not seen any record of anything like it in the Consortium files. She would try to get access to the records of the scientists that kept track of the Godong and see what they had to say about it. She would also have to check on the few Godong that worked for the Consortium. It might be easier to talk to them.

The mine records indicated that there had been plenty of pearl in the upper caves before the recent crisis—a lot of pearl to have moved in a short time. Who beyond the Consortium had the resources to do that? Someone trusted? Consortium staff? Was that why most of them were offplanet and replaced? One of the people left from the original staff was Chalmers himself. Investigating him would take some discretion.

Going deeper for more pearl made sense. That looked like the only hope for the Consortium to have even a minimal supply of pearl soon.

In any case, after she sent her report the League would have to decide if the Consortium could keep its control of the planet, in light of its habitability and the existing settlements. With clear violations of their contract the Consortium might not be able to continue mining pearl, especially if official colonial status was declared. It wouldn't be the first time the League had to supervise the shutdown of a Consortium franchise.

# Chapter Eight

While Sonja was finding her way back to the mine, Dr. Omar Harold stood on the edge of a cliff of rugged volcanic stone overhanging the moisture of the rift valley. Below and around him were the comforting wispy clouds that hung there perpetually.

Pulling down his eye shade against the intense glare of the sun, he turned his gaze to the vast range of mountains that stretched to the north beyond the dry plain with its scattered farms of modified earth crops. He loved this planet with all its life-threatening challenges because of this open, uncluttered space. It was so unlike the hostile, human-poisoned forests and deserts of Earth. Standing in this vast quietness was the reward of his day, a healing moment to prepare him for the return to the damp claustrophobic darkness of the cave where his research took place.

He sighed and climbed down the network of ladders to one of the honeycomb of volcanic vents underlying the plain. After a few more hours of this shift he would be able to return to the Earthdome for a satisfying meal and workout to ease his cramped muscles.

In his research module back in the cave, he removed his environmental suit, trying not to be irritated again by the human insensitivity that was the cause of his vigil. This research should have been done long ago before the exploitation of the planet.

It was an old story. Once again expediency had caused the powers-that-be to overlook the vulnerabilities of indigenous life-forms. Now, too late, the Consortium deigned to study the life-form that the farmers called workgrubs—the largest life-form on the planet. The slow and bulky creatures moved with a wide lumbering gait on two toeless feet. Because of the lower gravity they did not need an internal skeleton and their uprightness depended on semi-rigid exoskeletons. They grew to three to four feet high and almost as wide. They had three to five arms attached to a wide squat torso—the number of arms and tentacle fingers was a random genetic variable. Their thick luminescent articulated white exoskeletons deflected the sun's deadly rays. A small bald head on a narrow neck had slits from which they could extrude eye, scent and mouth stalks. They took in oxygen and other gases through skin pores.

Perfect workers for the fields, they functioned well in the oxygen-poor atmosphere and could even carry a human, though they could be steered only by physically turning an eye stalk in the direction one wanted to go. They needed little moisture on a planet where every bit of the precious water pumped up from deep wells was needed.

Omar again reviewed their history, searching for the clue that would lead him in the right direction. In the early days after farms had been established to supply the Earthdome, the creatures had appeared in the fields of genetically engineered crops. Fortunately, farmers noticed that earthcrops were poisonous to the grubs and that they ate only the local plants that thrived because of irrigation. A perfect symbiosis.

At first the population of workgrubs had seemed to be an endless resource lured by the easy source of food, so that those that retreated to the caves were not missed. It was all very convenient. The grubs ate voluminously for their short lives, worked without causing any problems and then crawled into these caves perhaps to breed and then to die.

But the population of workgrubs was getting smaller every year and the numbers of young grubs that wandered into the farms were fewer and fewer. When the farmers complained, the Consortium finally hired him, Omar thought too late.

One of the intriguing things was the speed of their disintegration when that could be observed. He had not been able to recover more than a few shriveled husks. And the minerals of the husks were not those normally associated with carbon-based life. But the farmers were only interested in how grubs reproduced and what it was that was preventing that from happening.

It was almost impossible to study them live. They combusted in a cloud of vile gases and quickly evaporating liquids if their normal health was interfered with in any direct way. There were theories about their structure, tying their volatility to the dryness and low gravity, but no one had figured out how to do the necessary research without destroying them…yet.

He had found egglike structures in the cool moist caves where he was working, but he also had to study those from a distance because they disintegrated quickly if handled. Omar thought privately that there was a certain justice; now the farmers would have to purchase expensive robots.

It wouldn't be the first time that humans had destroyed a species. If the Consortium had investigated when they first arrived—but economic developers were not known for their sensitivity to local flora and fauna. He really couldn't fault the farmers—they had to survive in harsh conditions.

The farmers blamed what they called vampires for the disappearance of the grubs. A phenomenon, perceived by farmers as flying creatures, appeared at irregular intervals from crevices in the rocks near the fields. Omar collected a few quick pictures of pink luminescent bat-like shapes in the volcanic gases deeper in the cave where he worked. As far as he could tell it was an illusion created by electromagnetism associated with the heat and gases from deep beneath the caves. As far as he was concerned the situation was a natural flux in the population or caused by the change in the grubs habitat caused by farming Earthcrops.

Before him now in the module was a portable life-monitoring system including a visual interpretation of a creature's life processes. Next to that image would be printed any tentative translation of any possible thought process into a version of human language. He grimaced. His bosses at Galactic Science would consider this a waste of exceedingly expensive equipment. He already knew these creatures had the intelligence of an Earth ant or bee. Still, that didn't mean they should go extinct.

A buzzer sounded, startling him out of his reverie. It wasn't the end of his shift. What could they want? He activated the receiver. It was his supervisor, a non-scientist bureaucrat he hardly ever had occasion to speak to. Scientists were pretty much left alone to do their work. What could the man want? He waited while the secretary went through the mandatory protocol of the bureaucratic hierarchy. Was that whistling sound in the background a privacy jam? He sat up straight, his interest piqued.

"If you turn on your unit's external view-screen you will see there is a vehicle waiting for you."

"But I am in the middle of—"

The man had already cut off his com. Omar quickly cleared his viewscreen. Sure enough, there was an official hovi a few feet away from the cave entrance. He zipped into his environmental suit. It was annoying at moments like this that the atmosphere on this planet was so inhospitable, the mix of gases and dearth of oxygen hard to tolerate. He set his observation equipment on auto record; Omar was too good a scientist to take a chance on losing data.

Of the three people inside the waiting vehicle, he recognized only the supervisor. The others were in the plain white suits worn by Consortium officials. Omar took off his helmet and stood waiting, aware that they were studying him.

They questioned him at length about his research and the supervisor said, "You appear to be the scientist most appropriate for our task. We do not have time to send for others. We will require complete discretion, however. You will agree to a memory delete."

Omar took a deep breath. "Why should I?"

There was a rustle of indrawn breath at his impertinence, but the woman smiled. "I am sorry, but in reality you have no choice. We need your help for a few days. If you agree to cooperate we will guarantee that the deletion will be minimal. It will be done by the best technicians so as not to interfere with your competence as a scientist. And, of course, we offer other rewards. Your own research grant, for example—a generous stipend for the rest of your life—"

"And I won't remember why I got it."

"There will be no confusion. You will believe you won it and so will your colleagues."

"And if I agree to do what you ask for no reward but to leave my memory alone?"

The woman turned to the others. No words were spoken but in a few seconds she turned back. Did they communicate directly without sound? He had heard there was some sort of implant the elite used to communicate—something called intiception.

Finally she said, "We have agreed that your cooperation is paramount. Go back, finish your shift, pack up your research equipment and leave it outside the cave. When you return to your station you will find that you have received vacation time. A vehicle, an ordinary hovi, will arrive. You will leave with your bags packed as if going for a fortnight holiday."

The woman nodded in dismissal as if Omar's existence was forgotten. In a daze of anxious speculation, Omar put his helmet back on. His biggest worry was that they had agreed too easily. Did that mean he was doomed to a memory deletion anyway? As if the supervisor heard his thoughts, she turned back. "We don't make false bargains. We know that if you don't trust us you won't work well. We will keep our side of the bargain...if you succeed."

# Chapter Nine

As Chalmers had requested, Sonja went to meet the two new techs—a scientific expert on detecting sentient presence, and a lay expert on the indigenous life-forms used for preparing the mining recruits—that she was to supervise. She stood in the doorway for the brief moment it took to evaluate them before introducing herself. The man reading some sort of high tech microcom would be the scientist, clearly one of the tiresome breed of people wholly without awareness of the nuances of behavior that made life interesting and worth living. Still, scientists were an essential part of any investigative team.

But Sonja thought there must be some mistake. The other person, a small woman with pale pink skin, roughened in places as if someone had gone over it with sandpaper, was dressed in a sacklike coverall and slippers. She had gotten up and was approaching, smiling and staring impolitely as if Sonja herself were some sort of zoo animal—typical low-caste earthrat behavior. Sonja momentarily felt contaminated by her very presence; there was protocol even on such a remote planet. What was going on here? How could the Consortium be employing an earthrat in such a highly sensitive position? For a split second Sonja wondered if this was some sort of cruel joke—some sort of insult by her enemies? The Eminence had addressed her as daughter; she couldn't believe she was expected to work with an escaped sewer earthrat. No wonder there had been so little information about her.

The creature stopped a few feet from Sonja and spoke. "Nombei, Nombei O'Brien. I'm a resident of the valley colony." The remains of a clipped earthwarren dialect bruised Sonja's ears.

Sonja froze for a moment. This woman had the naive openness of a mental patient; didn't she know? She took a deep breath. Part of her job here was to investigate illegal colonization. "You know, of course, that the League has not cleared this planet for colonization."

"Well perhaps your final report will include a recommendation to bring this planet officially into the League. If you included the farmers and the squatter groups in the desert there are enough people here."

"No one has made an official requests of that sort."

"We've tried. The Consortium refuses to allow us to send a request for a hearing to the League. But now you're here. You'll see that there are many of us surviving outside the Earthdomes. Or will the League go to the expense of moving us offplanet if we are declared illegal? Cheaper to call us a colony."

Sonja didn't bother to hide the irritation in her voice at the woman's rude presumption. "That's not what should be concerning you now."

Nombei still held out her hand.

Sonja contained her irritation. She had not overreacted in the presence of the Godong; she wouldn't let the presumption of a mere earthrat get her off balance. No matter what the circumstance one did not lose composure. She had worked before with people she knew to be warren caste, people like Lydia—often very intelligent people. But the ones she knew had worked hard to fit in—to disappear into a higher caste. Without surgical alterations of her squat pear-shaped body, blue eyes and rough pale skin, this O'Brien was identifiable anywhere. Sonja found herself inadvertently wondering what it would take to make this woman presentable. She was clearly still young, with potentially good skin if darkened. A cut here and there. The eyes were good—natural sea-blue was really quite rare.

She took a deep breath and took the hand, smiling with regulation politeness. There was no threat in that face rather like a piece of raw fish. She patted the proffered hand, gave it a little squeeze and saw the slight flush of pleasure in the woman's face. Whatever she was, Sonja had a convert, one that would do as she was told—someone who could be safely ignored. The investigation of the illegal settlements was part of her job. This woman might actually be of some help there.

But the woman's open and vulnerable expression made her uncomfortable…so easily exploited. It made her too aware of her own love of power. She tried to keep her voice neutral as she said, "Of course, as a representative of the League, I'll consider the readiness of the planet for official settlement status once the current crisis is over."

That left only the scientist to deal with. Scientists were predictable, although they could be opinionated and stubborn. This was one of that breed of ageless men who are in love with their creepy-crawlies. Sonja had a flash of him making love to a marsloth that almost made her laugh.

Best to start on the right foot. She moved away from Nombei. The seated man continued studying his records and did not look up until Sonja spoke, introducing herself, not quite able to disguise her irritation at his obvious rudeness. The awkward, too soft man looked up from his reading with an expectant but disinterested expression that showed his indifference to people and to the sort of social details that Sonja knew to be an essential source of information about any situation. The man squinted at her briefly, saying, "Omar Harold."

Sonja walked to a desk, mentally reviewing the information supplied for her about these two. Annoying how they always left out the most pertinent information. Earthborn did not begin to describe the earthrat's origins. Sonja was used to science staff who were educated elite from Earth or from colonies. One could always be surprised. She reviewed why these two were considered the best people for their jobs.

When she turned back to them she was smiling. She perched on the edge of a desk leaving a good view of her shapely legs particularly for Nombei; she always blossomed under her kind of adoration. It was a trait she had to control in herself.

"You probably both noted when you flew in that the refinery and the mine are at a standstill. We have an emergency situation here of galactic proportions. Whatever information we gather will be fed to the best minds all over the galaxy for a solution."

Nombei said quietly, "I know nothing about that. My job is to clean up pearl addicts. Having no more pearl available would be the best thing that could happen to them, once I've cleaned them up. The Consortium can always find some other ways to get richer."

Sonja carefully did not react. It was best to address the concern. "The ethics of pearl use are not at issue here, although the League has declared pearl a harmless recreational drug. You should be concerned that the Consortium not be forced to abandon the planet so that settlement survive long enough to warrant colony status."

Nombei said, "I still don't see how I can be of any use."

"Some pearl users, those that have developed symbiosis with the plant life in this region seem to be immune to the mineral poisons that prevent the mining operation from going deeper. I am told you've depelted some of these people, very successfully."

"I wasn't informed that the Consortium intended to use my patients as miners. I made no poison tests. I have no idea what sort of chemical poisons—"

Omar tapped a finger on his jeweled vidplayer. "As the Investigator said, that research has been done. Although I do agree it is premature to expose miners to volcanic gases and poisons again without further tests."

Sonja let her impatience show. "The situation is urgent; Consortium reserves of the refined product are not sufficient to supply legitimate customers. High quality pearl is still available deeper in the cave. All mechanical devices…disintegrate—"

Nombei interrupted with a question. "How many miners have been killed by these poisons?"

"None have died."

Omar asked, "If pearl is so profitable, why hasn't someone synthesized it? If it is really an inorganic substance, that shouldn't be hard."

Sonja smiled winningly at Omar, glad for a change of subject. "Whatever its chemistry, it is too subtle. The Consortium's scientific team is hard at work, trying to sort that out. Meanwhile, we need to get to pearl found deeper in the caves."

Nombei asked, defensively, "And are beggars really more likely to be able to get at it, or are they just more expendable?"

Sonja decided not to encourage the creature further and ignored the question, turning to Omar to ask about his research.

Nombei moved closer and before Sonja could speak. "If the beggars can get pearl, why bother to have me clean them up? They're far tougher and more resistant covered with pelt."

Not controlling her impulse to sound condescending, Sonja said, "That should be obvious even to you. Raw pearl would be contaminated by the beggar's pelt. You should be proud to be part of such an effort. I'm told no one else could have done such an exquisite restoration. I understand they'll soon be ready."

"You make it sound as if these people are some sort of antiquated household furnishings I'm restoring. They're not ready for anything. Their skin is not in a healthy state; there's not a whole skin among them. And there's too much pain for them to be conscious for more than a few minutes."

Sonja was surprised at the creature's barely suppressed anger. This Nombei was like a hoschalk defending its young. Sonja did not interrupt her outburst. Let her vent her anger; she would cooperate the sooner.

Nombei went on more quietly. "There's no evidence that their minds are recovering—not to mention their general health. If I'm to prevent extensive scarring—"

Omar interrupted Nombei dismissively, and impatiently directed a question to Sonja. "The physical welfare of beggars is not something I have expertise in. What could you possibly want from me?"

Sonja's eyes went out of focus as she controlled her own annoyance. Quite a pair, these two. She hoped their skills were inversely proportional to their personalities. "It is difficult to collect information about what is happening at the mine. Apparently your equipment is not subject to the electromagnetic interference in the caves. You, Dr. Harold, will set up your equipment to monitor our attempt to gather pearl."

Omar nodded. "My module is almost entirely organic. I have minimized the use of electronics as well as the materials vulnerable to the caustic nature of these caves quite successfully. But until now I have not needed to go as deep as the mine caves. My research subject, the creature they call workgrubs, prefer the moister caves above the valley."

Sonja smiled. "You were also picked because you're used to working in caves. Most of the research techs can't tolerate the environment there. You will have to carry everything in and set it up yourself of course."

"My equipment was specifically designed to function under difficult circumstances, but it was not designed—"

"I understand, but this is an emergency."

"My research is with a local life-form. My equipment monitors life processes. I know nothing about pearl."

"Your job is to help find out what or who we are dealing with in the theft of pearl. You have studied the phenomenon the farmers call vampires. What the miners say they saw and smelled in the mine before they fell unconscious has some of the same characteristics.

"The vampire phenomenon, however unusual its electrochemical structure, is not alive. It is likely the death of workgrubs and the occasional appearance of vampires are coincidental. There may be poisonous vapors associated, but I was not able to detect them. Most likely, vampires are an electromagnetic result of volcanic heat and the aquifer—underground storms—something like lightning storms on Earth. Very little is understood about this planet's geological water. At most the workgrubs are only incidental victims of electrical phenomenon, not natural prey of an unknown life form. I have not found believable evidence that there were attacks on workgrubs."

"If people are taking pearl, your equipment is exactly what we need to detect them. And you will analyze and keep track of the vapor or poison or whatever it is that has been disabling miners."

Omar shook his head in disbelief. "You are telling me that someone or something is taking or destroying pearl and the entire Consortium establishment can't find out how or who?"

Sonja sighed. "It's just a matter of time now. It's your job to decipher the evidence and separate myth from truth."

Nombei said, her voice calmer, "While he's finding that out, my charges need time to heal. It will be a long time before they will be able to resume normal life, let alone face hazardous fumes or whatever it is."

The Nombei creature was almost begging now; she could be managed. Dr. Omar would be more objective. Sonja would speak with him separately.

Omar said, "All the life-forms we have found on this planet have simple organic cell structure—the workgrubs and the leaves and the plant life—however unlike ours. The workgrubs are the most intelligent life form and they have the intelligence of an ant."

Sonja said. "Precisely. Most likely humans are behind this. Not only can you read alien life-forms, but you can detect the thieves."

The next morning when Nombei walked in to check on her charges, she was shocked to see them sitting up and talking to Investigator Shankar and Dr. Harold. They were asking questions of her charges that seemed irrelevant and they did not even bother to look at her.

Investigator Shankar finally turned to her and said, "If you will just wait outside, or better yet, in the office down the hall, Dr. Harold has some questions for you also."

Nombei sputtered, "But they're not ready—"

"I disagree." Shankar smiled complacently.

When Nombei reached for Pella's wrist to test her pulse, Pella pushed her away roughly and said, "Do as you are told woman and go away. We have what we want."

Nombei could see from Pella's eyes that they had been supplied with a healthy dose of pearl. All her efforts had been wasted. Nombei was annoyed and angry at herself for having been so stupid as to believe that there had ever been any hope of curing them of their habit. Frightened now, especially for Pella, Nombei couldn't help herself saying, "You'll ruin all my work. Their skin is still healing. If they're on pearl again, they won't eat and they may damage—"

Omar tapped his recorder impatiently and said, "Stay or go, but kindly remain silent."

Sonja Shankar stared at Nombei disdainfully, as if she were some sort of insect, then said, "Relax, you've done your job better than you know." Her voice became threatening. "You had better start appreciating how lucky you are to still be here. You might even learn something if you pay attention." Then she turned her back.

Nombei went into the over-bright hallway and stood for a long moment. It had all been a terrible mistake. Pella and the others were going to be nothing but sacrificial guinea pigs. She wondered what they would do with her now they might not need her any more. That woman, Shankar—she was just too perfect. At first Nombei had thought that she might be an android. Her body was attractive as if it had been designed to please others. She had heard rumors that there were androids built for the convenience of the elite.

But Shankar was also smart. She had the smartness of someone who knew what it meant not to have power. She bothered to appease and manipulate and seduce—talents that people with raw power did not need. Nombei sighed. That wouldn't matter now. It was true she wasn't a trained medical person. They could turn her job over to other people, to the medical staff she'd been training. She wanted badly to go home. She couldn't take care of Pella now that Investigator Shankar was here. And that Dr. Harold terrified her with all his scientific authority—always testing, recording—the efficient scientist, interested only in information.

No doubt they were keeping her at the mine because they were afraid she would talk about what was happening. She wasn't stupid. The best option she was guaranteed was a mind delete. She didn't want to think about what ultimate fate they had planned for her. They must think that she might still be useful since she was still here. But whatever her fate, it didn't matter what she did or said.

When Nombei went into her office, Dr. Harold was already sitting at Nombei's monitor going through her notes. He turned when Nombei came in and said, "I know you resent what you think is my interference with your charges. I had nothing to do with them being awakened or given pearl. I'm just trying to glean what information I can from this mess."

"I kept my records as best I could," Nombei said resentfully. "I was never allowed proper scientific training. I don't even know the vocabulary."

"I didn't mean the comment as a criticism of your work or your record keeping. I was referring to the situation here."

Nombei sat down. "You must see that they shouldn't be given so much pearl now. Pearl is the reason they ended up beggars. Giving them pearl—there will be no chance of getting them off the stuff."

"I'm afraid I'm beginning to agree with you that your charges are being pushed too hard. And I did not agree with giving them pearl right away."

"But what can we do?"

Omar Harold did not look at Nombei and his voice was impatient. "Investigator Shankar is the one in charge. She's intelligent, though not a scientist. She works for the Galactic League so she is the only one who can intervene. You'll have to appeal to her. I think it is futile; the Consortium people are desperate to get to the pearl and are convinced that the people you cleaned up are well enough for their purposes. You are incredibly naive if you ever thought they were to be cleaned up for their health."

"You're worse than they are. You understand the situation. They'll kill Pella and the others and you won't try to do anything."

Omar sighed. "Let's not start out on the wrong foot. First of all, I'm not responsible for your lack of education or my own birth into privilege. I don't have any idea what you've suffered. It is clear to me you have done remarkably well considering the handicap of your birth. If we are to work together, I would like to step beyond that if possible. I agree with you that your charges are not well enough to do any challenging work, but they are clearly mentally functional and capable of beginning some sort of minimal orientation program. I trust we can work together to figure out what they can do. One must be practical. Frankly, without the intervention of the League and the resources of the Consortium, those people would have had no chance to escape their fate. Now if they do their job well—"

Nombei liked the man's straightforward style in spite of herself. "If we can agree on a program, will you go with me to talk to Investigator Shankar? Will you help me convince her that I should remain in charge of their care?"

Omar sighed again and then nodded, turning back to the notes.

# Chapter Ten

Sonja enjoyed the small hovi she had commandeered for her investigation. The slightly lower gravity of this planet made the vehicle very easy to use, especially on the wide open plain, though it gave her vertigo. She had been on other underpopulated planets where private vehicles were practical, but nothing like this one with its wide open mostly uninhabited spaces.

The Consortium infocoms had profiled the mine and refinery employees and the Earthdome inhabitants, all legal visitors and employees from offplanet, but contained little about the illegal squatter colonies. Like the Godong, because they had no direct access to pearl and little in the way of resources, they had not been as thoroughly investigated. She would start with the farms on the nearby plain that supplied the Earthdomes with genetically altered, Earth-type foods and so were tolerated by the Consortium.

Unlike the high caste residents of the Earthdomes and their employees who were dependent on the Earth environment replicated there, the farm managers and owners had adjusted to the local environment to some extent. Because of their relationship to the Earthdomes they were fairly prosperous with access to resources. Sonja had intended to question one farmer at a time at their housedomes, but mine officials had arranged a meeting with many of them at the main farm produce transfer station on the edge of the rift valley. She had no choice but to meet them as a representative of the League.

It was a small but noisy crowd that gathered around her in the big warehouse. Most of the farmers had the particular yellowish tint to their skin that this sun's rays gave and their bodies had the stretched, long, lean look from the planet's lower than Earth gravity. She saw little evidence of pearl use. And among them were a few children with the wispy height and narrow muscle and bone that growing up without gravity enhancement gave them. Clearly these people were here to stay and not concerned about the changes in muscle and bone that would make it difficult if not impossible to return to Earth-type gravity.

"Why has nothing been done about the disappearance of our grubs?" one woman was shouting directly in her face as if she were deaf. She regretted not bringing one of the officials with her, if only to keep this crowd in order so she could talk to them.

There had been a few notes in the briefing material about these farmers' problems because of the loss of their workgrubs. There were a few farm robots, but the farmers could not afford state-of-the-art models and the ones they had were clumsy and not careful or thorough, so the local weeds were beginning to overcome the crops.

A man shouted at her, "Governor Chalmers promised us he would get rid of the vampires, but we're still losing grubs and he's done nothing."

Other people shouted, "How about our proposal to use workers from the refinery while that place is closed? We could even use some of those unemployed miners, daft as they are." "You kill all those poor worksods for stealing our precious pearl? You send 'em all home?" "What're we supposed to do with all the stuff we grew for the Consortium to feed the miners?" "You guaranteed us payment for it." "When can we get some decent robot or some new farm machinery sent in?" "Why are there no more transports off-planet?" "My kid is supposed to start university offworld." "What're you doing about pearl riots—my son is in the Sector Four colony. How can I find out what happened to him?" "When's the Gov going to get us those genetically fixed-up farm animals he promised us to replace the grubs?" "And what are you doing about the vampires?" several of them shouted at once.

Instead of trying to address their questions, she waited until they finished venting their frustration and settled into an uneasy silence. The earnest and angry people before her didn't strike her as a bunch of greedy pearl thieves.

She said, "I regret that the Consortium has not come to your aid in the way you would like. But it *is* a private company not a government. If you were legal colonists, I could help you, but as squatters you are responsible for your own well-being here, just as the Consortium is."

There was silence for a moment, then a discontented murmur. A tall man raised scarred fingers. He had the deep coloring from this planet's sun that made his lean face look almost jaundiced; he clearly worked in the fields himself.

After she acknowledged him and the murmurs settled down he said quietly, "Jacob Brunner here. I'm the chosen spokesperson for the farm community. We know we were not supposed to have settled, but it was convenient to the Consortium to have us here. They made us believe we could eventually become a legal colony. We feed them and their workers, but we don't need them or their pearl. This is our home now."

"I'm sorry if you were misled. As it stands you have no status with the

League. It is my job to report to the League on the situation here."

"If the Consortium loses pearl and clears out, we still can live here. We don't need the Consortium...or the League," he added with bravado. "Even the Earthdomers would have to leave if we weren't to feed 'em." The crowd around him cheered their agreement.

Here was a motive. But why would he throw it at her so blatantly if they were the ones sabotaging pearl? She decided on the direct approach. "So you are removing pearl to get rid of the Consortium's need to be here?"

He frowned and shook his head. There were more threatening murmurs in the crowd. Sonja lifted her hand.

Brunner, the man took a deep breath. His lungs must be affected by constant exposure to the dust and weed in the fields.

He spoke a bit louder, his voice going raspy with emotion. "We are honorable people who have worked hard for what we have." There were nods around him and straightened shoulders. "We've always thought pearl was evil and we're not sorry for its shortage. Some of us have even lost family to it, or are refugees from its curse. But we don't interfere with our neighbors. Without the Consortium we have no market for our goods. We could feed ourselves, but, you're right, we are too isolated from the rest of the galaxy. Too many people would lose too much with the Consortium gone—like the poor workers at the mine. We don't want them to be shipped back to the stinking earthpit. Anyway, unless we get help dealing with the vampires we'll not survive. Without our workgrubs we'll be put out of business by the local weeds." There were nods of agreement around him and all eyes turned to her as the representative of the League with the ability to save them.

Brunner had been very sure of himself. Could they all really agree with him? Sonja was watching the crowd for dissenters. A few people looked away. She observed some signs of pearl use. She noted their faces for future reference. They were the ones to question directly. Ignoring his statement she asked, "Are you offering to return pearl in exchange for field workers? robots? A better price for your crops?" Omar had said the vampires weren't the cause of the workgrubs deaths, but she would never convince this crowd of that. Instead she said, "What if the Consortium agreed to control the vampires? Would you return pearl then?" There were puzzled looks. A few embarrassed or confused laughs.

A woman in battered coveralls stepped forward and stood next to their spokesman and said, the irony clear in her tone, "Too bad we didn't think of that ourselves—'borrowing' pearl. Not a bad idea. A lot simpler than begging the Consortium clones for help." The crowd murmured and nodded in agreement.

Another man said bitterly. "Look at your records. We don't have your pearl. We been harassed bad enough. They searched and searched. My son is still in a detention center 'cause he managed to get off-planet so they think he's some sort of pearl connection. He just wanted to have a little fun at a moonbase 'cause they wouldn't let him go to school off-planet."

Time to take the pressure off. Sonja smiled in sympathy. "I'm sorry this crisis has made things so difficult for you all, too. I would appreciate any information and help you can give me so we can all go back to our lives. I'll be talking with some of you individually to get more acquainted with the situation here. As a representative of the Galactic League I'll help you as much as I can. Record and give me your comments and complaints and I'll see what I can do. Thanks for your time."

# Chapter Eleven

Sonja went to dinner at Chalmers' invitation, an opportunity to meet and mix with the Earthdome elite. It was clear from the luxuriousness of the Earthdome it was quite possible that some of them might be able to afford to be part of a pearl-stealing scheme.

On her way to Chalmers' sector she stopped at one of the shops and picked up an outfit. She could tell by the assortment of fashions available that the elite here were not up on the latest fashions of the colonies which meant some of them had been here quite a while. She picked out something conservative, a silver beaded dress that would show off her enviable skin tones and lean figure.

She told the robot attendant that she would introduce herself and stood in the shadow of the entry alcove to assess the other guests. Chalmers was not to be seen. She was pleased to see she had been right in her assessment of what was fashionable here. Seventeenth-century English court fashion mixed with a hodgepodge of more current styles. As she had expected many in the room were serious pearl users and she did not see anyone who was obviously a Consortium official.

She was surprised at the number of people who did not have implants. It was hard to believe anyone here was not entitled to intiception. Had some people lost their privilege because they were outcast elite or were there people here other than the staff who had never had entitlement? She doubted the Consortium would tolerate many pretenders even for profit. Someone like Chalmers would not.

Surveying the room took just a few minutes, then she moved casually over to introduce herself to the first chatting group that noticed her. She did not reveal her role as League Investigator; they would find that out when and if she interviewed them officially.

After she had made her way around the room, a small black shape appeared at her feet, a wiggly bundle of happy greeting looking amazingly real. It couldn't be, of course; most pets had been destroyed or eaten in the wars and subsequent cleanup at the end of the twenty-first century. Live pets had been made illegal in the twenty-second century. A dog took up the same amount of nutrients and space and care as a human child. It was not an option to own one, especially among the elite who were supposed to set an example for those they ruled.

She squatted down to examine it more closely. It licked her face enthusiastically as she ran a hand over it to feel for the underlying mechanism. Nothing but soft furry wiggling flesh. She was startled. Even in the colonies pet animals were forbidden unless they were local. No doubt there were genetic material preserves somewhere so earthtype animals could be introduced in planet colonies if they were necessary for human survival.

It jumped up on the seat to be petted, a much more congenial companion than the stiff, overdressed crowd. She said as much to the dog who cocked its head as if it understood her.

A small voice said, "She likes you. She doesn't like everybody. Her name is Pet." Sonja looked up. A stunningly beautiful girl-woman stood next to her looking down with large blue-green eyes. One large stone that matched but did not outshine those eyes graced the delicate throat. She wore a simple white velvet dress that emphasized her flawless golden skin, the exquisite lines of her perfect breasts and her delicate curved neck and fine cheekbones.

She sat down close to Sonja and touched her face with graceful slim fingers that trembled against Sonja's darker skin as she moved them slowly down her cheek and neck. "He said you were beautiful. He was right." She smiled.

Sonja frowned. The luminous blue-green eyes, the elflike face, the lush red-gold hair pinned high on her head with a few curls against the exquisite throat… This woman was not a surgery or cosmetic-enhanced lookalike.

The woman smiled as she received Sonja's inticeptor question then sighed, "Yes, I'm real, Family. My great-great-great uncle is an Eminence, if that matters to you, officially Contessa Julianna Montclaire—the Governor's…wife. She chuckled as if that word amused her. Then she smiled seductively. "But you can call me Julie."

Sonja switched off her inticeptor, chagrined to have been caught off guard, particularly by someone from the Family, the definition of fashion and power, the elite of the elite in the galaxy. Unlike most of those around her, this Contessa represented a powerful clan. What would one of them be doing here? She was not a pearl addict. There were a few Family in the colonies, always in position of power, both for the League and in the Consortium, but this wasn't even a colony.

Sonja looked into the half-closed gorgeous eyes, the pupils dilated—she felt herself pulled in, turned on.

The Contessa picked up the little dog and kissed it hungrily. Then she looked into Sonja's eyes wistfully, again saying softly, seductively, "You are beautiful. Chalm said you were. Even though you're not…high caste. That doesn't matter to me."

Sonja pulled back defensively, almost deferentially. Were those eyes dilated by drugs or did this woman really find Sonja attractive? All of her alarms went off. She needed to be very careful. Sonja ran her eyes over the Contessa once more. She had heard rumors of problems in the Family from genetic manipulation. From the look of this one, she had been sacrificed to a lust for childlike vulnerability. Small face, large eyes, a waist that even Sonja's hands might fit around. Setting the fashion, especially in terms of sexual attraction, was a risky business with unpredictable consequences. Sonja was reminded of what she knew of ancient Chinese society with its fetish for small feet.

The Contessa withdrew her hand and pouted. "You don't like me."

Sonja smiled. "Maybe I like you too much." She had to admit she was intrigued by the wealth and power this woman represented and her obvious beauty and self-confidence, as well as her look of vulnerability no matter that it was contrived. Her obvious neediness itself was a turn-on. Usually Sonja was more in control of her sexuality.

The Contessa said rather petulantly, "Well you needn't think I'm so easy. Chalm sent me to seduce you. I'm sure he thinks it's almost as good as having you himself."

Sonja decided to gamble. Gaining this woman's trust might help in her investigation. Not much else had so far. An affair with the governor's wife could well get her some answers. And she was intrigued enough to play the game.

Now Sonja's smile was her most seductive. "I must admit, I don't much like your husband…Julie. I have to put up with him because, technically, he's my boss. But you're…nice and beautiful too."

Julie laughed. "You are bad. He said you were. That you say anything you feel like. No respect for authority. Why aren't you afraid of him…or me? He has people killed sometimes. I could too."

"I was sent by the League to do a job—and by relatives of yours, I think. I'm worried about doing my job right. He isn't helping."

Julie moved closer and whispered, "I know why you are here. Their stupid pearl. Don't think I don't know. I'm not supposed to talk about it, but I don't care. I can't have any; they all say it would kill me." She looked at Sonja defiantly. "I'm bad too. I took some, once just one little capsule; I stole it from my cousin. It made me very sick, but I liked it anyway."

Two brocaded feet stopped next to Pet, who looked up and growled. Of course, Chalmers had been listening to their conversation and didn't like the way it was heading.

He said, "Julianna, remember what we agreed about Pet. It's better for it to stay in your apartment." His tone had a curious blend of annoyance, indulgence, and authority, like a parent whose child has embarrassed him in public.

Julie didn't look at him. Her eyes were still on Sonja while she picked up Pet and held her tight, but her words were addressed to Chalmers. "She won't tell the League about having a pet; she likes me…and my puppy."

Sonja smiled at Julie and gently rubbed the puppy behind the ears. His wife—a liaison with the Family—would be a feather in anyone's cap. A reward to Chalmers? For what? A wife like this would certainly enhance his status anywhere, however unfortunate her genes. Sonja hoped Chalmers treated her decently.

Chalmers said, "Greetings Investigator Shankar. I see you've met my wife. Come along, its time to go in to dinner."

Julie's luminous eyes looked deeply into Sonja's and Julie whispered, "I'll find you later."

Sonja nodded and got up while Julie slipped away with Pet in her arms.

Julie wasn't present at the dinner table though a place was set for her. Sonja was seated next to Chalmers. She asked him why his wife wasn't at table. He looked annoyed as if she should already know the answer. "She has…digestive problems; she'll join us later," was all he would say. Then he turned away abruptly to speak to the person on her other side. She had the distinct feeling from his behavior that her encounter with the Contessa was supposed to have turned out differently.

The meal was a nice change from the rather mundane food at the mine, though even there the food was better than what most people still on Earth could afford, unless one were rich enough to buy fresh produce imported from the off-planet colonies. Ironic that this hostile dry planet could grow a better quality of Earth-based food than the vast island farms constructed of cleaned up soil, floating on the oceans of Earth.

Julie came up behind her in the lounge after dinner just as Sonja was beginning to think about finding an excuse to leave, tired of playing the naive newcomer. Most of what she had heard she already knew. It was useful to get a feeling for the Earthdome elite, but most them were hopelessly wrapped up in their obsessions with pearl, with material possessions and the difficulty of getting there, the restrictions posed by the Consortium's transport system and, most of all, by their terror of the natural environment of this planet which only a few had actually experienced outside the Earthdomes.

Sonja was led by Julie into a separate apartment and into a little private alcove where they could see the stars through the dome. Sonja asked her directly why she wasn't at dinner and why Chalmers had been so rude about it.

Julie flushed in anger. "They are embarrassed, but I don't care. Here, I'll even show you." She unfastened her dress in the front and pulled it open. Below the delicate breasts there was a translucent cover. Beneath it Sonja could see a nest of small tubes inside the concave skin surface where her stomach and intestines normally would be.

"I am missing some…guts," she said matter-of-factly. "I was born with practically none. They rigged this system up for me. Had to keep replacing it as I grew. It's all pretty boring. When it gets hooked up, artificially digested juices feed me—go into my blood. I get hooked up to all kinds of machines at different times. They tried growing me some guts but I'm allergic even to my own cloned cells. Fun, huh."

Genetic defects would make her a discard of the Family. Defects that were the result of trying to keep too close a control on a caste's genetics. Her defects had made it necessary to exile her. Sonja said, "Doesn't seem so bad to me. Eating and digesting and peeing and shitting. It's all such a nuisance. Seems to me it might be more convenient—"

Julie held a delicate hand over Sonja's mouth to stop her. "Just as good as an android. Too bad they didn't program me to run on electricity, or better yet plutonium. So much more convenient, don't you think? As it is, I hardly use any food and even very little oxygen. I'm very efficient."

"I'm sorry, I didn't mean to be insulting."

Julie closed up her dress. "I know. Nobody does. They just feel sorry for me." Then she said, bitterly, not looking at Sonja. "You see, it's all those generations of women bred to be sylphlike. Genes that reduced the size of intestines and stomach so we won't ever get fat. Tiny livers too. Livers get in the way of a slim waist, you know." Julie looked up to catch Sonja's reaction.

Sonja took Julie's hands and squeezed them sympathetically, knowing it was not really enough. "It doesn't look so bad to me. You don't have to put up with all the bellyaches and it is pretty portable."

Julie's eyes blurred a little, just the beginning of tears. She went on. "In the nineteenth century they took out ribs and wore corsets that cut your liver in half just for a slim waist—just to make you more attractive to men. This is so much more civilized, don't you think? Ironic isn't it? I can't stand men." She shivered and then smiled at Sonja. "Women are so much better."

"I'm sure they didn't intend for you not to be able to eat at all."

"You're right. I'm an error. This stuffing that keeps me alive takes up too much room to be fashionable. That's why I'm on this planet. Chalm is the only candidate who would put up with me."

"I'm sure they don't like your candor."

"I don't bother to tell most people the details, but you're different—Chalm is afraid of you. You must really be smart and maybe even honorable. He hates honorable people; he can't manipulate them."

"Why did you agree to be his wife?"

"Good question." Inexplicably Julie rewarded Sonja with a kiss on the lips and Sonja returned the favor.

Julie leaned back. "I wanted to get away from the Family. To them I'm some sort of embarrassing freak. He was coming here. I was bored. This is more interesting." She snickered. "I know what you think. How disgusting. But I don't have sex with him or anything. I like girls—women like you. He knows that. That was part of the deal." She kissed Sonja again. "And there's nothing wrong with that part of me, if that's what you're thinking."

Sonja wasn't thinking that. She wasn't thinking anything at all beyond how incredibly seductive and beautiful this woman was, in spite of her strange anatomy. Her own body was alive for the first time in a long time. It had been a while since she had allowed herself to feel so sexual. But Sonja did allow herself the luxury of voluptuous sex when it was appropriate. And this strange exotic creature, from the clan of the powerful and beautiful felt like a kindred spirit in her candor and rebellion, as well as a potential ally in her work. Sonja pushed aside the velvet skirt and ran a finger slowly along the smooth golden skin of the well-shaped leg, then she bent to kiss Julie's delicate toes.

# Chapter Twelve

One of the people that had caught Sonja's attention at the meeting with the farmers was a woman who had the opalescent sheen of a pearl user. She had looked less concerned and workworn as well as more prosperous than the others.

The next morning Sonja landed her hovi in front of a new housedome and farm shed that was in the middle of planted fields. On this farm the problem of the missing workgrubs had been partially solved by planting corn and vegetables in rows wide enough for the crude robot cultivator that was plowing up weeds without damaging the plants. That left a rather dense growth of local flora thriving around the stalks of corn and vegetables. Rather inefficient and a waste of good soil. It was expensive and time-consuming to convert the local soil to be suitable for Earth plants and soil reverted back quickly without constant attention. Fields of young fruit trees were planted the same way—again with weedy patches around their roots.

There was no household robot to greet her at the entrance; perhaps it had been sent into the fields. But the door opened automatically when she approached and she entered and went through a small but nicely appointed hall. Farming seemed at least profitable. In the central living space, the lavender-tinted woman lounged on a low couch watching a viewer on a screen in the opposite wall. Next to her couch were low shelves with stacks of coms. From the look of it she was having no trouble getting pearl; in a white china dish next to her was a supply of pearl capsules. She did not get up when Sonja approached to introduce herself, but waved at a drinks console in one wall. When Sonja sat down next to her, she reluctantly took the com-ring off her head and the image faded. "I like it on, otherwise I scare myself too much and it ruins the pearl feeling," she said conversationally. She squinted at Sonja. "We saw you the other day."

"Sonja Shankar. I'd like to ask a few questions."

"You're the one who accused the farmers of taking pearl. Not a bad plan. Trouble is, they're all too retarded."

"You haven't lost your supply yet, I see."

"I can get it for an arm and a leg and a small fortune." She giggled at her own joke, then said more seriously, "Sure, we're worried like everybody else. This farm cost us too much and barely turns a profit. If it weren't for Consortium investments— We knew better than to depend on those disgusting bug grubs from the start. I'm sick of it all. If it weren't for pearl— I sure hope you find it so I can have as much as I want."

"You said we. Where is your partner? Any others working here?"

She snorted. "Jake doesn't work here. He works in security at an Earthdome. He pays some of the neighbors to keep things running. It's all supposed to be automatic." She laughed. "If I didn't love my pearl so, I could almost wish the Consortium had to give up on this frigging planet so we could go home."

"Why haven't you left already if you hate it here?"

She sighed. "My pearl source is here. I may be crazy but I'm not farm-clod stupid."

Sonja refrained from mentioning that if she hadn't wasted her creds on pearl she could have been long gone. "And who might that seller be?"

"He's an honest businessman, just smart enough to save a bit of stuff ahead of time. Some people can see a drought coming."

"I can access your cred-rec."

"I'm sure you can. He runs a legitimate establishment in the valley. Huniman."

Sonja had read all about Huniman and his hoard of pearl. She was planning to visit valley and its independent settlers like him soon.

"Have you any idea who might be taking pearl? Heard any rumors about where more pearl could be gotten?" she asked casually.

"Everybody knows the Consortium wants to raise prices so they made up that story about there being a shortage."

"If that were the case, wouldn't I know it? Why would I bother to ask you about it?"

The woman's eyes were a little too bright. Sonja could see she was afraid that her supply might disappear but she kept up her bravado. "Consortium people always lie. Believe me, I've asked around. It's my worst nightmare that pearl gets too expensive. You could get me some." She smiled eagerly. "It would be easy. Go into business ourselves. You work for the Consortium; I know the—customers. We could take our share in product."

Sonja shook her head. The woman was hopeless in her obsession. But even she must realize how dangerous what she was saying was. "The Consortium would reward anyone who provided real information about the disappearance of pearl."

The woman suddenly showed her fear. "I don't know anything. Probably those vampires. It's them that ate it after they ran out of grubs."

"What do you know about the vampires? Have you seen them?"

"Big fluttery things; they can go through walls. Jake doesn't believe me but they come in here when he's out, hover around my head, spoil pearl feeling sometimes, take it away. Warm—smell like smoke and morbon jam. Big pink moths." She smiled her eyes closed.

The woman was hallucinating, hopeless. Sonja got up to go. "Let me know if you hear something."

Without responding, the woman turned the com back on and stretched out on the couch.

After a few more frustrating interviews Sonja went to see Jacob Brunner, the man who had been the spokesperson at the public meeting. She had managed to get some robots from the refinery that were not being used sent to farmers who had requested them. Brunner was one of them. The robots were not programmed for field work, but they should be able to do simple tasks and it would show her good intentions.

She found Brunner in his well-kept fields with one of the new robots. He had the back of it open and was staring at the works with a screwdriver in his hand.

"I wouldn't do that if I were you," she said.

He started and looked up at her. Throwing the screwdriver into a box, he stood up.

"Didn't they include the programming equipment with it?" she asked.

He nodded." They did, but I can't get it to work right. Been at it all morning. It still makes a mess." He waved his hand toward a small patch of overgrown vegetables. "It can't tell a kontgrape from a watermelon, not to mention all the local weeds."

The man was from Calsor, the planet where kontgrape was a native plant. Calsor was one of the earliest of Earth's colonies. The people there had domesticated some of the local flora. People used to Earth food didn't like most of them but Calsorans had learned to love them.

"I'm sure a memory chip must have been made for that. Don't you have one?"

"Yeah, but it was made for the metal robots we used to have. They were designed for asteroid mining and were too simple, so the chip didn't work. I never tried to use them."

"The discrimination information should still be good."

He went into a shed and brought back a box with some chips in it."One of the other farmers gave me this. She said it's got local weed discrimination."

The robot had been designed for work in the refinery where small motor coordination was primary. Sonja took out one of the robot's refinery chips and replaced it with one of the older chips. It malfunctioned several times while it accepted the new information. Sonja made some adjustments in its main memory and some modifications in the range of its mechanical motion. Then they sent it into the messed up part of the vegetable patch for a test. It sorted out the vegetables from the weeds pretty well and replanted the Earth flora in rather ragged rows. The weeds were left in a pile outside the patch. Then it sprayed the area with a water hose.

Jacob nodded. "Not bad, but the grubs would have eaten all the weeds and sucked the ground to get every last weed cell around the plants. What the robot left will grow back faster 'n a hoschalk can breed." The small rodent-like hoschalks on Calsor produced twenty or more litters in an Earth year.

She laughed. "You must miss Calsor. This place is pretty barren." Sonja made a few more adjustment but there were limits to the ability of this type of robot. They should import some that were designed for farming.

He shrugged. "Calsor was pretty much a dead rock when my great grandparents got there. Not enough water or even oxygen for a decent colony. It was a struggle. It took a lot of teraforming to make a comfortable life. Here, if the Consortium were gone, and the pearl gone with them, we could make something of this planet."

"You've been here a long time. What do you think is happening in the mine?"

"I think you got to look to sources. That stuff's been there for a long time. What put it there and why? They say its inorganic but that don't mean something live wasn't involved. How come it melts people's brains instead of killing them. You eat most rock, it don't do anything to your brain. Might make you sick, but wouldn't make you drunk happy. Happy comes from stuff that's been alive. You ever been down in those caves?"

Sonja shook her head. "I've seen the coms."

"I went down there when we first got here. Eerie. All that pearl shinin' with its own light on the walls. I would'a sworn it was alive. Eggs of something. Soft and warm to the touch. Then they started hacking it away. He shook his head. "I knew there was trouble ahead."

"The vampires—you think that phenomenon is connected to the disappearance of pearl?"

He shook his head. "What they call vampires never hurt anything. Just lights up when the grubs disintegrate—some sort of gas nobody understands. Messes up robot and machinery if they're around. Smells godawful. People need to blame something."

Sonja nodded. "Yes, it is too bad about the grubs. They're useful. It's not often people find a creature with which they can share such a healthy symbiotic relationship."

"They'll come back. We just don't get their breedin' pattern. People're so impatient these days."

Sonja dictated a set of instructions on how to program the robots so that Brunner could help the other farmers put the robots to work, then she went to check out the mine again.

After leaving the farm area, Sonja scanned the barren rocky area around the mine compound in her hovi. She could detect no sign of unusual activity, human or otherwise, beyond the mine perimeter. If pearl had been removed it was not clear how it had been done. It was likely Chalmers was right and it had been moved deeper into the caves. Did the thieves hope to remove it at some future date?

She sighed and turned her hovi back to the mine where she continued her analysis of statements by the staff. She interviewed a cook in the cafeteria who had connections with former Consortium employees, people with skills and resources. Another dead end.

She thought about what the farmer had said about vampires. If this wasn't such a desperate situation she would think it was funny—that it smacked of nineteenth-century spiritualism. Vampires were supernatural beings from Earth's ancient history that supposedly lived off human blood. They were destroyed by sunlight and silver bullets. Vampires, ghosts, and spirits. She shook her head. Back then when scientists had actually bothered to investigate the spiritualist phenomenon, they had proved it to be clever human trickery—a knee moving a table, an accomplice appearing behind a gauze curtain and speaking in voices of the dead.

These onplanet vampires seemed equally dubious. Now you see them now you don't. At best they were a sulphurous smell or pink shadows. They appeared unpredictably, hovering over the death of workgrubs, haunting the dreams of pearl addicts. No evidence of harming humans could be confirmed.

Tomorrow Omar would take one of the ex-beggars down into the mine to try and gather pearl and get a better analysis of any 'vapors' that might be there.

Meanwhile, it was time to check out the settlement in the rift valley. If there were thieves with connections on the planet, the valley was a place to find evidence of them, having been settled by ex-mine and refinery workers as well as the riffraff the Consortium tolerated from other planet colonies. It was the sort of place that the Consortium officials would overlook because of their class attitudes. Letting your tastes and prejudices influence your work was always the downfall of an investigation. It was her job not to overlook anything.

Because of the harshness of its environment the valley was a place that would have a built-in tolerance for newcomers. She would go there as someone no one would bother to trace. Disguises were a particular talent of hers. If she could do it right she would get a job and live in the community for a while until some of the longer term residents learned to trust her, but there wasn't time for that.

Questioning people as an official Investigator had gotten her nowhere. She would go as someone else this evening, check out the night life in the valley. But who should she be? She could go as a degenerate member of the elite or a disenfranchised middle level worker, but that person might gather too much attention. Finally she decided on "naive would-be entrepreneur;" it was always useful to appear vulnerable. It would tempt those in the know both to want to help her and see an opportunity to exploit.

Not too young but vulnerable, attractive but slightly seedy and with apparent newly acquired resources that the unscrupulous might covet. Someone who had entrepreneurial enthusiasm. Being from offplanet, she might know something about terraforming. A good cover.

She put on a fluffy blonde wig and a tight suit that showed the smoothness of her flesh and the curve of her breasts. Make-up went on that changed her face so that she wouldn't easily be recognized if she should meet any of the people who might know who she was. She would go as Darleen, a rather naive but ambitious recent immigrant and former lower grade Consortium worker.

Back in her hovi, she headed down into the thick mist covering the valley bottom that made manual flying impossible. The layout of the settlement showed up on the hovi's infrared panel as a series of small domestic domes around a few larger commercial domes that supplied food and other basic necessities. It wouldn't be hard to hide in this valley of eternal overgrown damp if you could survive the environment. It would take considerable resources to do that though, something that the type who settled here did not have.

She landed her hovi at Huniman's, the entertainment dome that catered to the more affluent, those that had the resources to indulge in pearl. Huniman's client base was broad and since he had been the first, he had long-term customers. Those were the ones she was interested in. Like most establishments of this class there was no background music or common entertainment. Everything, even quiet and privacy, could be purchased. Here she didn't need an inticeptor. Those who could afford one wouldn't use it.

Huniman himself was behind the bar. She remembered the recorded statement he had given when pearl first started to disappeared. He had huffed a bit in the interrogation. "I get my pearl from legitimate sources. Do you think the Consortium would tolerate my business if I didn't? Just because I have been in trouble in the past. Just because I had the good sense to stock up on pearl—"

The interviewer had asked, "How did you know there would be a shortage, that you would need to stock up?"

"I didn't know. I was just concerned that the Consortium officials might arbitrarily cut off my supply…for some punitive reason, like they did before when they didn't approve of my client list. I don't discriminate; anyone can get pearl if they have the resources to purchase it. Stockpiling pearl was just ordinary precaution."

Now he looked at her with a penetrating gaze, obviously trying to make up his mind about her. "What's your poison?" he asked, not taking his eyes off her.

"Oh, I don't know, something not very intoxicating…just a little Calsor Gold, please." It was an expensive drink but had to be sipped slowly, showing her to be both able to afford it and cautious about her ability to stay in control.

He gave her a generous portion of the thick yellow intoxicant in a delicate long-stemmed glass of authentic opalescent Calsor glass.

"You been onplanet long?" he asked.

She shook her head shyly, then looked down at her glass. "Came with my man. He dumped me for a co-worker."

"Sorry."

"Don't be. Got enough guilt cred from him to start my own business. Don't want to be a Consortium lackey anymore." She smiled and said, "Darleen's the name, Darleen Anderson. I know all about how to outfit a space. You know any people here need advice about decorating, outfitting their domes? I could use a partner or two, just to get started—"

Huniman looked at her for a long moment.

She leaned closer and whispered, "I hear investment in pearl is a good bet."

"When you can find it. It's pretty tight right now."

She glanced around the room. There were quite a few users and they looked affluent and content. Even some Earthdomers slumming.

He said, "I do well enough. I'm in the market to keep my customers happy. We're not talking a lot of profit, but I've been lucky." He shrugged. "A few here in the valley have seen the trade as a good investment, a way to save for a rainy day, especially for those who aren't users. If you can pry a bit loose from the hoarders more power to you. All pearl came originally from the Consortium traders. Since they closed down sales there's not much on the market."

"Anybody here who's in the business?"

He nodded to the booth opposite the bar, "That littler guy over there in the booth, he sometimes gets stuff from people who need to sell their hoard, though I haven't bought from him lately. Hard times I guess."

A slight man resembling the Godong, though he had a bigger face and paler skin, sat in the booth opposite the bar with two other scruffy looking men. Just the sort of people she was looking for. Sonja laughed and said, "Skinny little fellow. What planet is he from?"

"Calls himself Georgio. Good man. He's from a settlement out in the desert. Knows a thing or two about the planet. Works out in the open on the shuttle station."

She smiled. "He's cute."

Huniman shook his head. "There's no accounting for taste."

She put on a disapproving look. "What's that supposed to mean?"

He shrugged. "He can't help you, Darleen. Hardly earns enough creds to eat by the look of him. I can introduce you to someone that might be helpful for your decorating business."

"Who would that be?"

He nodded toward an older man in an expensive though out-of-fashion suit of synthetic fabric in the booth next to Georgio. She exchanged glances with the man. Then she plunked down a cred, picked up her drink and followed Huniman to the booth.

Huniman introduced her and she smiled coyly, explaining that she wanted to find a business partner. She could tell by the way he looked at her that he saw her as a double resource, somebody to be exploited first for her body and then for her creds.

While the man talked about himself and his prospects in the community, she leaned against the partition, listening with her enhanced hearing to the conversation in the next booth. It was not particularly interesting. They were speculating about what indulgences they would buy if they had enough creds.

It had to be Georgio complaining in great detail about what various substances would do to his body if he imbibed—alcohol was a form of sugar poisonous to him, and too much water would make him bloat.... Then he said. "I have to get out of this dump; the air is giving me a headache." There was a long silence.

Sonja quit listening for a moment. The man opposite her, leaning closer, was proposing some investment schemes.

She said, "I'd be happy to look over some of the properties you mentioned. Maybe we could meet tomorrow. How can I contact you?"

While the man fumbled in his tunic for an ident she heard someone in the next booth ask, "What does pearl do to you, Georgio?"

"I don't know, but I'm not willing to find out. My mother is from off-planet like yours, but my dad's people believe pearl is…some sort of sacred poison that would destroy us."

There was silence in the booth for a few minutes. "Sacred, some sort of god blood?" one of them asked. She heard them laugh contemptuously.

"God substance, god memory. They're scared of it." Then Georgio laughed. "But now it doesn't matter any more what it is. The stuff's gone. No more, nickta. Consortium's going bust. No more work. You'll be outta here, if you can afford passage; this planet will be dust on your heels."

"What'll you do, Georgio? Go home to your folks in the desert?"

Georgio said, bravado in his voice, "I'll stay here onplanet. I like it. I can't breath the air in Earthdomes or in transports—makes me sick—thick and disgusting. My people, we'll take over the planet, pearl trade and all."

"Your folks got pearl? one of the men asked excitedly.

"I shouldn'ta' said nothing. No they don't."

An image of the isolated red pearl she had seen in the Godong cave came back to Sonja. The man in the booth with her leaned toward her and put his hand over hers. "No need to dig around for ident; come with me now." She shook her head and moved back against the side of the booth.

The man in the next booth was whispering. She could barely make out what he was saying. "C'mon Georgio. Tell us where there's pearl. We'll all get rich. People'd pay plenty for just a little bit. Even the raw stuff."

"Dealing in pearl that's already refined—that's one thing and I'm not saying I know where any is. But there's no way to market raw pearl without getting caught. The Consortium's got the whole thing tied up tight as a—"

Someone interrupted, saying contemptuously, "You don't know nickta. This talk is a stupid waste of time. Somebody'll hear us and we'll get pulled in again. Let's get outa here." The others grunted their agreement. They all stood up to leave, with Georgio the last one out of the booth.

Sonja stood up too, seeming to take offense at the behavior of the man in her booth. "I took you for an honest businessman. I want a business partner not a boyfriend. I've had my fill of that." She bumped into Georgio as the man from her booth grabbed her arm and she made a show of struggling to get away from him. Georgio came to her rescue, offering her sanctuary in his booth. Sonja took a seat there and said breathlessly, "Thank you ever so much. Maybe you would stick by me till he leaves the club." The man from her booth moved off in another direction.

Georgio's two companions were near the door when they saw him sit down with her, and they too left.

She introduced herself as Darleen and explained to Georgio about her plans to start or invest in a business here in the valley. "Mr. Huniman over there said you know something 'bout the pearl trade. I know it's a good investment. My ex is a user so I know something about that."

She babbled on, establishing her identity as a somewhat naive new-comer. When she was finally silent for a moment, he laughed and shook his head, "Sorry, Darleen, but the way you're going you'll scare off any business person with a sense of self-preservation. And you'll likely end up being cheated by some local predator. Anyway, if your ex is an addict you know the downside of pearl. Why you want to mess around with that any more?"

She put on a pout. "Joe told me that I'd look like a sucker—somebody that needed protection. But if I don't talk to people how'm I going to get anywhere? I got to start somewhere."

"Settle in and get to know the neighborhood. Get a job here in the val-ley. Don't risk losing your nest-egg to a conner. And be careful, somebody might take you for a conner yourself or even a Consortium spy and you'll get fed to the vegetation out in the bush."

"I never…I got enough creds to get along for a while and I'm sick of serving people. I wouldn't know where to start getting a job here anyway," Sonja said defensively.

Her pout seemed to be working. He smiled at her. "Whatever you do you'll still be a server."

She didn't smile back. "I didn't come here to be insulted."

"It wasn't an insult; we all work for somebody. Even people running the Consortium have to answer to someone. In the end it's just whether you get enough creds for what you want—with someone you care about." He looked sadly at his worn, work scarred hands for a long moment. "I should talk. I'm here scrounging for creds while my dad's people in the desert work hard each day staying alive, but they know why they do it."

Sonja laughed derisively. "If you admire them so much how come you aren't out there scratching in the dirt with them?"

"Sometimes I wish I could, but I'm like my ma—I'd dry up and die out there. I'm too much like you—a bag of water. We come from a water plan-et you know."

"Sounds like you want to go to Earth. It's poison, water or not. You want to go be an earthrat underground, you can have it."

Georgio sighed. "I'd like to see it, but you're probably right. I'll never go anywhere. I'm probably stuck on this fucking dusty rock—whether the Consortium leaves or not."

Sonja made Darleen sound angry and petulant. "If everything's so bad here how'm I going to survive or meet people I can trust?" She whined, "I'm an outsider. I'd go to my home planet except I haven't got enough cred for that and my ex won't send me. Says he doesn't have enough. He shouldn't have talked me into coming if I couldn't go back. He promised—"

"Nobody's allowed to leave right now anyway. Not till the pearl crisis is over. Nothing leaves the planet or the transport station. But you don't know anything about what being an outsider really means," he said bitterly. "Even the Consortium bosses treat me as half human 'cause my dad was here when the Consortium came. They needed us to get established but now they treat us as if we're worse than earthrats."

"But if your family came from Earth—early settlers—aren't you entitled? We colonists who came out first when it was hard deserve more respect and rights than the earthrats who stayed behind in the poison and only come out now to take advantage of our hard work."

"You haven't been on this planet long have you? This never was a colony."

She shook her head. "And I wish I'd stayed home. I need enough cred to go back," she said sadly. "I've got to invest what I have or I'll never get home."

He looked at her a long time then said, "There's a guy I work for sometimes. He might get you some work."

"He in the pearl trade?"

"That and other things."

"Great. Take me to meet him."

"Come back here in two days, say about the same time as now."

She smiled. "Will do."

He got up. "I got to go now."

She searched for information about Georgio. It was easy to find him. Because of the isolation of the Godong there were few who were part human and part Godong. His mother was an offworlder who came to the planet as a cook at an Earthdome and had run away into the desert with a Godong man employed to build the shuttle station. After Georgio had been born, his mother had left him at the farm community because she believed he wasn't going to survive in the desert. He had been raised by a squatter farm family and educated in the farm community. There were some bullying incidents in school because he was so small, but otherwise he had become a model worker for the Consortium at their shuttle station where he was useful because he could tolerate the harsh conditions working in the open environment of the planet. There was no indication of his being involved in the pearl trade.

# Chapter Thirteen

When Dr. Harold and the O'Brien woman came into her office the next morning, Sonja could feel the earthrat's agitation. Something would have to be done about that creature…soon. The woman's usefulness was coming to an end and she was clearly going to be a nuisance, especially if she got Dr. Harold involved in her point of view. Even Harold made her nervous—watching her, judging her. It didn't help that Sonja's investigation was going badly. She still had nothing.

But she listened patiently to the woman's complaints, still thinking, this O'Brien mudrat…she was out of her place, an aberration of her caste, too intelligent and opinionated for her own good. Even with a memory delete she would be trouble. Sonja had seen it happen too often. Mind deletes did not work well on those who had grown up resisting their socialization. The habit of resistance was too deeply burned into the more primitive parts of their brain. But it was almost always best if one could avoid the recycler. It was a part of her job that she least liked—mopping up. The sort of difficult problems the League trusted her to handle sometimes.

She didn't bother to keep the annoyance out of her voice. "Personally I agree with you—pearl addiction is a weakness best avoided in one's life. However, it has proven to have the least harmful effects of any such substance yet discovered. And it is what your beggars want from us. You are welcome to try and cure them of the pearl habit. We will be happy to let you try to do so—once the current crisis is over. Remember, now that she has been restored to the human race, even with her addiction, your friend Pella will likely live a long time. Plenty of opportunity in the future to get her off the stuff."

Sonja could almost see the earthrat thinking. Its round blue eyes squinted, its soft mouth puckered up as if it were about to cry. She hated all this useless emotion. But she could see she had won this round; she wouldn't have to get rid of it yet. It would do as it was told a bit longer.

Nombei was saying plaintively, "If you won't let me do my job here at least send me back home."

The O'Brien creature suddenly, inexplicably, reminded Sonja of The Contessa, in spite of the pale, blotchy pink skin and bulgy small frame. It must be the blue eyes. "All in good time. In any case, another shipment has arrived—more beggars for you to clean up. They will have to stay in isolation with you until you get the pelt off them. That and training new staff should keep you busy for a while."

Omar Harold's requests were more reasonable. He wanted records and information he thought relevant to his research. He said, "I haven't been allowed to see the workers' health records. Those must be made available. And I'll want to examine any victim's remains myself."

"We will go over that issue later. Right now there is no time for such a detailed review."

Omar looked thoughtful. "I assume that I'll at least have access to the investigative records on the victims."

Sonja wondered if Omar Harold understood the inevitable outcome for him of this project? Perhaps he would require only a memory delete and could then be shuttled off to some obscure university campus to teach beginning bio for the rest of his life. "We'll be conferring with the rest of the staff here. They'll fill you in with what is necessary." Then she dismissed them.

Sonja decided it was time to look more closely at the refinery. Officially the only pearl refinery was on this planet and in Consortium hands. Even if someone did find a way to steal raw pearl, it needed refining. It was always possible someone had managed to set up a refinery on another planet. That would require an inside job, someone who knew the technology of pearl refining. But the experts were sure that any alternative refinery would leave recognizable markers in the pearl intoxicant produced. She had found no evidence that illegal pearl with such a marker had shown up on the market…yet.

Refining was not quite an accurate term. Pearl handling was labor intensive. Exposed to raw pearl, anything metal would dissolve, so robotics were out of the question. Refinery workers tended to be women. Men did better in the mine environment. Women resisted the poisonous working conditions in the refinery better and had the small motor coordination needed for pearl handling. Like the women who worked in the silk industry in earlier centuries—who ended up with one shriveled hand because they had to start the cocoons unraveling their silk by putting a hand in boiling water—the refinery workers were ultimately damaged by working with pearl. Pearl was removed from the prepared globules with carefully calibrated pipette-like reeds taken from a plant from the valley. Then toxic substances had to be removed by tedious decantation which atrophied muscle and bone, particularly in the hands of the workers. The toxic residue was discarded. She had been told it was dumped into deeper volcanic channels beneath the pearl caverns where it could not leak back into the environment. Some earlier investigator had suspected that the miners were being poisoned by leakage of those toxins into the pearl caves. But chemical analysis did not support that theory.

After the toxins were removed, the purified intoxicant could be placed, a drop at a time, into consumable capsules. Refinery workers were very vulnerable to pearl addiction. Most eventually became comatose and were cared for in the refinery. Miners were luckier. Handling raw pearl did not cause addiction.

Now the refinery was closed. After inspecting the closed facility, Sonja decided to question some of the refinery workers directly. She didn't trust the coms of interviews officials had given her.

A cacophony of dialects bombarded her ears as she entered the dormitory, though she had been assured that they all understood standard Galaxy. First she spoke to them as a group, noting the whole range of pearl addiction.

Many of the workers were from the earthwarrens like Nombei and were worried that they would be sent back. They were considered the best workers; they were more motivated as well as toxin-resistant. This work was their one chance to earn enough creds to escape their dreary lives on Earth.

Those from other planets were often felons serving their time. For the most part they wanted to be returned home, realizing however hard the life in their colony, it was better than this. Sonja explained that she was here to figure out how to get more pearl so they could go back to work.

After reassuring them she would try to help them, and take their complaints to the League, Sonja took aside three of the least addicted—one from each of the factions she had identified, two from the colonies, one earthrat.

She got nothing useful from the first two. They were so frightened by being picked out that they hardly spoke. The third, Reanna, was not a young woman though she appeared strong and in good health. Sonja wondered if she had also had some illegal age reduction work done.

Reanna was not at all intimidated. She sat in the interview room clearly enjoying the warmth—no need to huddle near an inadequate solar heater—while Sonja scanned her record. She had had illegal body enhancement, but the more serious crime that had gotten her sent here was that of posing as a member of a caste beyond the one she had been born into. There had been insufficient proof of any other crimes so she had been given the option of working some years in the refinery.

With Reanna, Sonja tried the sympathetic approach and smiled. "I'm sorry you haven't been made more comfortable. There's really no excuse. You workers are not to blame for the current crisis. I intend to make sure you get better treatment. You could help yourself by telling me what you know. The sooner we find out who is taking pearl the sooner you can get back to work."

Reanna studied her thoughtfully. Finally she said, "Can't tell you a thing 'cept we been locked up too long. Shoulda chose to go to the asteroid mine; I'da done my time by now."

Sonja noted that the dialect she used was probably the one she had been born to, probably exaggerated to make Sonja think she was not sophisticated or knowledgeable. But Sonja knew she had successfully passed as a member of a more privileged caste. "I see that you have a minimum two more earth-years to serve here."

"When they get us back to work," she said fretfully.

"Do you want to be a free settler here when you have served your term?"

The woman looked at her suspiciously, "That wha' it say there?"

Sonja shook her head. "There is nothing in your record about your future."

"Said I could start with a clean record on another planet." Reanna stared at Sonja thoughtfully for a few seconds, her eyes narrowed. "I know. None of us will ever get offplanet. Know too much about pearl."

Sonja looked at her noncommittally, noticing Reanna's caste accent was less obvious now that she realized Sonja had read her record. The best Reanna could hope for would be to become a free settler on this planet. The Consortium would not go to the expense of shipping her elsewhere or giving her the memory delete required to protect pearl. "You must have heard something about why they stopped refining."

Reanna didn't answer but just stared at the floor.

Sonja went on. "The good behavior part is true. I need some information if I'm to give you a positive rating for this interview. What do you think has happened to pearl?"

Without looking up and without hesitation Reanna said, "Rumor is it's the farmers. They messed around with pearl because they want us working in their fields now their worms are gone."

"They call them workgrubs. They've asked for robots now to help in the fields."

Reanna looked up, anxiously. "We'd be a lot cheaper and easier to keep up. They don't like machinery—the farmers."

"So if the farmers are stealing pearl why don't they give up farming and just sell it?"

"They may be weird wantin' to scratch in the dirt for a living, but not crazy. Consortium's got that pearl trade tied up like a roach in a billibug web. They know better than to try and sell it. I know; I got caught up in it once."

Sonja waited.

Reanna sighed and squirmed a bit in her chair. Then she said, not looking at Sonja, "What's in it for me if I tell ya somethin'?"

Sonja pretended to look through info on her screen. "I could get you transferred to an asteroid to work out your time, or…there is a project on Mars—a bit rough—they're terraforming. Don't know if they would go to the expense of transporting you. It's a new mine—or you might be able to work for one of the farmers here—scratching in the dirt."

Reanna leaned forward still looking down, her hand casually across her nose. She clearly expected official spying equipment in the walls. Sonja had disabled it but she didn't enlighten Reanna. The woman whispered so low that without her enhanced hearing Sonja would have missed it. "Anything to get out of this…dump station." She looked at Sonja. "I don't have a clue about how pearl is getting ripped off, but…you know the Gov? He's doing research on pearl."

"Chalmers?"

The woman nodded and leaned even further forward, whispering quickly, her lips still covered by a lifted hand, "He's the one messing with pearl. Needs the shortage. He had them take blood from us. Not from me— the ones with a lot of pearl. Even cut off pieces. Rumor is he's going to extract pearl out of peoples' bodies. Make a fortune, he will. All those high caste richies desperate for the stuff. And with his wife in the Family…they wouldn't touch him. What's a few dead workers? I think that's why they segregated us nonpearls, so they can get at the pearlies more easy." She looked at Sonja suspiciously. "That why you're here? Or are you a Consortium spy?" She moved back, her eyes fearful now. Perspiration had appeared on her face as she glanced around, clearly sorry she had said anything.

Sonja tried to reassure her, but Reanna didn't look convinced as Sonja said, "Even if he could remove pearl from people, that wouldn't begin to supply enough pearl to meet current demand not to mention League rules on the ethical treatment of humans."

Reanna shook her head. "That's just the point. Only those with the creds could pay his price and we know who they are." She smiled nervously. "You telling me your League would really interfere for us throw-away workers? The League don't even admit we're here."

"That's exactly why I have been sent."

Reanna laughed and shook her head. "You do somethin' for me, for us here, and I'll see what else I can find out."

Smart woman. Maybe somebody she could deal with. "The best I can offer now is to improve conditions for you. Give you more ability to take care of yourselves. I'll check back to make sure they do what I ask. If you do come up with anything more...substantial...about what happened to pearl, you can tell me what reward you want then."

Sonja checked out the section of the refinery dorm where the pearl addicts were being kept. Here were the middle level workers—those that would normally be removing pearl from the final layer of husk, diluting it and putting it in the capsules for distribution. They had all been exposed to pearl, exhibiting different amounts of opalescent lavender in their skin. When there was still raw pearl they had gotten enough of it to keep working effectively. But now without pearl they were losing essential muscle coordination.

Those who had worked the longest were in the worst condition, their muscles rigid, their bodies lean to skeletal and none were truly coherent. Even those with only slight addiction had some dementia. And there was not adequate care for the most disabled; the place was a disaster with those still functional not allowed to care for the others. What staff there was indifferent, even hostile. They regarded their job as containing the workers, not caring for them. Something had to be done. There were adequate stores of food, but it was not going to those who needed it most.

In a third below-ground storage room Sonja discovered workers made comatose by too much exposure to pearl—their thin, wiry bodies dark purple—stacked on shelves with narrow aisles in between. The simple-minded monitors attached to each seemed to indicate that they were alive, though vastly slowed down. The single human medic explained that their bodies hardly metabolized, their hearts beat remarkably slowly and they didn't appear to breath at all, although he assured her that they did. She was reminded of ancient Egyptian mummies she had seen in educational coms as a student. She walked through quickly. There were only a few medical robots to take care of the rows and rows of lean, cadaverous bodies.

Because of Reanna's comment and to the annoyance of the staff, Sonja took the trouble to compare the records she had brought with her to those on site. She counted and compared. Of those present when pearl began to disappear, three had died in accidents, two had been released from their contract and were living in the valley and three of the comatose people were missing. She demanded to know where they were. Embarrassed, the medic in charge finally said, "Dr. Chalmers has those individuals in his keeping. You will have to discuss their status with him."

She went back to the first set of workers, those who were the least affected by pearl, and worked out a deal with them. Any workers who would agree to help care for those who were disabled by pearl and its withdrawal would be allowed to move to the other section where living conditions were better. Then she went immediately to confront him about the conditions for the workers.

At the Earthdome, Sonja was kept waiting for almost an earthhour. When he did come in Chalmers was furious. "How dare you interfere. The arrangements for the workers was carefully worked out. You have destroyed any reasonable control—"

Sonja did not move. She simply waited until he ran down. Then she stood facing him. "The conditions in that dormitory prison you set up would not pass the regulations for even an asteroid felon camp. You have some seriously ill and possibly dying people there and you are responsible for their condition. Where are the staff required for that size operation? Why have I found none of the original officials for the refinery? If you can't take care of the workers properly, you have an obligation to let them care for themselves. I'll report this to the Galactic League and to the Eminences—"

"Unproductive workers are expensive to keep. Once pearl supply is restored things will return to normal. Haven't you read the reports?"

"Yes, I have—very carefully. Well enough to notice that at least three workers are missing from the roster of those permanently disabled though apparently not dead—those who will not be restored to active life once there is a pearl supply. What have you done with those three?"

Chalmers was suddenly dead calm. She could almost hear the well-oiled gears of his brain. His eyes were cold as he switched tactics. He turned and sat down at his desk, gesturing at her to sit as well. She remained standing, her arms folded. He would try to disarm her now by appearing to be considerate.

He smiled icily, now in complete control. "I appreciate your concern. It was clever to arrange for the workers to care for each other. I see no reason not to allow that. It's an economically sound temporary arrangement. But your management of the workers' welfare is not the solution long term. Pursuing the missing pearl would do more to restore people to productive work, the sooner to help them to work off their debts."

She smiled pleasantly, having won this round. "I've made some progress on that front, too. I know what didn't happen to it. That narrows things down quite a bit." She turned away to go and then turned back. "Just one further little idea that would make things easier for everyone and avoid trouble from the farmers. I propose responding to their request—let workers who are able and willing, work off their debt on the farms, at least temporarily. That will save the Consortium the cost of their care and supply the farmers with replacements for their grubs."

He picked up an old-fashioned pen and twisted its cap. "Even if I agreed it's a good idea to send workers out to the farms to keep them busy until we need them, I could not. My superiors in the Consortium wouldn't agree. The workers' jobs are too sensitive. Representing the League does not give you authority to act, only to investigate. I am still in charge. Whatever action you take must be approved by me. I'll overlook your insubordination this time, but in future before taking any action please consult me." He turned away, dismissing her.

She said, "Please contact your superiors and request the release of the workers for farm maintenance. And what about the three comatose workers missing from the refinery?"

"I have no idea what you are talking about."

No point exposing Reanna. "I understand you took them away. Why?"

Chalmers kept his face deliberately blank, but there was anger in his voice. "You're mistaken."

"I can't overlook any details, especially missing people and records about them. I must have access to all possible information. I will require access to your research records and your laboratory."

He was looking distinctly uncomfortable. "That's not possible. My research has nothing to do with workers and their welfare."

"Also I'll need access to the Consortium employees that have been transferred because of this crisis. Not only do we need their expertise, but I must interview them directly. I have the records of their interrogations but no indication where they were sent."

"All that has nothing to do with the current crisis."

"What I need to investigate, whether there is a crisis or not, is mine to decide."

"You'll have to apply to the Consortium management offworld. I don't have that information here."

She leaned over the desk. "Something tells me you know the answer."

His face flushed. "You are seriously overstepping your authority Shankar. I will not discuss this further."

She smiled. She had pushed him far enough for the moment; she could see the rage building. She left abruptly.

Though she finally got access to offworld records, there was nothing useful. The records showed that the replaced staff at the refinery and the mine had been moved to work at Consortium outposts on other planets. To interview them she could go there or try to do it by holotransmit. She suspected she would find Consortium employees with the identities listed, but that they would have had thorough memory deletes and reprogramming if they were indeed the same people. And there was no trace of the three missing workers. Chalmers released lab records showing nothing suspicious, but she had to assume they were not complete.

# Chapter Fourteen

Summoned by Dr. Harold, Nombei was allowed out of the isolation required by the care of her newest charges. When she got to the lab, the original group of depelted beggars were sitting around a table, so she stood outside the doorway, out of their line of sight for a moment. They were dressed in the green uniforms of the Consortium miners and she could see that they had filled out a bit and their skin looked healthier. It was gratifying to see them healing so well that at this distance they looked almost normal. Then she realized that, though she could hear their conversation fairly well, she could not understand what they were saying. She had heard that the beggars had their own lingo—a version of the common dialect spoken in the valley. Even when she recognized some of the words they were using, the meaning of what they were saying escaped her. They did not bother to stop talking as she approached but kept it up as if to taunt her.

Omar Harold came up behind her. "Interesting, isn't it," he said quietly. "Your beggars have developed their own dialect living as they did shunned by other humans. Probably one of the reasons they survive. At least they have each other."

Nombei had often wondered what Pella's life had been like after she left the refinery, but she never liked imagining her as one of the beggars. Now she didn't want to think about Pella's comforting relationships or whether she had sex with other beggars.

She turned to him trying not to show her hurt feelings at being ignored by Pella. "Just tell me what you want me for."

Omar looked at his watch. "Come to...my office."

Nombei turned abruptly and followed him into what had been her own office. Nothing had changed much except the addition of some equipment. Omar sat down at the desk. "The beggars have been oriented and can function normally in the upper caves of the mine. We are now ready for them to go down to retrieve pearl. Pella has volunteered to be the first one and has insisted that you be present. Please don't interfere in any way. Any interference will be a reason to remove you."

Nombei simply nodded, though it was hard not showing him how pleased she was.

Dressed in scratchy insulated silicon fiber uniforms and breathing equipment like miners, Nombei and Omar went to get Pella. Nombei was pleased to see the relief in her dark eyes when Pella saw her. It was all Nombei needed to feel reassured that Pella really wanted her there.

They went into the caves with hand-held lights, following a series of natural volcanic vents that ended in a cavern so vast it was not possible to see the ceiling. The walls closest to Nombei reflected the artificial light in every imaginable color and shape almost as if they glowed. She stepped closer and could see that it was the shells of pearl, coating the stone that reflected the rainbow rich texture.

Omar had assembled a silicon-coated research module in the cavern. Nombei followed him into the module and found a place to sit in the cramped quarters. There was a large visualizer at one end of the module. Nearly every other surface was covered with a bewildering assortment of meters, control buttons, keyboards, recording and interpreting devices.

Pella waited outside while Omar adjusted his equipment and explained to Nombei that he had already analyzed the background ambiance of the cave. Now they were going to track Pella's progress deeper into the mine and analyze the changes in the cave environment to find out what was interfering with the collection of pearl.

Pella did not hesitate for a second when Omar indicated she should go down into the deeper caves. It was almost as if she were eager to go into the hot blackness. Nombei watched the warm red image on the screen as Pella moved through the rocky cavern below.

She pointed to the screen—to a series of kaleidoscopic flashes. "What does that mean?"

Omar's voice was impatient. "You don't really want to know."

Nombei frowned. "Yes I do." Omar sighed and turned away, disinterestedly launching into an obscure and technical lecture about the history of his equipment as he continued to work.

After a few moments Nombei softly put a hand on his arm. "I really do want to know."

Omar stared at her for a moment, evaluating.

Nombei said, "Your language, it's too technical. Surely you can tell me in ordinary language."

Omar dug through the drawers under the monitor and pulled out some coms and a manual. "Work on the vocab. Then ask me again."

Nombei tried not to waste energy being angry. Omar had seemed more sympathetic earlier. But what could she really expect of someone of his privileged caste, no matter what he might claim. She picked up the manuals and began to read.

After a few minutes she looked up at Pella's image still moving into the caves. This session was supposed to be brief, preparing Pella for conditions deeper in the caves, so she was not supposed to go further until the next day—but it looked as if she was already all the way to the chambers that would have pearl.

Then Pella's form bent down and picked something up. She was not supposed to try and collect pearl yet. "Aren't you rushing this?" Nombei asked.

Omar turned away from the visualizer. "We have been preparing her for several days now. She seems quite ready. The analysis has gone well so far and I have still not detected anything unusual."

Pella's shape stooped again to work at a globe of pearl, gently rocking it back and forth to remove it, Nombei noticed a diffuse light-red shape, like a fluttering insect, appear in one of the corners of the visualizer. She asked, "What's that?"

Omar turned back to the visualizer and hurriedly pushed a series of keys, working for an enhancement of the image, but it was still an ephemeral faint fluttering form, with layers of undulating pastel colors. Another shape appeared. The form on the visualizer that was Pella stood as if frozen in time, holding the globe that glistened now as if it were alive.

Omar spoke quietly to Pella. "Come back. Something has appeared just to your left. Move back up the passageway! Pella stooped slowly putting the pearl back, then moved away from the fluttering shapes. Omar repeated, "Come back, now!"

Pointing at some yellow spots on the visualizer, Omar said to Nombei, "These are the fluorescent markers she dropped that lead back here. Watch to make sure she doesn't turn off the path." Then Omar began moving quickly about the module from one piece of equipment after another. Nombei heard him ask Pella what the shapes looked like to her.

Pella did not answer right away. Finally she said in a voice that sounded staticky through the equipment, "I didn't see anything. I felt…a warmth, I heard…something soothing like water on rocks or birds. Now they're gone."

Once they returned to the surface, Pella was hurried off; Nombei would not see her again until the next day.

# Chapter Fifteen

When she returned to the mine Sonja found a message from Julie, a formal invitation to tea printed on fauxpaper with a border of flowers in nineteenth century Victorian style, a drawing of a little black dog in one corner. Sonja looked at it for a long moment. Did she have time for this…dalliance? Did she really believe Julie could tell her anything, even if she was foolish enough to risk the…situation? It did give her access to Chalmers' household. But then she really had no choice—she could feel her heart beating in her throat as she answered the summons.

Julie was in her favorite alcove. In the dusky light Sonja could see the rocky rim above the steamy rift valley and across to distant white-capped mountains.

The little dog greeted Sonja, accepted her petting, then curled up between them on the little gold-embroidered love seat. Julie was wearing a flattering blue-green satin dress that matched her eyes. She said, a bit petulantly, "You've been very busy—too busy to visit me?"

"I wasn't sure I would be welcomed in this household after—"

"Don't start lying now. You know I don't care what Chalm thinks."

"Does he know I'm here?"

Julie shook her head, looking like a Dolmara Catlizard that has just eaten the family pet tarantula. "And I made sure there are no recording devices, this time. He usually doesn't bother, but with you—" She leaned closer and whispered confidentially, "I'm supposed to find out about you—keep track for him. He hasn't a clue I'm on to his game. I'm sick of him and his conspiracies."

Sonja took a deep breath. She would have to be on her guard. She remembered her resolve to be honest, and her rationalization that it would get her more information. But really…she did want to trust Julie, even try to help her. She recognized the sentiment was informed by sexual attraction, but in the end she would be the one in control.

Sonja smiled. "What you call lying is part of my job. I'm not sure I can tell the truth in any way you would recognize."

Julie laughed and kissed her almost gleefully. "Saying that is more truth than I have heard in years. Nobody dares tell me the truth. The more I demand it the more they lie, thinking to protect themselves. You do understand how much I need…someone like you. Someone who doesn't have to lie to me because they are afraid of me." She laughed bitterly. "Even Chalm always lies. He can't help himself. He doesn't really know what truth is. He couldn't tell the truth if his life depended on it."

"I can't imagine what your life must be like. I know what you mean, though. I would like someone in my life I could be honest with—that could be honest with me." Sonja was shocked to feel herself flush. She had thought to say it to win Julie's trust. She hadn't known until she said it that she really felt that way. Once again she reminded herself to be careful.

Julie went on sadly. "And you can't really trust me either, because of who I am. You're right. But I don't expect you to reveal any secrets—even though that's what Chalm expects me to get from you. I've done it before, but mostly out of boredom and because he threatens to take my dog away."

She leaned against Sonja seductively and touched her lips to Sonja's gently. "But this moment is purely for my pleasure. I don't care about Chalm…. I'll tell you anything I know. Every secret. And I don't care what you tell me or don't tell me."

It was all too easy. She kissed Julie, a long slow kiss. Her lips were…so soft, electric.

"A game," Sonja said in a whisper against Julie's ear. "A kiss for a truth."

Julie laughed and kissed Sonja.

"So tell me, then, what happened to the missing pearl?"

Julie looked thoughtful. "You think I don't know anything. You're right, I don't know much about pearl except that a lot of people would be better off if it hadn't been discovered in the first place. What I know won't help you find it."

Sonja kissed Julie again. Her ability to think in words was melting away.

Julie laughed. "I wonder if I had something important to tell you whether you would hear it? Most people only see me for what they want me to be and don't listen to what I say. You all think my brains were left out along with my gut."

Sonja shook her head, but she had to admit Julie was probably right. Would she give much credibility to what Julie thought? At best she expected to get gossip, leads, an overheard comment from Chalmers or his staff, but she didn't expect Julie to understand the situation. Was she wrong?

Julie wrapped a soft silken quilt around herself. "What I know is that pearl is too important for its loss to be just an economic crisis for the Consortium. What truth I can give you is just some questions."

Sonja sat back, waiting.

Julie kissed her softly and asked, "Why did my Uncles send just one person, you, to investigate this late in the crisis? Why the secrecy? Other intoxicants are sold openly on the market. If their supply was threatened the Consortium would send an army to catch the thieves or would close down the operation and go elsewhere for profitable substances. Even Chalm does not know why the Consortium, the Family, cares so much about pearl. He thinks they're making such a fuss because they're addicted and sees it as an opportunity to get ahead himself."

Sonja leaned over to return the kiss, but Julie turned away, whispering. "I want what you promised."

"It's true you are incredibly beautiful…and sexy…and smart."

Julie did not look at her. She studied a vein in her delicate hand, waiting.

"They are good questions but—"

"But not good enough to earn some truth from you."

"What do you want to know?"

Julie smiled and moved closer. "Never mind. Your body will have to be truth enough for now."

After Sonja left the Earthdome and returned to the sterility of her quarters some part of her mind, the part not still wrapped up in a satin glow of pleasure, cursed her for a fool. Even if Julie wasn't part of Chalmers' schemes, she was too protected and too vulnerable to be a good source of information.

Also, she was beginning to care too much for this child-woman. If Sonja did get incriminating evidence against Chalmers through Julie, she would have to use it. She didn't like to think what he might do. And if Chalmers was behind the pearl theft, even Julie's family would not help them. She wanted very badly for Julie to be innocent. And that was a problem. Sonja would have to make herself stay away if Julie was to be safe, guilty or not.

# Chapter Sixteen

Omar Harold was going over the recordings, watching the session with Pella again. On the visualizer the fluttering images began to form and then grow stronger. This time Omar turned on a range of output formats he had not used before. One never eliminated a possible source of information, however remote.

He was even more convinced than before that what he was seeing had to be electronic projections of some sort. Human-generated, of course, very cleverly done.

Omar dampened the frequencies of Pella's life functions and human thought patterns to try and identify the fluttery shapes for what they really were. Curiously enough, faint consistent thought-like signals did show up—but not like any human signals he had ever seen. Had he misread the life function meter? Still, in spite of the life-like images on the visualizer, there were no life functions detectable. Except for Pella there was nothing alive there. He checked once again that the signals were not coming from Pella. The signals were clearly coming from the fluttering shapes. If people were projecting this phenomenon he could not figure out how. The only detectible source were the things themselves.

He switched on the translator, then worked to adjust the system, did some tests, and focused on the strongest emotion-tainted signal. There was a sudden spike on the meters. He readjusted. The readings were in the ranges he was used to from the workgrubs...only much more complex. Workgrubs here in these dry hot caves? But if they were, their life function should show. And the environment of those caves would destroy workgrubs. They were born and went to die in the cool caves at the edge of the rift valley. He banged the life function equipment in frustration. Was there something wrong with it? He did a check. It had to be malfunctioning. But he could find nothing wrong.

He reviewed the recording several more times, then sat staring at the readout panel. There was no evidence of anything living, yet signals that usually meant some sort of thought process were still strong. Here in the cave, not projected from somewhere else.

He focused in to get more details. If only he had the full capacity of his machines at homebase—this damn portable model—

He switched to the text mode to see if anything showed up that might be interpreted as symbolic. A burst of images, strange, unfamiliar…not texts or recognizable images but regular patterns. He switched to auditory. Nothing but crackling….Wait—a high pitched scratching sound. Were there repeated sound patterns? With the decoder he did an automatic search for matching patterns which might be symbolic.

The machine reported more regular repeating complex patterns. This had to be what Sonja Shankar was looking for—some sort of communication, purposeful or accidental, by whomever was systematically sabotaging and moving pearl. There could be coded messages here, if he could break the code. Excited, he scanned for an analysis.

Finally, after a several hours of frantic research, Omar sat stunned. If this was a symbolic system it did not resemble any that had been encountered so far in the exploration of the universe. No matter how clever people were, he doubted that they would be able to invent anything like this. Omar took a deep breath. He realized he wanted it to be a whole new system to decode. He smiled. It would take a long time, of course. But what a project!

But if this was not human-generated— He frowned. No creature he was aware of could live in those overheated depths.

Just finding a living organism that could thrive in this environment would be a feather in his cap. But this thing was not the organic, carbon-based life he had encountered before. Perhaps he had come across some sort of archaeological recording, a residue from some long forgotten civilization. Perhaps the trouble in the mine was the result of some residual protective devices left by some long dead species—

He turned back to his equipment, pleased with his theory, dreaming about the accolades he would receive for decoding the newly discovered history of a long dead civilization.

He sighed. There would be no way to tell the accuracy of any translation that this machine might approximate now. The problem, as with most human-manufactured equipment, was that there was the intrinsic prejudices of human holographic thought process built in. This machine tended to interpret in human terms. He wanted badly to have access to his home laboratory with its more sophisticated equipment.

Still, such a discovery would make his reputation in the competitive world of science. He settled down to work. Native to the planet or alien here, it did not matter to him. What mattered was its newness to humans and its complexity. It could mean a lifetime of exciting, engrossing research.

As the visualizer surged and throbbed before him, he wondered how long it would take before he could report this to the scientific community. He would have to come up with a plausible theoretical framework. Had some lost civilization invented the intoxicant pearl for their own use? An intriguing idea.

Then he remembered the circumstances. The dream faded. The Consortium would not want to believe a sentient intelligence was on the planet. Any evidence of a possible new sentient life form, long dead or still alive, would bring a full investigation by the Galactic League, not one lone investigator like Shankar. They would likely declare the cave protected archaeological remains. That would mean the end of pearl mining. The Consortium officials had obviously suspected something. Was that why he was here? Would he even be allowed the chance—time to fully analyze the data. Suddenly he was frightened. Would they even let him make a report to his other scientists or the League? Suddenly he remembered they hadn't brought him here to translate and do basic research, he was here to identify whatever it was so they could find a way to destroy—

And what did the…intelligence sending these signals have to do with pearl? Now he hoped they were not native to this planet; then, if the Consortium destroyed what was here, it would still exist somewhere.

He went back to his analysis, a bit desperate now. The Consortium obviously suspected human sabotage. It might well be in his interest not to change their minds about that. It would give him more time. If only he had someone to trust—to talk to. If there was sentient life other than humans involved…if only he had more time.

Omar finally left the module very late, exhausted. He hadn't made much progress in his analysis.

Nombei was in the office still poring over the manuals. Omar ignored her and lay down on a couch and closed his eyes. They ached dully and he felt nauseated. He knew he should try to eat, but the thought of reconstituted Nutro was too much and the cafeteria would long ago have been closed.

After a while the smell of hot, fresh cooked food touched his nostrils and he looked up to see Nombei spreading a clean cloth on the desk and putting out a plate of hot stew with fresh vegetables.

After Omar had revived a little, Nombei began to ask questions. Omar realized that the woman actually had learned some technical terms. Maybe the creature could be of some help. It would be good to have a little assistance now with this overwhelming turn of events.

# Chapter Seventeen

Julie showed up at the mine the next day in a small but stylish personal hovi. A very nervous official showed her to Sonja's office.

Annoyed at the interruption of her investigation, Sonja came into her office ready to scold Julie for her indiscretion. But before she could speak Julie looked up at the walls, shifting her eyes questioningly. Sonja had checked already for listening devices but Julie was right to be cautious. She waited for Julie to speak.

"I haven't been here before. It's not as bad as they say." Julie laughed. "Now that nothing's operating and most of the tiresome officials aren't here. I know. I was told you weren't to be interrupted. But you work much too hard. I've come to take you on a little outing." When Sonja shook her head, Julie said teasingly, "We won't be gone long. Come on, I'll give you a ride in my little machine. And maybe you'll even find a few clues."

Sonja had looked at just about everything within a several hundred mile radius of the mine in her investigation, as well as studying earlier searches, but the way Julie looked at her made her suspect that there was more to this little tryst than just a luncheon outing. It would be rude to refuse and might draw too much attention as well, so she smiled and said, "Thanks, I could use a break."

Between the mine entrance and her vehicle, Julie took her arm and whispered, quickly, "Chalm found out from the staff that you visited me yesterday. I thought they were loyal to me. I...sent them away."

To Sonja's look she said, "Don't worry, Chalm will find other work for them. He'll be listening in the hovi. We'll get out somewhere. I brought you some food. You can have a picnic."

Out in the open desert with the mountains purple and white in the distance, Julie shivered even in her thermal environmental suit. But she pulled off her mask and very proudly showed Sonja that she could breathe without its extra oxygen. "My metabolism is different. I don't need as much of anything. Just like being designed not to need so much food. I use less water, too." She valiantly laid out Sonja's lunch on the flattest rock she could find, all the while talking quickly. "Chalm got mad because I didn't tell him about our little tea party yesterday. He can be very nasty when he lets himself be."

Sonja frowned. "He wouldn't hurt you?"

Julie laughed. "He's mostly bluster and empty threats as far as I'm concerned. He's too afraid of my family even here. He'll take it out on some poor service person, no doubt. Then she looked down sadly. "I would have left him, the situation, already if I had any place to go. But the Family wouldn't support me, alone. They can't be bothered. He threatened to take away my dog and send me back to the Family. He wouldn't dare send me back. They would dump him faster than a robo can clean a pit. But dogs are not approved by the Family. The Family would just ignore me if I complained, and he would get into trouble with the Galaxy authorities for letting me have a dog. He says I can keep Pet if I get information out of you. Can you say something in the hovi on the way back that will get me off the hook?"

"What do you think he wants to know about me? We're supposed to be on the same side, solving the same problem."

Julie shrugged and touched her lips to a fruit, sniffing it longingly, then handed it to Sonja. "He wants something that will get rid of you, I think, something he can show the authorities that will get you called off. He says he wants to be the one to solve the problem and that you're too smart for your own good."

"I thought about your questions. The answers to them won't find the missing pearl. What is it that he is afraid I might find out?"

Julie looked at her wistfully. "You're just like the rest. You don't care about me. You and Chalm. All you want is for me to get the other one in trouble. Neither of you really cares about this planet or the Earthdomes or the miners or the poor rats in the refinery, or the poor squatters out in the bush. You only care about winning the competition to solve the problem for your bosses. He doesn't really even care about that. All he cares about is how much profit he will have when he's the one who gets more pearl. Admit it. What you want from me is something that will get him in trouble. You even think he might be the one stealing pearl."

Sonja smiled. "And you care about all that—the miners and the refinery workers and—"

"You're treating me like a child, just like Chalm, as if I couldn't know or care what's going on. I envy the people out in the bush. They have something to work for. Even the miners and the refinery people have something they want that they can work for. You could make that possible for them. Tell your League people that this is a habitable planet. Give the people here a chance to make this a real colony. The Consortium doesn't want that. It would threaten their control of the pearl trade. I want you both to fail finding pearl. Then maybe—" Julie turned away, looking out over the hills.

Julie was right, right to be angry. Whatever little bit of trust that had been building between them was threatened. But the real trouble was that Julie was wrong about one thing—Sonja did care about this woman. Not only because she was beautiful to look at and sexy, but because she was tough, defiant and smart and wanted to know the truth. Julie was closer to being her own equal than most people she met.

"What you say is partly true. But it's much more complex."

Julie didn't look at her, not really listening any more. But Sonja went on. "But to prove I really do care, for you and your honesty…. I will say something he thinks he wants to know about me in the hovi so you can keep your little dog."

Julie looked up, her eyes wary. "And in exchange?"

Did Julie really know what Chalmers was up to? Chalmers would not have given away that much. He must know he couldn't trust Julie not to talk about it. But Julie could find out if she wanted to. And she would want to. Sonja decided to plant that seed of curiosity. She said, "Perhaps, I shouldn't tell you anything. It'll just get you in trouble."

Julie's eyes opened wide in mock horror. "Trouble. Maybe he would even send me away." She smiled, "I wouldn't mind. Especially if they let me take you with me."

Sonja said, "Are the rumors true—that he's cutting up workers to get pearl—that he intends to use the recovered pearl to make a fortune?"

Julie frowned. "That's a frightening suggestion. I don't know the answer, but he might be desperate enough even for that. Try to put that in your report to the League and I wouldn't bet a cred on your chances of surviving very long."

"Killing off a League official would cause him too much trouble."

"You don't get what an isolated piece of dust this planet is. Since the pearl crisis nobody gets off or on unless Chalm lets them. And nobody talks about it, even in the Earthdomes. Might get their pearl rations cut off."

"One thing you must promise me, whatever you find out."

Julie waited.

"If you get in trouble, or think you need help for whatever reason—if you are in danger, please let me know. Please let me help you."

Julie laughed. "The noble knight to the rescue. What could you do? Find me sanctuary where I could survive and they couldn't find me? I don't think so."

"The League would protect you if you gave them information—"

"The League is a joke. You work for the Consortium just like Chalm. You work for my family. They own you."

"The League is an independent organization with the welfare of the human race as its mandate. It doesn't belong—"

"Are you an android or something? They said you were smart. Intelligent— maybe even brilliant. Did they design in some loyalty gene or just program you real well?"

Sonja shook her head; of course she was programmed, trained. She knew the League was not totally above reproach. But—Sonja felt dizzy. The Eminence's words came back to her. However over-simplistic her comment, Julie was right. The Eminences were the head of the Family and they ran the Consortium. Julie was saying that they controlled the League, too.

The combined contempt and despair in Julie's voice had a more profound effect than the words. This from a woman she had thought little more than an adorable but simpleminded child.

Sonja had never really questioned her ability to deal with any situation. Surely there was somewhere Julie could go and live the way she wanted. "Have you petitioned the Family for sanctuary? They could afford to set you up in one of the colonies."

"They tried that before I met Chalm. I couldn't keep my mouth shut. They don't like to be embarrassed. If they think I've crossed them, then I'll have an unfortunate accident. It won't be hard for that to happen—just a few septic bacteria in my feeding tube. That was the fate Chalm saved me from. Don't look so upset. He's not so bad. We have a working bargain—so far. After all, there isn't a colony of people like me out there…soulmates." She laughed bitterly.

Sonja thought of the Godong. Maybe Julie wouldn't be so bitter if she saw that there were people as different from ordinary humans as she was, who were glad to survive even without her resources.

"Come on. I'll introduce you to some people I think you haven't met yet, who you might find interesting—people even you don't know about on this planet."

Julie came around the little cloth she had laid out and put her arms around Sonja and said softly, "Yes, entertain me. You can do that at least."

Sonja told Julie to land the little craft in the spot she remembered from her earlier visit near the almost invisible huts. She climbed out and placed a vessel of water and the remains of the overabundant lunch on a rock. Then she sat down nearby and waited.

Julie stared at her, mystified. "There is nothing here. Nothing but rocks and dust."

Sonja smiled. "Just be patient for a moment."

After a while a narrow face peered out from behind a rock. It was Babe, the child Sonja had met on the earlier trip. Julie gasped and Babe approached cautiously. She came up to Julie and touched her hair, then her dress.

Sonja said to Babe, "Julie wants to meet Mammon. Can you take us?"

Babe whispered to Sonja, "You can't stay. I'm not supposed to talk to you. Some think you offended Gawaya and that you are dangerous. The security people came after you left and took some people away."

"I'm sorry that happened. I'll try to find out where they are and bring them back."

Julie took off a jeweled bracelet, handed it to Babe and said, "Please, we won't stay long."

Babe ran back to one of the huts. Some people filed out and stood chanting fiercely as if their visitors were evil spirits.

Julie asked, "Why is everyone so thin? They're like skeletons, no meat on their bones. Worse than me."

Sonja explained about the genetic engineering that allowed them to survive on the planet without artificial equipment. "Their bodies are designed to need less water and food. Our kind of diet would kill them."

Why had she brought Julie here? Julie did resemble them with their lean, genetically altered forms, but in so many ways she was their opposite.

Babe came back and picked up some of their offering of food and water. "Come on. Mammon will talk to you."

But Mammon was quiet when they went into her hut. Sonja said to her, "This is Governor Chalmers' wife, Contessa Julianna Montclaire." Julie stepped closer.

Mammon stared at her for a moment. "Do you have parents from the Godong?"

"What do you mean?" Julie asked.

Mammon pointed to Babe. "Except for those disastrously light eyes you could be her sister. You're not even wearing an oxygen mask."

Babe said, "But she would go blind here without staying inside when the summer comes and the sun is bright. And she looks so weak she couldn't even work enough to keep herself alive."

Mammon said, "Shush, Babe. The Contessa doesn't need to work to eat, I'm sure."

"I don't eat," said Julie bitterly, "in any way you would recognize."

Both Mammon and Babe looked puzzled. Sonja intervened. "Julie does resemble the Godong in some ways, though she came to be this way for different reasons."

Julie turned to Babe. "What do you like to eat?"

Babe said defensively, "We have lots of things to eat. There is water underground here for our earthcrops and we eat some of the local plants."

Julie sighed. "You're lucky. You have a place where you belong. A place that's yours with other people like you."

Mammon smiled. "You understand a lot, Contessa. This is a place to belong, to be happy with little…if your husband would just leave us alone to live our lives the best we can. Maybe you would persuade him."

Julie nodded. "I'll do what I can. Would you let me visit again? I'll bring you medicine and water, and food."

"Best you stay inside your glass wall, princess. Charity is a dangerous pastime, however amusing. We're better off taking care of ourselves."

Babe quoted proudly, "We are one with the desert. Gawaya gives us the strength and stamina with the gift of this place. We thrive where others would wither."

Mammon said to Sonja, "Security people came here after you left. They gave me medicine but wanted information about you."

"They took people away," Babe said resentfully.

Mammon shrugged. "Just escaped workers on their way outplanet. We couldn't feed them anyway."

"Outplanet?"

"Surely you know about the settlements over the mountains. The Consortium tolerates them if they make it that far."

Sonja nodded.

"They didn't steal your pearl, either. They're lucky if they have enough water to stay alive and have clothes on their backs and a few tools and seeds to scratch in the ground."

Sonja did know. She had seen some of them on her circle around the planet when she first arrived, and the governor's people had investigated them thoroughly. She'd seen the reports. Mammon was right, they didn't have the resources.

The chanting outside was getting louder and there were many more voices.

Mammon looked sad. "You frightened the Gawaya worshippers— they think you offended her trying to touch her, as well as provoking a visit from the security force. Best you leave now."

Before they got to the hovi, Sonja said to Julie, "Your test will be not to tell Chalmers you've been here."

"But then how can I help them? Why did you show them to me if I am not to help them?"

Sonja laughed. "I don't know. You wanted to know more about the planet. Maybe I thought you might need their help." An absurd idea, but Julie looked at her thoughtfully.

# Chapter Eighteen

Omar and Nombei watched the bright figure that represented Pella on the visualizer as she moved quickly and surely down the passage. Then the image stopped abruptly when Pella put down the basket and stood quietly as the fluttering shapes appeared, but this time they swooped and gathered around her, touching her.

After a few minutes recording Omar spoke urgently to Pella, "Remember, you must collect some pearl this time." Pella did not respond but stood quietly. Omar looked at his com. Was it not working? He repeated his message. Pella still didn't respond. Instead she reach out to the shapes, moving her hands as if stroking them. Omar barked, "Now." Pella stooped, quickly put a few pearls into the basket, and moved slowly back up the passageway. The shapes continued to flutter around her and she slowed to a stop. Suddenly the shapes disappeared and the image on the visualizer that was Pella brightened as if the fluttering forms had been swallowed up by her body. She twisted for a second, then fell, lying still. Omar said urgently, "Get up."

They heard Pella whisper, "I can't. Won't…they want the pearl."

Omar hissed, "It' just hallucination because of the fumes. Get some pearl and come back."

Pella whispered again, "They told me; they want it…back."

Omar sat back silently for a moment, then he said quietly to Pella, "Leave the pearl, then. Come back now."

Nombei held her breath, her eyes on the unmoving image on the visualizer. Omar repeated his words firmly. The fluttering images reappeared on the visualizer as if they had come out of Pella's prone body and her image faded slightly. Pella got up slowly. She did not pick up the basket of pearl but instead of going back the way she had come, she moved slowly down the passage following the fading fluttering images, her arms reaching out to them.

"No," Omar shouted. "The other way." Pella ignored him. A red light on the console began to flash. Again Omar shouted, "Come back to us— the other way." Again Pella ignored him. Under his breath Omar said, "I hate to do this." He put his hand on a lever under the light. "You know I have to make you come back," he said, almost to himself. Still Pella persisted in the wrong direction. Omar moved the lever and Pella crumpled. Nombei gasped. Omar said, "Get up now and come back here." Slowly Pella got up and turned, but stood unmoving. "Move." Pella did not move. Omar sighed and again moved the lever that would force Pella back up the correct path.

Nombei said, her heart pounding in her throat, "What happened?"

Omar just shook his head and said, "Watch her and make sure she follows the markers." Then he moved over to the recordings to begin an analysis of the events.

Once again Nombei felt the guilt and pain of her actions; she had saved Pella—for this?

As soon as it was clear Pella was back in the main cavern, Nombei climbed out of the module and ran to her. When Pella saw Nombei she began to fold. Nombei got to her just in time to catch her before she hit the ground. With an arm around her, Nombei helped her walk, grateful now to feel her alive and breathing. But even in the uneven light of her handlight, Nombei could see that Pella's eyes were glazed over. Her skin felt feverish, and there was a peculiar smell, a chemical smell to her skin. It reminded her of the pearl refinery and the peculiar stench that came from the vats.

Then Pella began whispering wildly. The sensual excitement in her voice frightened Nombei. "They went inside. They can go into my mind, my body. So wonderful, so beautiful…so alive. They're alive…forever. Even pearl was never like that."

Nombei said, "What, who are alive? What are they?"

Pella smiled, "The Mothers. One and many." She laughed quietly, kept laughing while Omar hurried over to them.

But rather than trying to call the surface for help, he sat Pella down on a bench near it and ask her, urgently, "What happened? What did you see this time?"

Pella stared at him blankly, her eyes glazed over now. Omar shook her and she collapsed like a rag doll. "Tell me!" he shouted

She roused herself and pulled her arm away, hissing angrily, "You hurt me! You made me come back."

He was still shouting. "You knew that could happen if you went the wrong way. You were going down, not up. There are no markers yet that far down; you could have been lost or died. I'm not sure how far I could track you. What did you see? What happened?"

"I couldn't see anything." Pella looked away and began to shudder as if she were cold, although to Nombei, who took her hand again, her skin felt feverish. Pella turned away from Omar, whispering now, "They went away…gone. They were here…" She put a hand on her chest, "…and now they are gone." There was a desperate sadness in her voice unbearable to Nombei.

"Who…what?" Omar asked.

Pella turned to stare at him. Then her wet, still lashless eyelids lowered. "You want to kill them…destroy them…steal their…pearl." Then Pella was quivering. She pulled her hand from Nombei and reached both hands toward Omar's throat. They all three struggled for a moment, then Pella collapsed unconscious.

It was Omar who was shaking now, but his voice was cold, commanding. "We'll have to carry her."

Back on the surface, after the robots carried Pella away, Nombei was not allowed to see her. All she managed to get out of Omar was that Pella remained unconscious, almost in a coma. It was not the coma typical of accident victims, but rather similar to what had happened to other miners who had gone deeper for pearl. When she asked the medics about it, she was told that those miners had eventually regained consciousness, but, either had little memory of the events leading up to their condition, or were delusional. None of them had ever been able to return to the mine without falling back into unconsciousness. The official had said, "It is exactly what brought the mining to a standstill in the first place."

Nombei wondered what 'delusional' really meant. Very likely the miners had experiences similar to Pella's. She said to Omar, "What Pella said didn't seem delusional to me. I believed what she said—that something went inside her. She wanted to follow it. We saw it too."

They were sitting in Omar's office and he was staring at her, eyes out of focus as if he were looking inside himself and did not even see Nombei. He whispered, "She said that, but it had to be hallucination caused by the fumes. There is no *they* as far as I can tell. Nothing alive anyway. Perhaps some echo from an earlier time or somewhere else."

Nombei asked, "What do you mean?"

Omar shook his head as if coming back to the present. He smiled, embarrassed to be caught off guard. "Nothing, just some silly theories, just daydreaming."

Nombei was whispering now. "What do you mean—echo from an earlier time?"

Omar smiled self-consciously, glanced up at the walls and shook his head. He was right, of course those in charge here would be listening. But Nombei wondered why Dr. Omar Harold didn't want them to know about his theories.

# Chapter Nineteen

Sonja decided the most likely place for some clues to what Chalmers might be up to would be in his lab. But another official visit would be as useless as the last one. Whatever scheme Chalmers was into he needed to hurry it up considering the pressure to resume the pearl trade.

Chalmers was having another dinner party to which she was not invited. Plenty of time for a look at Chalmers' lab while he was entertaining.

She went to the main Earthdome on the pretext of an evening's entertainment in the public rooms next to the lab. She took a private room for the night and rented some of the entertainments that did not require human participation—nothing that would shock or surprise anyone. As far as the staff was concerned she was taking a much-needed break from her investigations.

She had looked up the original plans for this Earthdome. As in the layout of most such places there were hidden service tunnels around each of the public and private rooms connected to the kitchens and storerooms as well as the security section. Around each section were a double set of tunnels. The lab lay at the edge of a section and the public house she was going to visit was in the adjoining section. She was pretty sure that the tunnels around Chalmers' lab were still there, though probably sealed off. Getting into the tunnels was a tricky business, but just possible.

Once inside the room, she turned on the holo she'd ordered so the equipment would have a recording of her participation. At the time she'd designated, a server rang the little bell that warned her he was coming through the server entrance, then entered the dining alcove though its red velvet curtain. She was relieved to see that the server was human not a robot. Everything a robot did was automatically logged. But this was a classier establishment understanding its client's need for privacy.

She stood over him as he uncovered the dishes, then she tasted them and sent some back, hanging over him seductively as he exited, so that she could read the code he put into the small readout lock on the service door. As she had predicted, the eyeprint readout was turned off because of the recent replacement of staff due to the crisis. When he returned with the new dishes, she continued her act of the spoiled and obsessed citizen, and when he came to take away her half-eaten meal she pretended she had a fetish about server clothing and bribed him to let her put on his. She put him naked into the big red satin-covered bed and locked him into the restraints. She could see from the lascivious look he gave her that he would wait patiently for her return. Then she went into the dining alcove, put on his clothing and keyed herself into the tunnel, carrying her dishes on the service tray. She checked the side of the tunnel that should be next to the lab, passing other preoccupied servers in the half dark of the tunnel. If they did suspect something it would take a while for the service personnel to dare to report her. All the entrances on the lab side were sealed—welded shut. No doubt they had alarms as well. She went back to her own alcove, returned the clothing and sent the poor man on his way somewhat confused. But he would not mention the clothing she had borrowed to save his own neck. He would end up on an asteroid if they found out he'd overstepped his role.

She waited until the earthtime-obsessed techs and dome citizens would be most likely to take a break and sleep, then entered the service tunnel again. There were no servers in sight. If she was lucky she could open a sealed entrance to the lab in a section where no people were working at the moment. Just a little time, that's all she needed.

She dismantled the alarm system, one of the first lessons in her training. The seal around the door was a more difficult problem. She tried cutting it with her laser. No luck with the seal but the door itself was vulnerable. She cut a hole just big enough to squeeze through and was in the tunnel running along the side of the lab. The doorways into the labs were not sealed off. She'd thought the tunnels were only used for emergency. The tunnels were in fact being used as access to the labs.

There were a few labs with lights on. She tried the dark ones first, but found nothing useful. Chalmers had told her he put everything in this part of the lab into the analysis of pearl. It seemed a waste to try to synthesize it, but she could find no evidence that was not what he was doing. She wondered how he managed to get enough pearl to continue his research during the crisis.

There was one lab devoted to experimental toxins and another one to various explosive devices. What in Scorpio did he have in mind?

Finally she found a refrigeration unit in the tunnel itself in an area sealed off from the rest of the tunnel. She'd already been inside the lab too long when she finally managed to break the code on the unit. What was left of three pearl-comatose people lay on shelves inside. She thought about Reanna's comment that Chalmers had taken blood and even bits of flesh from refinery workers. What she'd been told were attempts at synthesizing pearl might well be something else. If Chalmers was convinced he could salvage and sell pearl from the bodies of pearl-poisoned workers, then the unavailability of the real stuff might actually enhance such a scheme. Did he even intend to keep his recycling plan from the Consortium and get rich himself? No wonder he wasn't cooperating with her investigation. She should have guessed earlier that anything he didn't want officialdom to see he would hide in the tunnels. She would expose Chalmers' nasty research. But it was not necessary to prove that to the League. Doing research with the bodies of the workers was sufficient. This should go to the Galactic League's ethics committee. She would try again to send in a report as soon as she could get to moonbase and she would request that they forward a complaint to the Consortium about Chalmers' treatment of the workers. She suspected now that her difficulties transmitting a report were not accidental.

She took some comsnaps quickly. Looked for lab notes She was suddenly aware of the sound of people running in the distance. Opening the refrigerator might have set off some sort of alarm she hadn't detected, but probably someone had discovered the hole she had cut in the door. She slipped down the tunnel in the opposite direction from the sound. The tunnel took her around to the outside of the lab. Luckily the guard on the outside door had been distracted by the commotion and was away from his post. She slipped into the public corridor and waited until he returned. Then she rushed up to him and waved her identification at him saying, "What's going on here, soldier?"

"I don't know Investigator, some sort of breach of the restricted tunnel, I understand."

"Has this been reported to the Governor?"

"No, the Major said not to bother him unless it was necessary."

"Call him."

"But, my orders were—"

"Call him now." The man saluted, turned and went to an emergency call box.

It gave Sonja a certain satisfaction to wake Chalmers in the middle of his earthnight. He merely grunted his agreement that she should take charge but said he was coming in. She presented her credentials to the Major and found that it was the cut door that'd been reported by a server. So they didn't know that the refrigeration unit had been opened.

When Chalmers finally arrived, sleepy-eyed and angry, the Major apologized for disturbing him. Chalmers eyed Sonja suspiciously, but said nothing in front of his security people. She left him inspecting the cut in the door and checked out of her room.

Chalmers might eventually find out she had been in the public rooms for the evening. She was curious what Chalmers would do if he ever figured out that she knew about his secret research. For the moment she would not mention her little exploration in the lab.

Meanwhile, she would need to do something to keep Chalmers away from the refinery and its vulnerable workers. Instead of returning to the mine she took her hovi directly to the refinery. She found Reanna had organized the workers to care for themselves and they were functioning quite independently of the few staff and fewer guards in residence. Sonja was glad to see that Chalmers had taken her suggestion of reducing staff. There was no pearl here to protect at the moment and where could the workers go were they crazy enough to try to leave the refinery. She explained to Reanna that she might have been right about Chalmers' use of the comatose workers and that she might need to recruit other workers to help resist Chalmers' plans to use them.

Reanna laughed. "You're telling us to commit suicide. If we did anything like that, they would put us in the recycler faster than a hoschalk—"

"The authority of the League is behind me. I authorize you to—"

"Easy for you to say. They wouldn't fry you. The League is nothing here."

"I'm just telling you there is no one here who will protect you. You have to do it yourselves. I'll do what I can."

When she tried to take a shuttle to moonbase to send in a report she was told that the shuttles were temporarily shut down because of a security breech at the Earthdome. When she tried to contact Chalmers he was unavailable. She contacted moonbase by com and left an encripted message to be forwarded to the League, wondering if even that would get sent. She had an hologram appointment with a Consortium official scheduled for a few days from now. Chalmers wouldn't dare interfere with that would he?

The next evening she went out to keep her date with Georgio, disguised as Darleen, taking the usual precautions not to let mine staff know where she'd gone. Undercover meant just that. Any sources of information she found had to feel secure. If she had the luck to contact anyone who knew what had happened to the missing pearl, they would have the means of detecting surveillance equipment.

Georgio was standing at the bar with a man in a silver cape and soft boots made with the skin of a canta lizard from her home planet. The boots looked familiar—just like the boots she had once given Mark. She looked at the man more carefully before she approached them. It was Mark, her schoolmate, the one who had helped her with the Godong. He'd been onplanet all the time. That was why it had been so easy to contact him the first time. She should have figured it out then.

She sat down next to him. She wondered if he had known all along that she was Darleen. There was certainly no reason to think she could fool him now. He knew her too well.

She saw the humor in the situation. He studied her for a long moment and played along with her Darleen persona, taking her to a booth and sending Georgio for drinks. "I should have guessed it would be you. I'm actually not disappointed, though I had planned on the creds I was going to squeeze out of poor Darleen, Georgio's great find. Pickings have been lean lately."

"I thought you weren't interested in the pearl trade."

"I lied. Do you mind?"

"Still some out there, then?"

"Huniman has a stash—and connections. If you are looking for a new source you're out of luck. Nothing, not even crude, showing up in the black market. Why do you think I'm stuck on this piece of turd planet?"

"I didn't know you were."

Georgio came back with their drinks and Mark waved him away. He took her hand. "It's a miserable existence here, but I've got one compensation, a suite here at Huniman's. We can have a good time." He looked down at his drink. "It may be our last. You're in trouble here, you know. The powers that be are desperate to get rid of you."

"Chalmers has sent out the word, has he? It doesn't matter. He knows I can't stop him doing what he wants here. I can't even get reports through. You got access to holotransmit I can use?"

He shook his head, but still didn't look at her. "Consortium's got it all tied up right now. That's why they want to get you, before you make a report. You're not safe, Orris blossom. I'll bet you even came here without any backup. You should be more careful."

She was disappointed and feeling really tired. Maybe she should go to Mark's suite, if only to take a break. "Don't worry, Mark, you're safe. They don't know where I am. You're sure you haven't got anything for me?"

At last he looked at her. "Lets go to my rooms and have some fun while we can."

She sighed. "I'd better go. I hoped Georgio would—"

"Show you where the missing pearl was hidden?"

"I know, nothing is that easy. But I wanted something, a lead."

He looked away. "Just for you—I can show you something. It's not much, but—"

She grabbed his arm. "You've been holding out on me."

He smiled but looked away again. "You could say that. Or saving you."

"Which means?"

"It's dangerous. I like you well enough to warn you. Go back to your safe, security-force protected mine."

"You're teasing me. When have I ever been afraid of a little risk?"

He didn't respond, but got up and took her arm.

It was Georgio driving Mark's hovi. Why wasn't she surprised? Georgio gave her a worried look when she got in, but said nothing as they left the complex. She felt sleepy. She would just take a little nap.

Sonja woke up in the dark. She was lying on something hard, she was naked and it was chilly. There was a tiny light source off to her left, very close. She moved toward it and bumped her head which already ached—something strange had been in that last drink.

She felt a jolt of fear and felt around her. She was in a very small space, but felt some air coming in. She followed its path above her on the smooth surface, touched a tiny vent. She checked in every direction—a very confined space. The surface under her was body conforming, but for someone larger. Gravity felt normal. She was in some sort of medical or restraint capsule.

Mark had drugged her, but she hadn't been harmed. What was he after? She'd always assumed he indulged in black market goods. How else did he live so extravagantly? But everything about a League employee was traceable and therefore not safe to sell. Even her inti implant wasn't worth enough—not enough to risk the wrath of the League.

She suppressed her rising panic. She had to relax—to think. She was dispensable as far as the League was concerned. But her training and outfitting had been expensive; the League would note her absence and follow up on her disappearance. But when?

Then she tried to reassure herself. Of course, it had to be a little joke of Mark's to show her how vulnerable she was. She sighed. Best to just wait. After all, she hadn't had any real rest for a while. After what seemed like an eternity of worrying she finally fell asleep.

The next time she woke up it was to a light so bright she wanted to shield her eyes but her arms and legs were restrained by straps.

Mark was looking down at her through a window in the capsule, his unsmiling, brightly lit face barely familiar. "Now you really are mine," he said, satisfaction in his voice. She heard this distantly through some sort of intercom. Then he did smile briefly. "You don't look scared. You really do trust me. You shouldn't."

She sighed. "I trust your sense of self-preservation."

"Oh you think the League will care if you disappear."

"You'll be the first place they look."

"But there will be no evidence of you, thanks to you."

"They'll know you were the last person I saw."

Then he laughed. "You took care of that for me. Remember, I was once one of you. I had the training; I know the drill; protect your sources, make them feel safe because you aren't."

"What's in it for you? The Consortium paying you to get rid of me?"

He said, "I know about the nano-computer thingy in your body—cell based technology. Maybe even quantum. That alone is worth a fortune for somebody who knows how to use it. But League techies can't read it where you are. Shielding on this capsule is state-of-the-art. They won't be able to find you even if they want to." He patted the capsule's thick, hard surface.

"What do you want?"

"Nothing *you* can get me."

"The  Consortium did hire you to get rid of me," she guessed.

"You're just too good at your job—the one for the League. The Eminences don't think you're doing what *they* told you. They tried to tell you. You had no choice but to cooperate. Pearl, you know, its their life blood. Can't mess with that."

He sighed, but his sympathetic smile was false; a glint of triumph was in his eyes. "I know, we were buddies—sex and all. But, Orris blossom, I'm the guy that got kicked out of the institute, the one not good enough, not like you and what was his name—your best buddy, the one you liked best—Jason. Especially that Jason." He leaned closer, his voice a whispered hiss. "I heard he was here onplanet, visiting your lover, Viol."

Viol…Jason. He was reaching. Neither of them could be anywhere near the pearl planet. She felt a surge of hope. He had said here onplanet. That meant they hadn't taken her very far.

When Sonja said nothing. Mark said in a gleeful rage, "He's dead, you know—the real Jason. The one here is just a clone—a copy, not even an agent, just a look-alike to please Viol. Looks a lot like the old Jason. Five years ago they burned that Jason—all of him—contrary brain, perfect tan, brown eyes and blond hair. He was a traitor to the League—tried to leave the service." Mark laughed. "No little nano-computer left from that sucker to get anybody in trouble."

She felt a profound sadness. She did care about Jason. She hoped Mark was lying about his death. But particularly if Jason were alive and not a clone she would never see him again. Agents trained together in the institute never worked together even when they hadn't known each other well. It was against League policy. Mark had been an exception because he never became an official agent.

Mark laughed for a long time. Then he leaned even closer to the window. "Now you know how I really feel. I've waited a long time for this day." His eyes narrowed greedily. "I wish I had all of you here, so smug, so successful. But you'll have to do."

"So why haven't you burned me already?"

"And miss this opportunity to let you know how I really feel?"

"So what will you use? Burning is risky; the temperatures you'll need to destroy—my equipment and recordings—are detectable. An explosion would give you away. Is this a space capsule? Going to put me out in space in deep freeze? Recoverable records still in my brain?"

The window snapped shut and she was in the dark and silence again. She shouted, "How long are you going to keep me here? I have to pee." She felt an automatic toilet unit move up between her legs. At least he could still hear her. There would be a feeding device, too, if she asked for it. She shouted, "You could at least take off the restraints." The ones on her arms and neck loosened. He was not in any hurry to kill her. Not much comfort if she was stuck here forever.

# Chapter Twenty

Omar took more of the former beggars into the caves. It pleased Nombei, in spite of her worry about Pella, that Omar again brought her along. It was an admission that she'd learned enough to be useful.

Nombei had spent every waking moment she could with the texts and guides that Omar had given her. She didn't begin to understand it all, but what she did understand was amazing. The equipment in the module incorporated all the latest understandings gathered from the study of other brain systems discovered in the galaxy. The translations were compromised in their analysis by the limitation of humans and their unique thinking processes. But this new equipment could even translate some alien mental images, memory complexes, and holograms into human language phrases.

She'd often wondered if her leaves were more intelligent than anyone thought. They seemed smart to her. She wondered what this machine would say about them.

What was Dr. Harold looking for in the caves? If there were something intelligent besides people what did that mean…? What had Pella experienced? Maybe it wasn't hallucinations induced by fumes.

The man insisted on being called by his beggar name, Ghoul. He had the typical short stocky build of the earthwarrens and his skin was still healing from the pelt, a mottled, scarred wreck, but he was cheerful and relatively sane, joking about how this was a lot better place, cushy, compared to beggaring in the valley's jungle-bush. Except for his accent, he could have been Nombei's cousin.

They went through the same routine that they had gone through with Pella, but Ghoul had none of Pella's reluctance. He went down as quickly as possible, gathered some pearl and getting out even before the fluttering shapes began to form on the visualizer. But he obviously felt something as he ran up the passageway. He came all the way back followed by a blast of heat that almost knocked Nombei over when she went to help him.

He had managed to bring some pearl back with him but fell unconscious at their feet. They took him to the surface to the robot medics.

It wasn't till the next day that he was coherent enough to talk. Omar asked him what he had seen and experienced and he said, "Moved too fast to think. Didn't see nothing but black and red hot rock. Suddenly got damn hot. Hot as the center of a black hole. Stunk too. Sulfur and brimstone." He laughed and said, proud of himself, "My brain, she got addled, lights and all, but I'm used to that with pearl."

When Investigator Shankar was not at a scheduled meeting, Omar sent the report about their progress collecting pearl to Governor Chalmers. Later in the day a member of Chalmers' staff showed up with congratulations on their success in retrieving some pearl. "We are pleased that you are ready to accelerate the pearl gathering."

Omar was annoyed. He didn't usually care enough to dislike officials, but this one's presumption was irritating. He didn't want to discuss the evidence that there might be some sort of nonhuman intelligence in the cave. He didn't want to think about what the Consortium might be tempted to do. He said, "It's entirely premature to do anything but observe at this point. The beggar barely managed to stay uncooked. The first one is still delirious. I need time to determine—"

The official's eyes narrowed. "There is no time. Our techs say the cave is getting hotter and more poisonous. We must move quickly if we are to save what is left of pearl."

Omar asked, "Do you know who's stealing pearl? Are there people—?"

"Investigator Shankar has eliminated the possibility of sabotage by local people—you have not given us conclusive evidence of outside human intervention. Our probs indicate that what pearl was removed was not significant. What we primarily require of you now is your work with the beggars to gather pearl."

"Is there no one on Governor Chalmers' staff with sufficient experience of the caves to monitor the beggars?"

The man's face blanched. He shook his head.

They were all afraid of the caves. That gave him a bit of advantage. Time to push. "I haven't finished my research. I agree with you, there is nothing alive in the cave—in the conventional sense, people or otherwise. But I have observed some sort of inorganic electromagnetic phenomenon, perhaps generated by heat and chemical reaction in those hot caves. The fumes do cause some …illusion, even delusion perhaps. But there is something else. There are organized signals—an implication of symbolism, deliberate—"

The woman's eyes narrowed. "We've followed your research. We know what you've seen."

Omar turned away, offended. But he should have expected it. What could he say? Why should he be surprised that they had his research notes long before he was even ready to state a thesis?

The official said threateningly, "We can find another technician to follow through with the program."

"But even the fact the living things have been spared when machines have not implies intelligence. And I've detected…what appears to be an organized symbolic system…triggered by the presence of humans in the caves. Omar took a deep breath. "It seems possible—pearl might be…some sort of archaeological residue. Left by some intelligent life—"

The official stepped closer and Omar moved back, afraid that the woman might try to touch him. The woman's voice was low now, almost sweet. "Good. Now we want you to find out what it is and how we can stop it…without destroying pearl. Congratulations. The Governor is very excited by your work. We'll be following your progress…closely."

The next morning Nombei was shocked to find that Pella was the beggar waiting for them in an environmental suit. Pella did not turn to watch them as they approached but stood very still, facing the passageway into the mine that she would soon be entering. Before they went down the narrow dark passage Nombei looked into Pella's eyes. They were open wide but were out of focus as if she was seeing nothing. Nombei said. "Why are you here? If you go down you'll just fall back into a coma."

Pella hissed. "Leave me alone. I want this." Now her eyes held an angry glint that Nombei had seen before—the day that Pella had left—so long ago. Nombei felt tears in her throat as Pella turned her back.

They walked silently down the long passage following Omar's lamp. Once they were near the module, Nombei again confronted Pella urging her not to go down.

From the doorway of the module Omar said impatiently, "She won't be harmed. It's her own decision to go down today. Come in here now. I'm ready to begin." He went in.

Pella had already gone around Nombei and was going steadily toward the passageway. Nombei slowly climbed into the module. Pella's warm red shape was already visible on the screen moving down. Halfway down she stopped and sat down.

Omar hissed into the com, "What's wrong? Keep moving." There was silence. He said under his breath, disappointment in his voice, "I should have used a different beggar." When Pella didn't move he said, "Come back. I'll send someone else." Pella still did not move. Omar sighed. "I don't want to hurt you—"

Pella stood up slowly. What was she doing?

Omar almost shouted, "Damn her to a black hole. She is taking off her suit! I won't be able to bring her back like last time. She'll die of heat prostration before we can get her out of there."

Nombei's heart started to pound and she felt helpless as Omar continued shouting at Pella.

Pella was ignoring him. She sat back down, a bright red shape huddled on the floor of the cave.

Then Nombei heard faintly, "Good-bye Nombei. Thanks for trying. I'm going home now." Then there was a flash on the visualizer and the light that indicated Pella's com went out.

Pulling on a thermal suit, Nombei headed for the door. "I'm going to get her."

Omar handed her a com and light and a thermoblanket with a respirator. "Follow the lights that mark the passage. Keep the com on and cover her with the blanket. It will keep her alive till we can get her out of there."

Nombei hardly noticed how she got there, but found herself next to Pella's suit staring at a white shape on the cave floor. She reached down. A powdery white ash formed the shape of what had once been a human. She squatted, staring for a long time at the curve of a white powder hand, a perfect work of art…until Omar led her away.

Nombei sat watching the enhanced record of what had happened to Pella over and over while Omar went to report to the mine officials about this new turn of events.

As Nombei watched Pella's form fill the visualizer, every detail of her body pulsed in rainbow colors. She sat, her long legs folded under her, her arms upheld as if she were waiting to embrace someone. The translucent flying forms gathered around her, almost seeming to caress her. Then she stood, reaching out to them. Again there was the brightening flash and Pella disappeared. Again Nombei saw the white ash. Pella was gone—really gone this time. Dead. Somehow the fluttering things had killed her.

Nombei let her rage push back her grief. She wanted vengeance. The things had lured Pella back, then killed her. None of the other miners had died that way. Others who had gone for pearl had been left alive, if sometimes in a coma or mad. It wasn't fair. Why did Pella have to be different? It was Omar's fault, too. He shouldn't have sent her.

When Julie did not hear from Sonja she went to the mine again looking for her. The staff confirmed that she'd been gone a day and a half and had left no instructions or messages. No one at the mine seemed concerned, though Sonja's hovi was in its place. When pressed, the staff said it had been returned unoccupied in the morning. Julie left a message for Sonja in her apartment and told the staff to inform her as soon as Sonja got back.

When she got no messages by evening, she went to Chalmers.

All he would say was, "For once I am not responsible for your misery. I have no idea where she is. Snooping around where she shouldn't, no doubt."

In her dark capsule Sonja had had plenty of time to think about how to get herself out of her plight. Clever of Mark to take her clothes, but he wasn't as up on the latest technology as he thought. She did have a cell-based nanocomputer with information that included the construction of capsules. She explored the inside of the capsule with her supersensitive fingers looking for door seams, locks, codes. It wasn't a typical medical capsule, used for maintaining patients until they could get intervention—which would be was powerfully constructed and complex. This was more like a punitive capsule used to contain violent criminals for transport. There were only four or five types of those being manufactured. Unfortunately the codes for opening the doors of this type of capsule were randomly placed. Fortunately her inticeptor was sensitive enough to feel the slight electromagnetic force used to keep it locked. When she'd traced the slight crack of the door with her finger she ran the edge of her ear along it until she located the locking mechanism with her inticeptor. Very sophisticated. Probably supplied by the Consortium just for this job. Clever of Chalmers to find out that Mark was a friend and recruit him. She spent a long time trying to read and decode the locks.

The capsule was well constructed, but she was not defeated. What Mark had also not known was that she had recently been outfitted with tiny lasers in a fingernail powered by her own body's cells. She hoped she could generate enough power to open up the door a crack so that she could read the lock better. Using the lasers was a slow process. It took a long time to recharge with the limited electrical power her body cells produced.

She finally did read and decode the locking mechanism. Now it was time to tell it to unlock. If she was on a planet's surface she could just step out. She was likely on a planet because she could feel some gravity. The surface of one of the moons would have had practically no gravity. If she'd been launched into space, when she opened the door at least her death would be quick. Even if she were on an asteroid she would die quickly from cold and no oxygen. She waited, her heart beating wildly. Maybe Mark would come back. She would wait just a little longer.

While Sonja waited, Nombei and Omar again sat in front of the monitor in the cave. Nombei had said nothing more about Pella. She had decided to keep her anger, blame and sadness to herself. Pella was gone. In reality Pella had been gone a long time. The brief rescue from being a beggar hadn't been Pella's wish.

So when the next beggar was sent down, Nombei sat passively watching the wispy forms ooze through fissures in the rock and fill the chamber with their fluttering energy, as if it had not been what had killed Pella.

Omar began analyzing, leaving the monitoring of the beggar's progress to Nombei.

When the beggar found a pearl and put it in her basket, the shapes hovered near her. When she started back up, the shapes did not dissipate but got brighter and followed her up the passage. A small red spot appeared in the center of the visualizer. Omar worked to adjust the monitor as he said, panic in his voice, "It can't break down on me now."

Nombei said quietly, "They are coming closer. Maybe they're trying to communicate."

Omar shook his head, but he stepped back.

They watched the spot slowly grow. Nombei reached over and dimmed the visualizer.

Omar froze for a minute. Then he shook his head. "It looks as if they're trying to take over the machine."

Nombei said nothing. She would almost be glad if the machine were destroyed—all their efforts ended.

He stared at the visualizer for a long moment, then began frantically to turn off most of the systems, but leaving a channel open at the lowest level.

The spot grew, filling the visualizer with a defuse red tint; then jumbles of letters and symbolic images appeared, but distorted as in a bad dream. Sheets of color, images and shapes, took form as if the machine had a life of its own.

Nombei touched the visualizer and the images gathered around her fingers. She laughed. "It tickles." She scrawled hello on the visualizer with her fingers. An image of the word was left there. She took Omar's hand and did the same. When he finished the word faded and then appeared in warm orange. She touched the visualizer again. The screen felt warm. Then a tingling went up her arm and she pulled away.

They looked at each other. "What now?" Nombei asked.

"Back to basics, I guess. Who knows what's happening? It still could be people causing this," Omar responded.

"Pella said they could get inside her mind."

Omar shrugged. "Try some other words."

"What shall I say?"

"Touch the screen; ask them to put something on the visualizer—something simple like the color blue, but don't speak."

Tears came to Nombei's eyes as she touched the visualizer. Send Pella back to us, she thought. All the while she was visualizing Pella coming back down the trail—imagining Pella entering the module, embracing her.

Suddenly Pella's face appeared on the visualizer drawn in shades of blue. Nombei gasped.

The image took form slowly, fading in and out, wavering. Then the image of Pella spoke slowly and carefully but distinctly—as if she didn't quite trust that she would be heard. "I don't want to come back. I belong here—leave me alone." It was Pella's voice, but uneven, staticky. Then her words appeared in written form on the visualizer.

Nombei pulled away her hand as if she'd been burned. The image of Pella disappeared.

Omar touched the visualizer slowly, thoughtfully. Abstract shapes began to appear. Then nothing. He adjusted the screen and the image of the beggar reappeared standing rigidly near the module. Her basket was empty.

Nombei was in shock. For the first time since Pella's death she began to sob uncontrollably.

Omar said, anger in his voice, "Stop it. The woman is gone. That was just some sort of memory, a recording of her image being manipulated."

Nombei quieted, but she shook her head and whispered, "No, it was more than that. I think she's really there. Someone's holding her prisoner."

Omar shook his head in turn. "She can't still be alive. The ash that was left was analyzed. It was organic—human. There is no reason to believe Pella didn't die…although she would be the first miner that did."

"What do you mean?"

"If the records are to be believed no one else has actually died while trying to get pearl. Even going deeply into the caves, they have come back temporarily demented or they fall into a coma. The beggars are more resistant to the poisons so perhaps— It looked as if Pella wanted to die; she took off the protective clothing. She would have died from shock and heat before we could have gotten to her anyway."

"So why did she appear on the visualizer now—so real."

Omar shrugged. "If Chalmers is right and human thieves are behind this, the thieves transmitted some sort of holographic recording of her." He rubbed his eyes thoughtfully. "But I can't believe we wouldn't have some clue to all this new technology if some people had come up with it, and I don't have any indication that there is transmission coming from outside the cave. I think there is some sort of archeological protective device, some residue of a previous civilization."

# Chapter Twenty-One

When Sonja finally opened the capsule, the cold that came in was planet temperature; she'd been right about the gravity. It was dark where she was, but not as dark as the capsule. She stepped out shivering and breathing hard. She would have to find clothing and a source of extra oxygen soon or she wouldn't get far.

She could see that she was in some sort of hut. It smelled like a Godong hut, dry, and dusty. She neither heard nor felt anyone present. The only sound was of the machinery that serviced the capsule. She found the console that controlled it and noted that an alarm had been set off when she opened the door. Not much time.

She found her clothes piled in a corner and pulled them on. Outside the hut, there was a little starlight showing a few more silent huts nearby. Then she heard footsteps running, just one set. They'd been pretty confident that she couldn't get out. She slipped behind one of the other huts, away from the sound and waited.

One small person entered the hut. A light went on and there was a guttural cursing and then silence. She moved closer and could see through the open doorway that it was Georgio. He was at the console. Sending Mark a message? She got him from behind in a neck hold, his arm tight against his back. "Where is Mark? How far away is he?"

"How did you get out? It's not possible. Did he let you out?"

"Yes, of course he let me out," she said. "What did you think, he was leaving me there forever?"

"He never meant to do that. But I'm glad you're out. I was in one of those once for a little while. I nearly went crazy."

"Maybe I should put you in there now."

"I meant you no harm. Mark said it was for your own safety. So they wouldn't kill you."

She almost laughed. "So he didn't do it to sell me to the highest bidder?"

Georgio shook his head. "I don't know. He said he would help my father's people if I did what he asked. They have so little."

"Where is Mark?" Georgio shook his head again. Sonja moved him toward the capsule and lifted him in. He struggled but she pushed him down. She was activating the strapping mechanism when he finally said, "I left him at an Earthdome. I'm supposed to get him tomorrow."

"You have his hovi?" Georgio nodded. Sonja couldn't believe her luck.

Sonja set the timing mechanism on the restraints in the capsule so they would release after a couple of hours and left Georgio looking forlornly up at her from the open capsule. She took Mark's hovi back to the mine.

When she got there, the staff told her that Julie had been there looking for her the day before. She contacted Julie's apartment at the main Earthdome and Chalmers answered. There was silence when she identified herself. Finally Chalmers said, clearly annoyed. "Where have you been, Shankar? You've got Julie in a state. Now she's gone out in the desert looking for you."

"Just doing my job…Sir."

"Well, if you'd been here you'd know Dr. Harold has had a breakthrough. One of the beggars managed to collect pearl without going off his head. And we finally have some chemical analysis of the gases, the poisons slowing us down. I'm working on a way to clear out the poisons right now. We'll have a supply of pearl in no time."

"Please let me know when Julie gets back."

"You two have quite a thing going. Haven't seen her so…excited about anyone since she got the stupid canine." He laughed. "Don't bother to get involved Shankar. She's going back home to Earth as soon as she gets back here. Now that there's going to be more pearl to refine, we'll allow space travel. Can't say I'll be sorry to see her go."

Then Sonja made an attempt to locate Mark. He wasn't at Huniman's. She checked the coms of people going in and out of the resident entrances of the Earthdomes and didn't see anyone in the last few days that could be Mark. If he wasn't at an Earthdome—?

She would deal with him later, once she could contact the League. He was likely no longer a real threat. Whoever had hired him wouldn't be happy that he'd failed. And now that she had Mark's hovi, where could he go? She sent a crew from the mine to pick up the capsule she'd been kept in. Presumably Georgio would be long gone from its vicinity. She wasn't sorry about that. He hadn't wanted to hurt her. The capsule turned out to be the escape capsule for Mark's hovi, not a space capsule at all. Very high tech, but not as invulnerable as he had claimed. He would claim the whole episode had been intended as a joke if she ever found him. Most likely someone like Chalmers had wanted her out of the way, at least temporarily. Why? What was his new plan to get to pearl?

Sonja was worried about Julie. She hadn't returned and her staff would not forward any messages. Finally they told her that Julie had gone to visit a cousin at a smaller Earthdome on the other edge of the valley. They said she did not want to be contacted. Had Julie taken refuge there because Chalmers was threatening to send her offplanet? Or was she angry at Sonja for disappearing, assuming it'd been a deliberate snub.

First she needed to make a trip to the moon to check for offworld messages and to try once again to send in a report to the League. She was told that Governor Chalmers had put a security restriction on all communication offworld and she was still not able to send her report.

She left a message at Julie's cousin's asking to visit and was granted an hour the next day.

The next morning she was ushered into a delightfully pleasant though modest room upholstered in white silk that blended nicely with the white snow visible through lavish windows. Seated flatteringly near a satin curtain was a Julie look alike but with more normal human proportions. Sonja introduced herself as a friend of Julie's. "She left a message that she would be here."

The woman smiled politely. "I am always happy to meet my cousin's friends. But you must have misunderstood her message. I haven't seen the Contessa for months."

Sonja exchanged pleasantries with the woman, hoping for more information, but got nothing. Like most members of her class she was expert in polite conversation that sounded authentic but meant nothing except to fulfill the social vacuum. She excused herself for pulling out her communicator and called Julie's apartment. Then she played the recorded message.

The woman flushed and said with an uncharacteristic touch of anger in her voice, "It has to be some sort of tasteless joke; typical of her, telling her staff that she would be here. We are not exactly on good terms, you see. I'm sure she is home and just doesn't want to be seen. If you know her, you shouldn't be surprised at that. She is not very presentable. Our quarrel, if you must know, is because she won't take any advice about how to improve herself."

# Chapter Twenty-Two

Nombei sat staring, her eyes unfocused, while Omar worked with the recording of the session where the image of Pella had appeared. He sat up suddenly and took a deep breath. He took off the helmet that had allowed him to experience what had been recorded from Pella's personal monitor—what Pella had felt just before she died.

Nombei asked, tiredly, handing him a cup of tea, "What is it?"

He turned up the atmospheric filter so its whine might mask their conversation if there were any listening devices still intact. Then he took a sip, leaned toward her and said rather wistfully, "I felt I was flying, but it was comforting and…I can understand why Pella felt they were alive. There was a great appeal, much like pearl itself I would guess. Still I think what she experienced was from some sort of device, from some earlier time. With an archaeological record to be translated and understood."

"But they seem so alive. Existing now—communicating with us."

Omar sighed and nodded tiredly. "There is nothing alive out there now. Perhaps they did reproduce, care for their young and their old and had a culture and a history of shared experience just like other organic life-forms. But all we have located is what they left, a recording device, defensive perhaps. There will be records of their existence but that's all."

"Are you going to tell the officials? They'll find a way to destroy…it, your record, or whatever it is, because of pearl."

"I'm sure the Consortium suspected all along that they were dealing with intelligence. Why else would they bring me in? They expect me to collect information to help them destroy it. It doesn't matter to them whether it's alive or in the past or or just chemistry. All they care about is pearl. I've got to find a way to inform the Galactic League before—"

Nombei's face changed, paled. She said vindictively, "They killed Pella. I'm glad they'll be destroyed."

"Don't be a fool. The woman wanted to die. I wonder what pearl was to them? Why it so desperately wanted pearl protected that it would set up a way to move it and poison anything taking it? And why it took so long for that defense to kick in? If I could just find a way to get pearl without interference, buy some time so I could study—"

"Could it have been a energy source for them? If they were alive they'd have to get energy from something? Or maybe pearl is its eggs?"

"It's not alive, certainly not now."

"Why don't you ask them what they…were?"

"I won't do more research until I find a way to get word to the Galactic League. I won't take a chance on helping the Consortium destroy them."

Nombei snorted. "The Consortium will never give up the sale of pearl. It's too profitable. They won't let you communicate with anyone about this."

Omar put down his cup, "You think I don't know that."

"So let's ask the questions."

Nombei volunteered to put on an environmental suit and go into the cave not to collect pearl, but to bring them out. When the fluttering forms faded Nombei returned to the module and watched while Omar analyzed what he had recorded. This time Pella's image was not on the visualizer, but what resembled human language was there—letters, words instead of simple abstract images. Single words in standard Galactic English. Words like polish, tend, burnish, gleaming surface, crust, skin, clutch-of-ovaries, external-memory-eggs.

Omar adjusted the system, allowing it to sort for grammatical structure, to search for meaning. More words appeared scattered across the screen like the crazy writing of a child. But the words themselves were not childlike as they sorted themselves in different patterns.

Then a sentence formed like a mathematical formula unravelling itself, different words fading in and out and around each other in different colors as if the shades of color would change the meaning.

*Tenderly, proudly, with infinite satisfaction. Husk of shed soil-skin, shredded and tucked in around to make the nests, even softer, more protected. Nest-mine, the envy of younger ones filling this cave with spiral mounds of newness.*

*"Reflection. In childhood-mine. This hollowness has been only a few nests with the wrinkled puny eggs of those…compatriots-other maintainer-mother-single parents—too weak or too stupid to survive in the crowdedness of grand-grand-grand-mother hollowness.*

Omar was totally absorbed in the process, forgetting the obvious danger. Soon the electronic signals were translating directly into standard Galactic English on the visualizer, and Pella was seen less and less.

Nombei was glad. Each fresh sight of Pella was just as shocking and painful as the last. She wanted to accept that Pella was truly gone.

The words turned from golden lettering on a black background then to blackness with stars and white lettering.

*"Fearing. Now—so-near—you-new host-aliens, drop in shiny, not-living caves from ancestress heaven. (misty light red clouds appeared on the visu-*

alizer behind the words.) *Terror. Heaven-sky was the place of the fearful ancestress.*

Omar shook his head and switched to Pella's native language to see if the thought framework and nuances fit better. A faint image of Pella's face appeared and faded. She spoke in her own language with a cloying sense of effusive emotion clinging to the words. He set the machine to translate her words into Standard Galactic English and spent a few moments adjusting for his own understanding. There was always the danger that in spite of the shielding, their own minds would influence the outcome. The system was sophisticated enough to record alternative interpretations for future study. He could choose the one that made the most sense to him now.

Pella's image spoke and, simultaneously, text appeared on the screen with alternative meanings. *"There was much discussion-debate among the elder-elder-elders that still deigned to be grub-tenders. Subject—about the risks of the you-new sweet-smelling hosts. They argued-discussed that the promised golden age had come or not."*

Omar smiled at the gold and rainbow fantasy from a nineteen century painting appeared, the best visual approximation the visualizer could manage.

*"It would be now as in those days when the host was fat with sweet-tangy nectar before the deserts had taken so much away into death-dry heat. Some saw you-new host as proof-justice that the ancestresses has forgiven them after so many thousand-eons seasons of deprivation."*

Here Omar commented that the word ancestor had a feminine ending attached to it, an annoying redundancy in English since the original word an-cestor meant female predecessors and there was no evidence of dimorphism here.

*"But others see that you-new sweet host from the sky are-were-will—be evilness. Taking the memories. Destroying the egg-bookbeads. Devils sent by the oldest-oldest-oldest ancestress—punishment—angry over slothful nurturing. Others anger-demanded that the collection-community propitiate the ancestresses. They-imperative-must go to the blackness void that speaks. 'Telling cave.' The eldest egg-memory of each nurturer must be life removed—sacrificed."*

An image of thousands of shiny translucent black spheres appeared on the visualization monitor. Information about pearl, this planet's chief controversial economic resource, had rarely been recorded. And the emotional meter was off the scale now. The equivalent of human hysteria.

*"For the first time in memory there was a…"* (The words disagreement, war, conflict flashed in and out of the text visualizer.) *"…in the community. Some went to the telling cave for the 'time of sacrifice'. The golden-age-collec-*

*tive-faction stayed in the home cave and some of them even occupied the sacred space of the old nurture mothers who had gone to sacrifice. Those that came back told that even from the first egg of the first mother there was no-speak-nothing about this new tempting host. Not even from the oldest ovoid-bookbead was there anything about the new delicious tasting host-you. Those that came back said that the ancestresses were displeased and would punish. They would open no more eggs—would not allow themselves to be gorged with the evil-wealth-of-sweet juices of the new host. The anger-war-dissension is not healed and there is no answer-solution-resolution.*

*So for the first time in memory clan-collection-community is divided. Those that see you—new hosts as punishment of ancestress-wisdom carry their bookbeads deep. There is emptiness pain-regret-sorrow. You—new host—take our memories. Where are our eggs-bookbeads? All-is-recorded-in-the-telling-cave."*

The text stopped and the visualizer became a blur of unpatterned color that surged and throbbed in tune with the emotion meter.

Nombei sighed. "All I understand from that is that they don't like us much. Pearl is something important to them they don't want us to have."

Omar shook his head and smiled. "Some of them think we are sweet."

"You're telling me they like the way Pella tasted?" Nombei hissed.

"I don't know what to think." Omar said, his eyes wide and out of focus, staring at the screen.

# Chapter Twenty-Three

Even confronted with Julie's cousin's statement that Julie wasn't visiting her, Julie's staff at the main Earthdome politely but firmly implied that it was Sonja who was not telling the truth.

Finally Sonja went to Chalmers. He laughed. "The Contessa is sulking and her cousin is indulging her in her temper tantrum. She left because I said she had to give up that vile animal. Her doctors think it is bad for her health with its unsanitary, disgusting habits. There's a reason why they were banned years ago. She'll just have to get used to it, get a robot pet for company. She can afford it."

Sonja was suddenly angry. Maybe Julie was playing with her.

Then he handed her a copy of some of Omar's notes about his research. She and the mine officials had been given copious summaries and conclusions by Omar, but clearly the man was not reporting everything.

Leaning too close and smiling, Chalmers said. "He could very well be sabotaging your efforts to get pearl with the beggars. Maybe he even killed one. Doesn't want interference with his precious research. But you wouldn't mind I'm sure going down into the pit and checking on his research."

He was right. She would have to go over some unanalyzed raw data herself when Omar was not around—find out what he was hiding. Omar Harold was the stubborn type, enamored of his science.

She landed her hovi and went down into the mine in the middle of the night. The guards were used to erratic work hours in this emergency situation. She climbed into the module, but all the records she found were a repeat of what she had seen. She searched further. Yes! She was in luck. Omar had left some of his raw data recordings not in the main memory, but cleverly left unlabeled in the blank infocom bin.

As Sonja had thought, there were materials that Omar was hiding. She sat back to watch the coms, fast forwarding them as they followed a figure into the caves. The walls of the deeper cavern appeared on the visualizer, showing a rich layer of opalescent pearl. The red-outlined figure stopped in front of a series of narrow fissures in the pearl beds as if waiting for something. There was no sound and the figure did not move for a long time. Then it bent down and began to pry at a purple globe.

Then there was a hissing sound. As in earlier records something like water vapor was oozing out of fissures in the rocks—steam? The vapor formed the usual misty, fluttering, translucent shapes, tinted orange-pink.

The scene faded and a word, hello, formed slowly on the visualizer in orange. A cute trick. Of course any beginning student of artificial intelligence could do it, but why put such games on a hidden infocom? Then, her exhausted mind was bombarded—meanings independent of language, echoed as the word hello rewrote itself and images and meanings entered her mind like bright confusing dreams. She felt the excitement of flying, flowing through the cave, then into the night sky. She shut down her intiception in a panic. Her whole body shook. Was there was something alive, something intelligent, but not human? She'd never imagined anything, anyone more intelligent than she was. Now this thing felt as if it were inside her—her mind, thinking faster than she could.

She squeezed her arms tightly around her body as if to ward off the feelings, the images that still swirled in her brain. After all this was just a recording. The source was no longer actively in touch with the module's equipment, or was it? She shook her head as if to clear it. Was she the one who was going insane?

She turned off the equipment and sat staring at the blank visualizer. Had it been real or some very powerful illusion? If it was real, was it an intelligent sentient life-form? She shivered. Did the Consortium officials suspect…did the Eminences? That was why Omar Harold and his equipment were here. She should have known. How could she have missed the clues? She shook herself. Of course it couldn't be. It was just very clever, very smart people inventing an illusion. But she had to admit that the idea of a new intelligence, a previously unknown sentient excited her.

She realized why Harold hadn't told anyone about this new evidence. No wonder he had been so secretive. He knew if the Galactic League found out about sentient entities here, the Intergalactic Assembly would immediately quarantine the planet. No more pearl could be mined until an investigation was completed, and then maybe never if pearl was found to be integral to the social fabric of the new sentience, or even part of a sentient's archaeological record.

Did Chalmers suspect? And what about the Eminences? Did they know something too and intend to keep this secret—indefinitely? But if they suspected, why had the Consortium allowed her to come? Was Mark right that it was just so they could convince the League that every effort had been made? How it would have panicked Chalmers if he thought there was evidence of sentient intelligence.

She felt like a fish dropped into the mouth of a carnivore. It was a no win situation. If she saved pearl for the blue-lipped Eminences and the rest of the addicted elite and evidence of an intelligent life-form was destroyed, she would be a number one intergalactic criminal. If she didn't—

She felt her face flush. That was that why so many of the employees here had been removed—all mindblanked or dead by now. That was why her reports hadn't gotten through.

She felt like such a fool. They had sent her here so they could present a clean report to the League, prevent an intervention. They assumed that if she were to find out the truth she would cooperate in a coverup. That was the reason for her audience with an Eminence before she came. And now what choice did she have? No wonder someone had hired Mark to take her out of circulation.

Greed for pearl. The sight of the quivering blue-violet fingers of the Eminence came back to her and she shivered. How dependent were they? What would happen to her world if the Eminences should fail to…function? Everything she knew, all that made her feel powerful, might be gone. In the past she'd never doubted her ability to succeed whatever she tried. Now she felt as if everything would crash around her. Could she? Whatever the truth she had to do her job. But for whom? Even if she could report the situation to her League bosses, she wasn't sure what they would tell her to do. She was obligated as a League employee to do everything in her power to try and protect intelligent life-forms until the League could make a decision.

She felt an affinity new to her. Something, someone as intelligent, as aware as she. More so. What if they were real, alive, an intelligence to share observations, thoughts, insights with—to learn from. She couldn't give that up. She wanted badly to save them.

She reviewed more of the recording. Omar Harold's notes further along on the com stated that he thought that it was the beggar Pella's death—something that had not happened with other miners—that had triggered the communication. Humans mining pearl had provoked some mechanism protecting it. This intelligence had somehow disabled the miners and moved the pearl. But since there was no evidence of organic life anywhere in the cave, one could only conclude that the original entity was long gone, extinct.

On the record Harold asked, "What was pearl to them? Their eggs? They talked about nurturing. But then they had said memory, taking the memories. Was pearl just some sort of memory beads, records, or was it both eggs and history? In any case, the original creatures are no longer here. It appears what is left here is an artificial intelligence—some sort of archeological artifact capable of protecting pearl."

Sonja sighed. She had so wanted them to be alive.

But once more she was optimistic. Of course the Eminences did not know of the evidence of a intelligent entity—archeological or not. She was ashamed of doubting them. Fortunately, tomorrow she was to have a conference with an Eminence from moonbase. Chalmers might prevent her reports to the League from getting through, but he wouldn't dare prevent her conference with a Consortium elder. She made copies of the relevant records. Those should convince the Eminence of what must be studied and protected. There had to be some way to preserve this evidence of intelligence and still mine pearl. It was just a matter of taking the time, making the authorities understand. She would make the case.

The appointment with an Eminence had been set up before she arrived onplanet. Sonja was eager for the interview after her night of collecting evidence and constructing arguments. Surely with all their accumulated wisdom, the Eminences would come up with a reasonable solution. A new intelligence, even if it was a constructed one was too important. There had to be time for study. Attempts at communication. And maybe somewhere its creator still lived.

On the Consortium moonbase she was ushered into the presence of an Eminence. The holographic transmission was so good she would have sworn it wa real.This time the Eminence did not approach her but waited in silence, not moving as she began her report.

After a few minutes the Eminence moved toward her waving a quivering, translucent hand impatiently, and the amplified voice boomed angrily, "You have failed us, and obviously do not understand the urgency of this matter. You were allowed to come to the planet because we trusted you to help restore the mining of pearl and you have failed!"

The thin translucent fingers trembled more and began fluttering as the surrogate mechanism that would send a sensory holograph came toward her. The cool fingers of the machine touched her throat and moved across her torso, pinching and jabbing. The Eminence's holographic fingers hung just before her eyes, shaking uncontrollably as the Eminence whispered hoarsely, "We will tolerate no more delay. We will have fresh pearl…now."

Then the coded message the first Eminence had given her began to decode. The message was something she should have expected. The Eminences depended on pearl to stay alive. Pearl was not just a pleasure drug, it could be used to prolong life indefinitely. She thought of all those comatose workers. There must be people all over the galaxy in that state— if one could call that living. But somehow the Eminences had figured out how to use pearl for longevity without becoming frozen, comatose. She wondered how many of those in power were using it that way—a closely held secret. On Earth and the colonies everyone assumed pearl addicts eventually died. The thought that somehow those minds controlling the vast and complex network of the Consortium, keeping it running smoothly, were dependent on pearl for their life, their consciousness, and perhaps their sanity, horrified her.

She remembered what Mark had said. "Pearl, you know, it's their lifeblood." So the Consortium wasn't just out for profit.

The shaking hand danced with agitation. "We must get the pearl…the thieves, blow them up, poison them. Now."

Still she persisted. "We have not determined exactly what the phenomenon is that is preventing access to pearl. As you've seen from the report, the technician, Omar Harold, believes what the miner encountered to be evidence of formerly unrecognized intelligent and sentient lifeforms…and I agree with him. There needs to be more research—"

The trembling hand waved dismissively. "We are not stupid. We have known about this theory for some time. An absurd idea—the ramblings of defective minds. The stuff is inorganic. The League long ago accepted that. The mining must be resumed. We will tolerate no more delays."

Sonja's intelligence struggled with her conditioning. She recognized her worship of the Eminences as an early imprinting on her psyche. What would happen to her when she resisted it? She gathered herself—took a deep breath. She understood what the Consortium would do if she didn't cooperate. They might already have tried to eliminate her. Of course they hadn't let her reports to the League get through. Right now was the time for triage. She must stay calm—think what to do. "There are other solutions than destroying them. Dr. Chalmers has gone forward with research into artificial pearl and says he's near—"

The quivering hand waved dismissively. "He did send us a sample of an inferior product. The pearl recovered from people is better but still inadequate. Perhaps there is some profit in it, but it is useless to me—to us." Even though she understood there was no use bringing up ethical considerations, she said, "His research on the recovery of pearl from the bodies of comatose workers is unethical—those people he dismembered were still alive—"

"Why do you bring up these trivial issues?" The shaking hand waved dismissively again. "Chalmers has assured us the volunteers were not revivable, but that is beside the point."

She felt a profound sadness. How could she ever have been so naive? Jason had tried to warn her. The Eminences were not as she'd been taught, brainwashed, really, to believe. Of course they and even the League leadership were not entities beyond the crass weaknesses of mere mortals, interested only in the well-being of the whole human race—they were human, greedy and self-absorbed, interested in preserving their own immortality.

She took a breath and tried again. "As I said, the exact nature of the interfering phenomenon has not been established. Even to destroy it you must know what it is. Previous attempts to deal with it have failed, and the prevention of mining has continued. I believe the technician Omar Harold has communicated—"

"It is stupid to try communicating with gas and rock—or with ordinary thieves. Pulling in that organic life technician was not our idea."

The mechanical fingers entwined in Sonja's hair and pulled her face closer. The eye, glazed with need, felt as if it might touch her face. "The data Dr. Harold collected has been analyzed by others. Dr. Chalmers is assembling a team of experts. They will blast to vent the caves soon. Whether or not you will be…dismissed depends on your cooperation with that process. We will allow you to continue trying to collect pearl before that happens. The only way to prevent more extreme measure is to restore the supply of pearl. Chalmers assures us once he has removed the…vapors we will have unrestricted access to the lower caves. We find no reason not to agree with him."

"But—if such drastic measures are used, the source of pearl itself may be destroyed and we may never learn how it was produced."

"Dr. Chalmers assures me that there is at least twenty year's supply of fresh pearl in the lower cave, more if we restrict its distribution. Plenty of time to figure out how to synthesize it."

The hologram disappeared. It had been a disturbing encounter. To see an Eminence so out of control— The elders of the Consortium with their superhuman intelligence, their age, their experience, had been the gods of her universe. She'd been taught that the Consortium leadership stuck scrupulously to the Galactic League's ethical guidelines.

She sighed. Perhaps it was just this one Eminence. Yes, an aberration, one Eminence had finally gone senile. The others should be informed, the other Eminences would be different. But in order to contact them without this one knowing, she would have to return to Earth and there was no time. And if this one knew, how could the others not? She had no real reason to think this Eminence did not represent them all.

As she hurried away, she took a deep breath. It was important to put all this in perspective. After all, she always worked best under pressure. Of course some part of her had always known that underneath the facade of power that surrounded them, the Eminences were human. They had all once been people like herself, more intelligent and skilled than ordinary humans, but human nonetheless.

# Chapter Twenty-Four

That evening Omar was stopped by a security officer and taken to Chalmers' office in the Earthdome. Chalmers just stared at him for a long moment, his eyes wide with accusation while Omar said nothing.

Then Chalmers placed a printed copy of Sonja's report to the Eminence in front of him. Omar stared at it. Finally Chalmers said, angrily, "When did you plan to report on this new material?"

Omar was flustered. What else had he expected? "We wanted to be sure."

"Of what?"

Chalmers was a scientist, after all, he should understand if anyone did. "If we are to make a convincing presentation to the Galactic League for protection of the—remains, I needed to have all the evidence—"

Chalmers stood up and leaned over Omar. "Protection?"

"There were…sentient beings. From what I have seen, a very intelligent life-form, represented through the phenomenon we detected in the mine. We have made contact—this report is about that communication. Their symbolic system is—unique."

Chalmers laughed angrily. "An old fantasy. The farmers claim some sort of flying thing out of the caves, vampires. But what has this fantasy to do with the pearl theft?"

"They can't steal it. It's theirs. I believe they left some sort of device to protect it. We are the ones who have been stealing it."

Chalmers frowned and Omar went on. "If you viewed the com, you know what they were."

Chalmers eyes narrowed. "Something invented by you and your machines."

Omar felt helpless, desperate. "They had language, thought, they reproduced, lived as a community. When their energy and mass grew too large they combined as one organic being and re-divided into smaller units again, each encoded with the whole. Pearl was a necessary part of that process."

Chalmers smiled cynically. "Like some sort of gaseous amoebas?"

"Hardly. I think now that pearl could have been for reproduction, egg-like constructions, or a collective record of individuals that could be revived in future reproduction, or at least a record of their history."

"You are claiming that they recorded events like the rutting ritual of '27?" Chalmers asked contemptuously.

"That might be a very crude translation into English of a small part of the process. We are not really capable of experiencing their reality. The frequencies, the energy fields of our perception are too limited. That's why translation has been so difficult. They didn't know there could be an intelligence with our limited perception." Omar smiled. "We don't even have multidimensional existence."

"If there were something like that, so intelligent, why could we take pearl at all? Why didn't they defend it when we first arrived?"

"I think they existed in a much larger spatial-temporal context. Our presence on this planet is only a second in their terms. And…" Omar looked thoughtfully at Chalmers. "…their recording devices saw us as…attractive hosts for the original life-forms. One might be tempted the think those still exist, perhaps in the form of the farmer's vampires, consuming workgrubs. Although the term hosts does not imply the destruction—

Chalmers gave a snort of incredulity. "You call yourself a scientist and you have come up with this fanciful fairy tale? A pretty invention, this theory, but I'm not convinced. It's thieves—human thieves—that are feeding you all this fantasy."

"Miners have experienced the sentient mechanism directly. The miner that was burned up—Pella—"

Chalmers laughed. "No doubt she's part of the plot. She's joined the thieves down in the caves and they sprinkled some white ash in the tunnel to fool you into thinking she was dead. Now she's appearing on your visualizer. Not hard to do—project her image and pretend to be speaking for some mythical creatures."

"Why didn't your thieves' life energy show up on my monitor?" Omar asked.

"They did, you fool. They were walking around in some suit that shielded their body image, projecting the fluttery thing you saw on the visualizer."

Omar stared at him. Finally he said angrily, "I told you. This is a completely new symbolic system. There is no way that human beings could have invented it, even if it were possible to enter the caves. Shankar told us that she'd checked out all other possibilities. Was she lying?"

"I don't know what her game is but no doubt she can be fooled too. People or some new and mysterious entity, in the end it doesn't matter. We will protect the Consortium's interest in any way we can. We are developing a way to clear out the caves without harming the remaining pearl. When we are ready to do that, your job will be to lure it out—whatever it is—so we can get rid of it. That's got to happen soon; within the week we'll be ready. And you are not to mention this to Shankar."

"Certainly not, Sir. She won't even find out I talked to you."

"Good, then she won't try to interfere with my plans."

When he got back to his office, Omar said softly to Nombei, "Chalmers found out about our research. I've got to find some way to get information to the League. Will Shankar help?"

Nombei shook her head. "It won't matter. The League won't interfere."

"We'll just have to make her understand that this is larger than any temporary economic crisis," Omar said fiercely.

Nombei just sat shaking her head. Dr. Harold, for all his intelligence and education, could be so stupid sometimes.

When Nombei spoke she half-directed her words to the walls. After all, it was very likely they were still being monitored. One just forgot sometimes. "The woman isn't a person you can appeal to. She is some sort of investigative machine. The Consortium would see to it the League didn't take any chances employing a regular person for a job like hers. If she isn't some sort of robot, she was bred for the job—some sort of genetic—"

Omar said nervously, "That's illegal. It's been illegal—"

Nombei laughed. "What asteroid cluster time-warp did you come from?"

"I don't believe it's ever done any more."

Nombei went on. "You can't expect any help from her. She works for the Consortium." She shook her head. "You know, you should get her to work with you. With her engineered brains she'll have built-in code breaking capacity. Probably better than your machines. I bet she's a hell of a lot faster. Probably spends her spare time solving—"

The power went out for a moment and when it came back on the door opened and Sonja stood just outside, her finger lightly pressed against her lips, waving at them to come outside.

After the door slipped shut, she led them away. They moved to a spot in the cave where Sonja had made sure they couldn't be heard by monitoring devices. She confronted Harold, waving the unlabeled recording at him. "Why didn't you tell me about this…communication?"

Omar flushed. "I…I wanted to be sure. You suspect human thieves. I thought they might just be very clever. I thought…I wanted enough evidence to convince someone…you…to take this to the Galactic League. But Governor Chalmers knows about it too. I thought as a scientist he should appreciate the value— But he is too obsessed with getting at the rest of the pearl."

Sonja said nothing and Omar went on excitedly. "If you saw my research you must have felt it, too; there is—was a unique intelligence. Nothing about it resembles any life-form encountered before. The symbolic thought process, the forms of communication—totally unique."

Sonja decided she wouldn't give away any thoughts she herself might have for the moment. She nodded. The man was obviously tempted by the work itself. Like all scientific types he was greedy for acclaim, for the attention and status he would receive for such original work. She said coolly, "Yes, of course, I'll take responsibility for arranging a hearing with the League in due time, so that your evidence can be presented. Meanwhile, I expect you to continue your research. You will keep me fully informed and I'll need access to your records here and in your office from time to time."

Omar flushed again. "I would certainly appreciate your requesting information from me. There are rules of conduct—"

"If I could be assured that you'd no longer be hiding information from me, I would do my best to help you with your research. After all, that's my job."

Nombei asked, skepticism clear in her tone, "Your job for the League or for the Consortium? Who do you work for? The Eminence you gave our research to?"

Something seemed to snap in Sonja. She said, anger clear in her voice, "You fools…you mindless blobs of hot protoplasm…don't you understand? It doesn't matter what we think or feel. There's no time. The League and its ethics are far away. We…none of us will even survive this. It is too important to those in power. Mindscrubs aren't even reliable enough."

Omar and Nombei stared at her. Sonja took a breath. "Pearl means more than you think to the Consortium. The Eminences themselves are dependent on pearl to stay alive. You're here to find ways to keep them supplied. That's all. End of mission—end of usefulness. Whether you succeed or fail the outcome for you will be the same. You are disposable. The remaining length of your existence…our existence is directly related to whether they believe you will succeed at getting them resupplied with pearl—soon."

Omar took a deep breath. "Even you?"

Nombei said contemptuously, "Do you think she would tell us about it if it didn't apply to her too?" She turned to Sonja. "You mean the longer we successfully delay the longer we live?"

Sonja sighed. "I don't even know that." She leaned against the stone wall, her tiredness showing in her face, her anger subdued. "There are more like me. I'm replaceable. But even if I weren't, it isn't a question of business as usual. It isn't just the profits to be made or even the politics. I could get around those kinds of motives. They don't care about anything but pearl itself. Mindless appetites for that purple goo."

"What can we do?" Omar asked.

"At this point Chalmers is the key. The Eminences and the Earthdomers with any influence are behind him and his plans. Somehow I'll have to find a way to delay his more extreme measures. We must try to continue collecting pearl as instructed with the beggars to buy time."


Sonja went to Chalmers in one last attempt to gain more time for Omar Harold's research. He listened to her quietly for a few moments. She was saying, "It wouldn't take all that much time to establish the nature of the what Harold has communicated with in the caves—" when he interrupted her.

"What Harold says is that there is no evidence of anything alive down there. Even the pearl thieves are gone now that they have pearl."

Sonja tried to be patient. "I know you think what's down there is just some sort of poisonous chemical or vapor that is attracted by the presence of miners, but—"

He began pacing his office impatiently. "I am not proposing anything that will destroy pearl, whatever it is. There will be plenty of time to do research once we have access to the remaining pearl. It's very simple. There are inorganic poisons that need to be removed. I want to create a chimney to the atmosphere, whatever poisonous vapors that we haven't neutralized will be vented, dissipated through the opening."

"An explosion could set off a volcanic chain reaction—destroy the environment of the rift valley and even the Earthdome water supply."

"You know, Shankar, this planet has the most stable tectonics of any planet yet studied. There hasn't been an earthquake in centuries."

"Precisely. Such stability is very rare. We don't know what is keeping it in control."

"My staff has established that there's little risk. The hole won't be large, just a chimney from the caves to vent the poisonous vapors. Water may be lost but even that problem can be solved. We will monitor the loss and—"

Sonja interrupted, saying, "But with the help of—the intelligence Harold has contacted we can make a substitute for pearl for human consumption. We need time to—"

"Even if your mythical intelligence were real and Harold's demented hopes could be fulfilled, there's no time. As you saw for yourself, the Eminences are already over the edge. There are pearl riots all over the galaxy. The Consortium is in danger of losing its grip on its colonial enterprises. If it gets any worse the Consortium will send a security force here."

If she could get her reports through the League would send one—probably too late. "Maybe they should. Please, give Harold just a day or two."

"For what?"

"There has to be a better way."

"Even assuming that these poisonous gases represent something that was alive and intelligent, how do you know they don't eat pearl instead of producing it?" He laughed. "Harold seemed to think they might have some interest in eating us. Juicy hosts—didn't he say they called us that?"

"If you would just come into the caves, if you were in Harold's module when there were communications, I could show you—"

Chalmers stopped smiling and his face paled. He said, angry now as well as anxious, "If you had managed to gather a bit more pearl with those useless beggars—"

Sonja's frustration turned into anger at the man's stupidity. He knew perfectly well an intelligence was there. He'd seen Harold's records too. He was deliberately choosing to ignore the evidence. "There is intelligence, maybe even living sentient beings. You must give us more time before you risk destroying it."

His manner became suddenly more friendly, more expansive. "Let me show you something." He took her arm to pull her into his lab. He gestured imperiously to a covered cage. Sonja pulled up the cover and looked inside. Two intense brown eyes peered back at her; it was Julie's little dog.

He still held on to her arm as if that would convince her to do what he wanted. "Look, Shankar, if you cooperate with me now I'll promise to intervene with the League on your thing's behalf. You help me and you can do whatever triage you can with your archeological residue before we blast. I'll even give you a day or two." He smiled reassuringly. "Harold can try and convince the 'intelligent' vapors to release the remaining pearl and we will call off the blast."

"What do you want from me?"

"I need another sample of the poisonous vapors."

Annoyed, Sonja said, "Why not send one of your research people? I'll be occupied with my investigation."

"The very thought of going down in that filthy place gives us—" He shivered with a fake coyness. "From the coms I've see it's worse than the Earth's warren pits."

Sonja smiled her sweetest and said intimately, "Not quite. I'm sure there are none of Earth's creepy crawlies—roaches, worms, disease and human waste with deadly viruses, body parts and—"

The man blanched and let go. She had breached caste protocol, but he tried to look amused by her comment. "It will take no effort on your part. One of your miners can take it down to get a sample. Leave the damn canine down there till it draws some of the vapors. The cage has collecting and recording equipment that works automatically. All organic, too."

"Did Julianna agree?" She touched the little dog through the cage. "I don't believe she did."

He said, annoyed now. "Your League rules mandate it be destroyed. Julianna would be grateful to know it's still alive, if I could find her to tell her. Anyway, if you are right about your vapors being intelligent, they won't hurt it. I get my sample so I can check my analysis, Harold gets a bit more time to talk to your vapors."

"What do you mean, if you could find her?"

"You were right; she isn't at her cousin's. She hasn't left the planet and she isn't hiding out at home. I thought maybe you might know where she is."

Sonja shook her head.

"She'll show up when she gets uncomfortable enough. Her hovi only has enough supplies to keep her going for a few days."

Sonja decided not to push him about Julie. "Two days isn't enough time."

Chalmers laughed. "Have you got a better plan? Convince me the vapors will let us have pearl and you'll have all the time you want. I'll even let you arrange a hearing with the League."

"Give us more time and we'll come up with one."

"Two days. That's all."

Sonja nodded, curtly, then she added, "Have you informed the Galactic League what you intend to do in the caves?"

He looked uncomfortable. "Do you think I care what a bunch of inter-galactic busybodies think? There is an emergency here, if you hadn't noticed. A communication would reach the League long after the blasting is completed. Any way we won't be destroying anything, just clearing out the vapors. Just a little hole—and some chemical antidotes. What doesn't vent will be neutralized."

Sonja said nothing just turned to leave.

"And I want you to bring another one of the stored cadavers at the refinery to my lab— for testing."

"As you very well know they aren't cadavers, they're comatose because of excessive exposure to pearl. Even you don't have the right to do experiments with living humans."

"This is an emergency situation."

"Why don't you get some research volunteers from the Earthdome? There must be a few comatose people stored there."

"I don't think the Eminences would appreciate your interfering with their access to pearl. That was not what you were sent here to do. If I don't have the material I requested in my lab by noon today, I will send my security people—for you."

# Chapter Twenty-Five

With the help of two refinery workers Sonja took Pet in her cage and one of the comatose pearl users to the mine. She hadn't wanted to obey Chalmers' request for a research subject, but she knew she had to keep him away from the refinery for the time being. But she hadn't been able to bring herself to deliver the comatose worker to Chalmers' techs at the Earthdome.

Omar Harold and Nombei were already in their module in the cave. Sonja didn't trust the mine officials so she brought Pet in her cage and the workers with the comatose woman down into the cave.

Sonja climbed into the module. Omar had just sent a beggar down into the caves after a few pearls. Omar hadn't yet tried to communicate, but was just monitoring the beggar's progress. The fluttering images had appeared, but the miner was still doing well and had one of the precious globes in her basket. Sonja told Omar to send a warning to the sentients about the Chalmers' plan to blast a hole in the cave.

Omar encouraged the miner to return, then sent the message.

When the miner was back with a few pearl, the words "Go outside now" appeared on the monitor in a wavy red scrawl. They sat staring at it not fully understanding. A voice, tinny and remote, repeated the message. Then it said in Pella's voice, more clearly and urgently, "Get away from the module."

Nombei was the first to move outside, pulling Omar with her. Sonja followed.

When they were well away from the module the lights in the cave dimmed for a second and the module disappeared, imploded in a burst of blue energy. Turning, Omar threw his hands over his mouth to suppress his cry of horror at the loss of his precious machine.

Then a shape began to form in the hot vapor where the machine had been.

Nombei reached out to Omar, but he was backing toward the passage out of the cave. Then he stopped, his eyes still wide with horror. Nombei turned and saw that the form in the vapor was human. It couldn't be…Pella. At first a shadow only, but finally she appeared as she had when Nombei first knew her. Tall and strong, her long dark limbs glistening in the bright light. Nombei began to shake. It had to be some sort of illusion. The vapors where poisoning her mind. She looked at the Omar, staring too. "Do you see her too— Pella?" she asked. All he could manage was a nod.

Sonja said, "Amazing. A visual of the beggar. They don't seem to need your visualizer. They…it learns fast."

Pella's dark eyes were sparkling a bright blue light. Then that blue light surrounded her body—a halo that followed as she turned to face the group of huddled people.

Her voice was familiar to Nombei, yet somehow amplified. "We wish you no harm. We have absorbed the mechanism for its information so that it is no longer necessary." Pella held out her hands open-palmed, smiled, and reached toward Nombei. "Show them how you can experience us without losing your human mortality. Bring me the pearl."

No one moved. Finally Nombei picked up the basket the miner had dropped and moved toward this new Pella almost hoping she, Nombei might be vaporized too.

Omar gasped and grabbed her arm, but Nombei carefully disengaged his fingers and moved on, putting the basket at Pella's feet and placing the pearl in her hands. Pella's hands were as cool and soft to Nombei's touch as they'd always been. For a moment she thought that Pella wasn't dead, that her death had been an illusion. Now she'd come back whole and herself. The kiss that Pella gave her was soft on her cheek. Pella said, "You see she is not harmed by my touch."

Nombei realized suddenly that she was no longer holding Pella's hands, though Pella hadn't pulled them away and the pearl was gone. She looked into Pella's eyes then. Pella was just an image in the vapor and smoke, not alive. In despair she reached for Pella's hands, again wishing to be a vaporous image like Pella, her human self a pile of white dust.

Sonja too moved toward the Pella image. She could feel her heart beating faster. She'd felt a kinship with these sentients even when she thought they were only a recording. Now the woman Pella, this apparition, had been sent by them. Somehow they existed now, were really present, not some mechanism left by an intelligent being but real, here—able to think, to learn and to act.

And if the earthrat Nombei wasn't afraid—hadn't been harmed… She moved closer and reached out a hand and Pella touched her. She felt only a gentle prodding of her mind, almost a question. Then all her suspicions, her fears, her obsession with control, everything in her training shut down.

But Pella moved away and an elongated arm reached over to the comatose refinery worker. The other refinery workers backed away, terrified. Pella stroked the comatose woman's face and body for a few seconds.

The deep purple tint seemed to drain from her body and her skin turned a healthier color. Finally the woman turned her head, her eyes open, and a beatific smile appeared on her face. There was a gasp, but no one moved.

Pella said to everyone, "You need not fear us. We wish only to welcome back that essence of ourselves which you name pearl and which you are taking from us. We have learned how to take that essence back…and to restore the human host back to its own original nature. Now each of those humans who come to us can choose their own path. Like the Pella you see before you, you can join us, leaving your mortal self behind as base minerals. Others may stay in their bodies, as will this woman who lost her conscious self to our history and who is now restored to active life."

Julie's little dog whimpered, and Pella reached though the bars of the cage and touched her, rubbing her fingers through her fur for a long moment. Then Pella smiled at them all again and disappeared.

Pet whined. An image of Julie distraught came into Sonja's mind. She let the dog out of her cage and Pet rubbed against her. Sonja had the illusion that the dog was speaking to her, but she couldn't hear anything. Yet she knew Pet wanted to go back to Julie.

Meanwhile, Omar and Nombei were trying to control the beggar who had collected pearl and was trying to run back into the caves when Pella disappeared. They had the beggar on the ground now shaky and demented, screaming for Pella to take her. Pet ran up to her and licked her face and she quieted.

The cave felt cold and empty. Nombei almost looked happy. "Now that they have been warned, the sentients are defending themselves. They know what Chalmers intends to do so they'll have to destroy him, maybe all of us. They could do it—the way they vaporized the module. They might dissolve everything that doesn't belong here. I'm glad. Better to end here as ash, but with Pella, than have a mind delete or worse."

"They warned us before the module was destroyed—They restored that worker. Pella's …death was an accident. They said they wouldn't hurt us." Omar said, his voice rising with uncertainty.

"Not yet," Nombei said. "Not yet. And they could destroy inorganic stuff and leave everybody alive. That's what I would do if I were them. All those Earthdomers naked in the desert." She laughed. "It would serve them right."

Then she shouted, "Pella come back, we have something to tell you." Her voice echoed emptily down the cave. Omar grabbed her arm.

The little dog came over to Nombei. She pulled away from Omar and squatted down to pat it. "You're right. She won't come back. I just hope they don't wait too long to do something."

A desperate, vain hope, Sonja thought as she left the two researchers whispering to each other. She picked up the little dog and headed out of the cave taking the cage. The others followed.

When they reached the surface, Sonja called Chalmers to tell him what had happened, explaining that the comatose worker no longer had any pearl in her system. He clearly didn't believe her version of events. She hoped the cage would have recorded what happened adequately to convince him of the reality of intelligent entities to be protected.

Chalmers was adamant. "I don't know what destroyed the module, but all that accomplished is to shorten the time I gave you. Without the module, Harold's research is finished. You've failed to collect pearl so the mine blasting will take place later today. Is the cage still intact? Send it to me—now. There's no time to waste. Make sure the miners are ready to go back to work once the poisons are cleared. Leave that tech, Harold and his rat assistant at the mine. They'll be useful to lure it—the vapor things—out again. We're almost there. I can smell it. Once the cave is vented, we can send down robots. I don't understand why no one thought of blasting a vent in the first place. When our analysis of the data you collected is finished, personnel not part of the blasting squad must leave the mine area immediately so the they can set up."

Sonja said, desperately, "The sentients are intelligent; they can act. We have to stop—"

"Don't be stupid, Shankar. Your brain was addled by fumes. It was all some sort of illusion, no doubt, created by your researcher, Harold, who is desperate to continue his futile project. Good try. This just forces us to act more quickly."

The man was hopeless. Sonja made one more attempt convince him at least to delay his plan. "Why would Dr. Harold destroy his module if he wanted to continue doing research? Pearl was taken out of a worker without harming—"

Impatiently he said, "That's even worse. Now more pearl is disappearing even from people. It doesn't matter who, or what is taking it. That's why we must act now."

"What do you want me to do?"

"Go to the refinery and make sure it is ready to start operations."

She sent off the cage and made a show of following Chalmers' instructions to prepare the officials and miners for their theoretical resumption of operations.

Then she went back to the refinery as instructed taking the three workers and Pet with her. There was considerable excitement and concern when the three refinery workers told the rest what had happened at the mine.

Chalmers called her soon after her arrival. She could hear manic excitement building in his voice. "We haven't a moment to lose. Congratulations Shankar, you lured the thing out and, before Harold's module blew up, enough data was collected with the cage to proceed. Don't even need the filthy canine."

"Then I'll return Pet to Julie. So you saw that they, the sentients are real. They—"

"I saw the module disintegrate. I saw a hologram speaking. I saw a worker open her eyes. Cute tricks. Harold is clever. Oh there is something there. Some phenomenon being recorded. My techs are working on a procedure now to destroy it, whatever it is."

Sonja was silent. Chalmers had seen what happened. And still— What could she do? She realized that if she was going to be able to do anything at all, she had to make him believe she would cooperate with his scheme. Not arguing with him now left her with some authority, although she couldn't imagine anything that would stop him. Even if she could contact someone offworld that she could trust there wasn't time.

Even on the limited visualizer of the communicator Sonja could see Chalmers was elated. He said, "You'll be glad you cooperated. As a reward for restoring pearl, you, as well as I, will have more cred than you can imagine—and think of the prestige you'll have, the power. It's what we both want."

Sonja was almost amused at Chalmers' gesture of generosity in including her in his scheme now that he thought he'd won. Of course, he pretended to include her only to keep her from trying to slow down his plans. She wondered what fate he planned for her in reality.

She said, quietly, "The refinery is being readied as you requested. I've contacted moonbase…to recall the staff." It was almost the truth.

As she switched off the communicator, Sonja was feeling hopeless—no way out. Can't help or save anybody. Even if she was able to contact the League wouldn't she find the same flaws there? She couldn't help the workers, or the farmers who might even lose their water source. She couldn't save Julie from her family and from Chalmers. Who in her life could she trust? Was there even anyone, trustworthy or not, who could help her now? She thought of Jason. Jason had tried to warn her in the beginning. He said he could help. Even as a child he was always trying to be fair, to enforce fairness. His teachers had treated it as a fault. She decided in desperation to try and contact Jason. But how?

She had to do something. She could probably contact Viol. If she was just sending a message to an old friend, it might get through. Viol might be willing to forward a message to Jason if only because it amused him. She would include a coded hologram with their secret childhood symbols. She contacted moonbase and had them send the coded message. Absurdly, unlike her reports to the League, they said it went through.

It was a desperate, futile gesture but she felt better. She did have a plan that might at least help the workers. Reanna had organized them so that the dormitory was working smoothly. Sonja had had time to think about what to do about taking over the refinery since their last conversation. When Reanna heard about Chalmers being distracted by his plan to blast open the mine, she agreed that she would cooperate with Sonja's plan to get a transport to take the workers to a squatter camp when they needed it. Sonja pointed out that the refinery had several vehicles at its disposal that they could get to if they were in control of the facility.

It had not been difficult to disarm the few security people one at a time and lock up the officials. Sonja assured the workers that if they were careful Chalmers would not realize that they were in charge of the refinery. He was too busy planning his blasting project. She convinced them that it was in their best interest to continue the charade as long as possible. She gave them what information she could and left them trying to decide where to find a place onplanet to escape to.

Then she took Pet and went to the chamber where the comatose refinery workers were stored. She needed a minute to think and it was quiet there. With the help of the refinery workers she could get some of the comatose people to Pella and the sentients to be restored. Should she take them to the mine now? But the officials there would tell Chalmers and she didn't even know how to contact Pella now that the module was gone.

She put the little dog down and touched her soft ears. What to do now. Couldn't return Pet to Julie. Why couldn't she have asked for a different assignment in the beginning? Then she had had a choice. But the person she'd been then, that Sonja, wouldn't have done it. She marveled at the limitations of that former self. So many blinders built in. When had she changed? How could that Sonja have been so…stupid? She laughed. She had been brilliant, talented and so stupid.

Should she try to run into the desert with the workers? She could still look for Julie, steal a transporter—join the renegades to become a pirate.

She'd met a few pirates in her career. She could succeed at that as Mark had; she would be even better at evading Consortium spies. But being a professional thief for the rest of what lifespan she could save didn't really appeal to her. The thoughts were so absurd she almost laughed.

The little dog was watching her expectantly. When Sonja's eyes focused on her, Pet began to wiggle—she imagined Pet wanted to play. Why couldn't she have been born some simple joyful irresponsible creature like this one? She could feel the tears starting, but it was no good feeling sorry for herself. Waste of time, and she didn't have much of it. She sat down and Pet jumped into her lap. She spoke to the dog again, desperate, suddenly exhausted but trying to think. "What can I do?" Stupid talking to a dog. If only she could take a quick nap and then— If only she could get Pella to come here to free the refinery workers from their slavery, their dementia, their pearl.

Finally she couldn't stand Pet's wiggling and let her go. Pet ran around in a circle and then stopped and sniffed at the floor. Then Pet ran to her and licked her face and she imagined Julie again, happy to have her dog back. Somehow she should find Julie to give her Pet—but Chalmers would take Pet away again. Pet jumped down and ran around in smaller and smaller circles and then stood there very still. It was a silly sort of game. The dog was waiting for her to come play…but she was too sleepy.

She was dreaming of Julie and Pet reunited, she and Julie and Pet leaving the planet. She turned to look and saw a red hot ball that turned into a red-hot gapping hole in space. She woke with a start and without thinking about it reached down. Was the floor getting warmer? Hallucinations now. But could the blast at the mine affect her here? She was miles away from the mine site. She didn't want to think about what was happening down in the caves—what might be happening to the two researchers she'd abandoned there. She had grown quite…fond of them. Even that annoying woman Nombei had some integrity.

The floor seemed to get even warmer. She closed her eyes, exhausted. There was nothing she could do. She could not even pretend to follow Chalmers' orders any longer. If she returned to the Earthdome she would eventually be arrested. No, at least here the refinery workers could protect her for a while.

# Chapter Twenty-Six

Chalmers actually went to the mine himself. No more taking chances at this stage; he would see this thing through himself. Now he stood in the cave supervising the blast setup. Rather than the minimal oxygen mask and filter and protective suits worn by his security force and techs here in the mine, he was completely encased in an elaborate explorer's environmental suit and helmet.

The destruction of Harold's module had caught Chalmers off guard. He hadn't thought whatever was down there had that kind of capacity. It had to be destroyed once and for all. Ironic that the solution was so simple. Blast open the cave and the poisons preventing mining would dissipate into the atmosphere at the same time whatever mechanism was producing it would be destroyed.

He was over his annoyance that Shankar had taken the dog. He hadn't needed it after all. Harold and his earthrat assistant would do admirably as organic lures for the stuff he was about to destroy. And he would convince Julie that Shankar was responsible for the dog's disappearance. Even Shankar wouldn't be a problem anymore. He'd left instructions that she not be allowed offplanet. He'd told her bosses she was dead, as she would be soon enough. He would deal with her when this task was completed and he had access to pearl.

When he was ready to blast, he called to Harold who was nearby with Nombei. Both were being guarded by security. "Since you're so enamored of the vapors and magma down here you can join them." He signaled for the guards to release them and was surprised to see them head down the passageway without being forced—so willing to be his lure and conveniently disappear. He had the beggar crew ready to go down as soon as the blast area cooled, which shouldn't take long once the caves were craters.

Below, Nombei and Omar moved slowly into the dark warmth of the caves. Behind them were the security people who'd been told to shoot if they tried to come back. When they could no long see them they stood for a long time huddled against the cave wall with just the faint light of a little lamp to comfort them. It could be just minutes before Chalmers set off his double blast of explosions and poisons. Nombei took Omar's hand. In desperation she called for Pella again, this time quietly telling her of Chalmers intentions—a one-sided dialogue warning the sentients to stay away or defend themselves.

Meanwhile, Omar cursed Sonja for deserting them—saving the dog over them. Then he said to Nombei, "Don't waste your breath. Pella showed how she could remove pearl from people's bodies safely. Her offer was not taken up. Destroying my module was a last gesture. Chalmers ignored it. The sentients must understand what he's trying to do; they have to give up on us humans and save themselves."

Nombei crouched down, silent now, despondent. This time it was Omar who took Nombei's hand. Ironically, at this moment when they both were going to die he understood that Nombei was in fact at least his equal as a human even though everything he'd ever been taught, either overtly or unconsciously, denied that. But Nombei had faced hardship and difficulties and even now was stronger than he would ever be.

She took off her face mask smiling at him. He did too. Hopefully they would die of asphyxiation and heat before the blast hit them. Silently they walked hand in hand further down the tunnel toward the heat and magma to join Pella, in spirit, if not in reality.

After a few minutes a thin, hot, red line appeared in a rock ahead. Omar put his arm around Nombei as the temperature began to rise in the narrow space. Omar could imagine hot lava breaking through and flowing over them.

They were losing consciousness in the hot airless space when Nombei heard the words, "I'm so sorry." The tears evaporated before they could run down her cheeks as Omar moved closer.

Nombei imagined Pella in the hot vapors that engulfed them, smiling her approval. Wisps of poisonous steam that might be Pella's hand crept toward them like a beneficent touch. Nombei covered Omar's head with her arms for the few seconds they would have alive together. Then they lost consciousness and did not feel or hear the explosion.

Below the refinery, Sonja was awakened by a blast of heat in her face. When she opened her eyes there was a small hole in the floor with an orange-yellow glow and the room was beginning to fill with hot gases. Sonja got up, her heart beating fast. Even so far away from the mine this had to be a result of Chalmers' work. It was just a matter of time now. Magma would follow the gasses seeping in and everyone would die. She had to get everyone out somehow. Was there time to get everyone on a transport? It was worse than she'd anticipated. She was glad for whatever terrible fate the Consortium might have in store for Chalmers after this, if he was even still alive. She imagined him slaving on some cold, airless asteroid.

But before she could catch Pet and leave the room the vapors began to condense and cool and Pella's glowing image coalesced in the middle of the room.

The little dog crouched near Sonja watching with luminous brown eyes, unafraid. Sonja was frozen with amazement at the power the sentients possessed. Pet ran to Pella and licked her hand as if she were still alive. Wasn't the spot where Pella appeared exactly where Pet had stood? She must still be dreaming.

Pella said, "We have to hurry; the energy from the explosion will dissipate soon. We must use it while we can. Bring the humans who contain pearl to me so that we can call back our history and restore them."

Sonja ran to find Reanna and between them they got the able-bodied workers to carry the rigid comatose workers near enough for Pella to touch.

A blue light surrounded each comatose worker and they seemed to quiver and become translucent for a moment as Pella touched them. Then their flesh became rosy brown like that of a newborn baby and they would gasp for breath, then get up slowly with a dazed look on their faces.

More and more refinery workers gathered around to watch—even those with different degrees of addiction and suffering the usual dementia. When the comatose workers had been restored. Pella spoke to the gathered workers, her voice hollow and echoing. "We are transforming our…recordings into a form not perceptible by organic life; there will be no more pearl. Those of you who carry pearl in your blood will step forward one at a time and touch me. As you have seen me do with the unconscious, I will take pearl from you, gently and without harm. You must chose if you are to join me-us or return to your human existence after pearl is removed."

After a moment a woman with lavender-tinted skin rushed forward and touched Pella's hand. Then another worker stepped forward and was also transformed.

As others stepped forward the image that was Pella faded. Only the hands remained as they touched those that came forward. Some regained their original healthy color and some disappeared like Pella, with only a little ash left on the hard dark stone of the floor. Those who were reluctant were urged forward by those who'd been transformed until no shadow of pearl was left.

# Chapter Twenty-Seven

Nombei came to consciousness, Omar still clinging to her, but instead of hot lava, untainted warm air touched her cheek and she could breath. After a few amazed moments she got up. The lamp still clutched in Omar's fingers was giving a faint diffused light which showed that the crack that had sizzled with deadly heat before was now a steaming opening. Inside the crack Nombei could see a passage slanting upward.

To her relief she noted that their environmental suits were only somewhat damaged. But next to her Omar choked and gasped for breath. Nombei gave him her filter and oxygen mask which was less damaged than his. When his eyes fluttered open he pulled away from her. "We're still alive."

"It seems so," Nombei said flatly.

"Before, I didn't mean—"

"I know. You clung to me because you thought you were dying, a moment of weakness. Anyway, we aren't out of here yet."

"You think the sentients—Pella—saved us?"

"It seems possible. Let's hope the air coming through that crack is from the outside and not from some tunnel filled with security guards."

They squeezed through the crack and trudged up the passage for what seemed like hours. The air still came down to them, but now from more than one passageway. The one they were in had narrowed so that they had to stoop to walk. They talked about going back and taking another passage but were too exhausted. Instead they stopped to rest. Nombei took off the cloying suit and lay on top of it naked in the warm dark. They both fell asleep.

When Omar woke he turned on the precious lamp for a moment to orient himself. He looked at the still figure of Nombei lying beside him in the dim light. His first response to the smooth white form was revulsion. His old mind told him the woman looked in her nakedness like a white slug with her too rounded contours and her smooth pale skin. Then Omar took a deep breath, remembering the feelings he'd had just before the blast. After all, he was a scientist. Why should he be influenced by society's irrational prejudices. Nothing alive in nature was ugly. Beauty lay in the specific adaptation of an organism to its environmental niche, as much as it did on social conditioning.

His prejudices about the proper form for the human body were wrong—too deeply influenced by his upbringing as a member of the academic elite where lean muscular bodies with narrow hips and small breasts for women were the approved style. Members of his class regarded any vestigial remains of the pretech age as sloppiness. After all, any defects which genetic engineering hadn't removed could be easily remedied by technology or will power. Nombei still had the wide rounded hips and breasts of her caste on Earth where pretech birthing was still practiced and genes were not enhanced—when reproduction was allowed at all—no doubt to save the cost of the technology used by the higher castes. He turned off the light.

Now the form before him reminded him of reproductions he'd seen of pre-twentieth century paintings. He'd been told they were considered beautiful in their time. He and his classmates had shuddered and giggled about what seemed to them grotesque images.

Now the soft curves and colorless skin evoked only compassion. The woman had a brain and good sense and a generosity that had nothing to do with her external shell—or did it? He could no longer separate the two qualities. A frightening realization was that he wanted to touch that cool smooth skin and be touched by those roughened narrow hands the way he'd been touched by the woman's mind and personality.

Nombei's eyes opened and she smiled. Even in the dim light of the lamp, the blue of her wide eyes showed. She got up and dressed herself and Omar gently took her hand and said, "Let's get out of here."

After what seemed like hours of walking and crawling through narrow low crevices in the damp dark, away from the heat and toward cooler air, Nombei and Omar emerged from a narrow fissure into the dim predawn light. They crawled out onto a shelf of rock above the rift valley.

# Chapter Twenty-Eight

Chalmers' staff at the Earthdome sent a communication to the refinery that the blasting at the mine was finished and they should prepare to receive pearl for refining within thirty-six earth-hours. Sonja sent a noncommittal acknowledgment and turned to find Reanna and several of the others waiting to speak to her.

After Sonja repeated Chalmers' message to them, Reanna declared, "We won't go back to work for him even if there is raw pearl, especially now that we understand what it really is." The others nodded in agreement.

An excited worker spoke up. "We control the refinery now—All we need is transport. We can take over moonbase and the interplanetary station, even try for a ship to get away—offplanet."

Sonja sighed. "The Consortium forces would be on you like a Moravian space raptor if you try to go offplanet. Pella said that pearl has been transformed so that it can't be used by people. If that's true, even Chalmers has to understand the pearl trade is dead. The League has to help anyone abandoned onplanet or move them to a colony."

Reanna snorted. "The settlers here maybe, but we are criminals now, even those of use who weren't before."

Someone else said, "Yeah, whatever we do they will send us to some forsaken asteroid mine or an ice planet colony to work off our time, or maybe just recycle us."

"I'll put a good word in for you," Sonja said. "A new colony will need all the able bodied people it can find. The League will understand that."

"And what makes you so sure Chalmers and the Consortium will give up so easily?"

"I hoped that Chalmers would blow himself up," Sonja said quietly. "But even without him we'd still have a difficult situation. I have to find out what's going on at the mine. Since Pella was here after the blast and was able to remove pearl from people here, we know Chalmers not only failed to destroy the sentients, but may even have strengthened them, maybe permanently. Convincing him of that, still might not keep him from trying to destroy them again. We must convince the Consortium that Chalmers tried to destroy the goose, but that her golden eggs are gone as well."

They all looked puzzled, then one of the women said, "She means as in the planet Horozo fable of the Talvano and the golden seed."

Sonja nodded. "An older, earthbased version. What you can do is to keep this place in order until I call for your help. See if you can put together a believable security force. There should be enough uniforms here. We may need to try and occupy the mine."

One of the women spoke. "Why should we trust you? You're a League employee."

Sonja nodded and answered, realizing as she did it how true it was, "You heard Pella. You saw what she and the sentients behind her can do. There is no more consumable pearl. The Consortium's pearl trade is dead. All there is left to do is to control the situation so that those of us still onplanet find some way to survive this crisis. If we work together we may live through it.

"Right now I need to find out the real situation at the mine. When I get back we will decide what to do together. Chalmers thinks he needs to let the blast area cool before anything else can happen. That gives us a little time."

She contacted the mine staff to say she was on her way and got in her hovi. She left the refinery workers in charge, with access to the medical supplies and other stores to help the recovering workers and to defend themselves. The mine workers had been locked in their dormitory at the time of the explosion. She was determined to help them too if she could.

Dawn was breaking as she approached the mine. In the faint rose-orange light she could see that the dome and buildings were still intact. There was a white glow from a small crater in the earth above the mine. She flew as close to the crater as she dared. Deep inside she could see seething magma, but there was no magma spilling from the crater, no dust, steam, or volcanic debris as she would have expected from a volcanic explosion. It was more like a festering wound, its edges pulling together as if it were trying to heal.

She called the Earthdome from her hovi and asked for Chalmers' office. He was in and would speak with her. She was connected and he said coolly, as if nothing were wrong between them, "Shankar…I wondered when you'd re-emerge. Staying away from the event was a smart move on your part. Some of my men who were down there had to be pulled out by the androids and are still unconscious." He didn't bother to suppress the note of elation in his voice. "But it worked. The cave is opened up and any fumes should be dissipated by the atmosphere." There was triumph in his voice now. "And without major environmental damage. Your worries about the water supply were unfounded. The water supply is still at its normal rate. By my calculations the area should have cooled and cleared out enough in a few days so that we can send miners down for pearl."

Sonja said nothing as she looked down again at the seething magma beneath a cooling edge and felt a profound sadness. It should all have been done a different way.

Chalmers went on. "I've alerted the proper authorities offplanet of our success. The first transport for the refined pearl is ready and waiting on moonbase. I expect you to get the facilities in order. The mine officials who were sent off during the blast will arrive back this evening. Then I will no longer need your help. You can return to moonbase and make your report."

He must still not know about the workers controlling the refinery. He didn't know that Pella—that the sentients were as strong as ever, or even stronger. Sonja took a deep breath. She certainly wasn't going to enlighten him at this point. He wouldn't listen anyway. She tried to sound cheerful. "Of course. Congratulations. I just flew over the crater."

His voice was a bit more edgy now, anxious. "We're monitoring it. You'll be glad to know our equipment has not detected any problems we can't handle—not even much water loss. Not too many casualties. How does it look?"

"Hot. Bigger than the hole you anticipated. Looks like a lot of white-hot magma down at the bottom. The mine buildings and the dormitory are intact and there's not the volcanics on the surface that one might expect with something that hot—no hot flowing magma or volcanic debris. No plume of steam or ash. Strange, it looks more like a healing wound than a volcanic explosion. I'll go down into the cave as soon as I can."

Chalmers said smugly, "Didn't I say that the damage would be contained?"

"I can't locate Dr. Harold and his assistant. Can you tell me where they are so they can help with the assessment?"

There was a pause, then he said, intending her to feel responsible. "You took the animal away, so we needed volunteers to lure the—vapors out."

Sonja sighed, feeling sad. She hadn't been able to save them after all. "So Harold and O'Brien are dead."

"Some sacrifices were necessary. You can return the animal to Julie."

And your security people will be waiting for me, she thought.

She said, controlling her anger, "So even without Dr. Harold to check for you, you have confirmed that pearl is unharmed?"

There was another, longer pause. Then Chalmers said, clearly controlling his annoyance, "The extra heat shouldn't have affected it. It's known to survive very high temperatures—having originally been formed by high temperature volcanic action."

"Certainly," she said guardedly. "I'll deliver Pet when I have a moment."

"Where are you going now?"

"I'll check on the mine staff that is still there—and the miners. Then I will continue getting the refinery ready as instructed…Sir."

He sounded relieved. "Signing off then."

She wouldn't dare try to contact Julie yet. He would be monitoring her calls. Anyway, Sonja had to admit she was enjoying the company of the little dog. She seemed almost like a person.

Sonja landed as near the mine as she dared. She needed to evaluate the situation there. If, as she assumed, there was just a skeleton crew, it wouldn't be hard to take over.

As she'd suspected, there were few guards present and those were there to keep the workers confined to their dormitory. She was relieved to find the remaining staff and the miners unharmed.

Sonja went down an old abandoned tunnel to get nearer the blast area. Surprisingly, it was not unbearably hot. There was nothing left of human construction anywhere in any of the remaining mine chambers or caves she could get access to. Like Omar's equipment it had all been vaporized. Nothing was left but some metallic ash showing her footprint in the floor of the cave. She returned to the refinery to collect Reanna and some of the workers.

# Chapter Twenty-Nine

Wrapped in some abandoned sacking Nombei had found in the cornfields nearby, Omar slept curled up against a rocky ledge. When Omar opened his eyes next, the planet's red-orange sun was just brightening the thin air and Nombei was pulling at him. "Wake up. We won't have much time before someone comes looking for these grubs."

Omar sat up. Two workgrubs carrying large cloth sacks were standing passively nearby on a path that snaked down and through fields of oversized corn. In the distant fields he could see other grubs bringing in the corn. That was all they needed, some farmer coming up to look for his grubs. The farm community was always suspicious of strangers, especially those without obvious means of transportation. They would be arrested as grub thieves—not a trivial crime with the current depletion of the grub worker population.

He reluctantly stood up. "The farmers will miss these grubs right away."

"Nobody's around. They left the loading system on auto. If we hurry we can get to the transfer station before any farmers show up." Nombei pulled him toward the work grubs. When Omar resisted, Nombei said impatiently, "They're not going to hurt you." She smiled. "You're not their normal food. Hurry up. They'll carry us to the transfer station. That way we can avoid the sensors picking up our tracks. The storage sheds for corn are near the edge of the rift valley near the main Earthdome. If we can get in the transport cars with the corn, we can get to the edge of the valley— closer to my dome."

"Your dome. You're crazy. Chalmers will find us there."

"They think we were burned to a crisp—vaporized. They won't be looking for us."

"What good will it do to go there? We can't buy transport without alerting Chalmers that we are still alive."

"My neighbors in the valley will help us."

"Why should they risk—"

"Even the farmers resent the Consortium. They believe the Consortium let them settle just because the pearl industry needed cheap food. The Consortium barely tolerates the valley community. Most settlers in the valley are former employees of the Consortium for good reason. Why should they turn us in? They would celebrate if the Consortium were gone—the planet would belong to them."

Omar was skeptical but what choice did he have. He climbed into one of the sacks and let the grub worker pick him up and carry him like a sack of potatoes, his face against its gray wrinkled skin smelling of corn husks and something nauseatingly sweet and dry. In spite of his research, he had never been this close to a live workgrub. Investigating the life of this planet he had always been protected by layers of plastic and metal and his intellectual and scientific perspective.

Fortunately there was nothing smarter at the transfer station than a class five robot. Nombei and Omar were deposited at Nombei's command on the pile of corn sacks waiting on the loading dock. When the robot had counted out sacks of oversized corn into a car and after the controlling surveillance camera had turned toward the task of filling the next car, they climbed quickly into the filled car, trying to keep out of sight of the surveillance devices. Nombei quickly built them a shelter out of the filled sacks—a hollow space. They made themselves as comfortable as they could. Anxiously, they waited for the cars to move or for farmers to appear. But none came and finally the line of cars moved.

Just before they got to the storage sheds the cars slowed. Wrapped in the corn sacks they rolled off the edge of the car onto the hard-packed desert ground. They would be registered by any surveillance device as bags of corn to be salvaged later. If they were lucky no one would ever look for them, assuming desert scavengers, escaped Earth rodents that infested the desert near human habitation, would make them not worth salvaging.

Nombei knew about an old abandoned road nearby. It has been left by the original planetary explorers who built it to get from the water-rich valley up to the cliff tops where there was land that could grow genetically-altered Earth crops. It switched back and forth steeply down the cliff into the rift valley. The way down was steep but not difficult until they were in the cover of damp fog and lush vegetation on the floor of the valley. Here Omar needed her help. Fortunately it was a part of the valley with which she was very familiar and it had a few recognizable signs that were kept clear to guide the residents. She wrapped their faces in sacking to temporarily protect their breathing from the spores but even with that she was practically carrying Omar by the time they reached her dome.

Marla finally answered Nombei's insistent buzzing. Nombei almost smiled at the shocked look on Marla's face staring back at her from the dome monitor. Finally the woman pushed the lever to open the door for them.

She helped Omar strip, then got him a respirator that would help clear his lungs of spores. Then she pushed him into a chemical shower that would remove the layer of life they had acquired on their long walk here. She put a respirator over her own face and stepped into another shower cubicle. There wasn't time to let a leaf clean her naturally, and who knew what noxious substances she might have acquired during her long sojourn away and in the volcanic tunnels that might poison them. She got clean clothing for them and led Omar, still suffering with labored breathing, into the residential part of the dome.

Marla, still looking frightened, said, "They told me you were dead. They transferred your assets to me—just today. They said you were attacked by one of the beggars you were trying to help. They've stopped the reclamation program they started for the beggars because—"

"Well, as you can see they were bending the truth," Nombei said dryly.

Marla looked away for a moment as if trying to think what to say. "It'll take a while to reinstate your assets. I'm sorry. I didn't—"

"Don't worry about that right now," Nombei said.

"You didn't already alert them that we were here, by any chance?" Omar choked out in a hoarse whisper.

Marla didn't respond. She was still looking at them as if they were ghosts. "They said everyone in the program was dead and the security forces had to—there were pictures on the news."

"We won't bother them right now, OK?" Nombei said. "They have enough to worry about."

Marla nodded slowly, her eyes still fearful.

"My friend here needs a little help. We were out there with damaged filters and suits. He isn't used to it."

"Oh my, you must feel awful." Marla rushed over to Omar.

He whispered almost conversationally, "Thanks. I'll be better after a little rest. I don't understand how you can stand to live in this dank soup all the time. I feel like I have mold growing in my lungs."

Leading him into the next room, Marla smiled uncertainly. She said, almost too reassuringly, "You get used to it. There is more oxygen here with all the photosynthesis and water. One can get along with just a filter after a while."

Nombei was amazed that Omar had made it this far. The thin oxygen, the heat of the tunnels and the cold dry cliffs were bad enough, but the dense spore-laden mists of the valley—

She got a cup of hot broth for herself out of the dispenser; even she should go easy on food. Now that she was alive and home she wanted more than ever to find some way to alert the Galactic League about the sentients—even if the sentients were already destroyed. She wanted badly to believe they weren't gone, that Chalmers had failed, that it had been the sentients who had saved them.

Marla was a good person; she wouldn't want to harm anyone, but she was timid, vulnerable to authority. Nombei checked the com for any outgoing calls but found nothing recent. She had no choice but to trust the woman, but she would have to be watched. Could she really trust anyone onplanet now? The euphoria of escaping from the mine was fading. Nombei suddenly felt exhausted, lost and nearly overwhelmed by hopelessness.

Then she took a deep breath. She refused to be defeated. Nothing had really changed. The Consortium had never intended to let them return to their previous lives. But that just meant they had nothing to lose by trying to survive, or even by trying to contact the League. At the moment Omar wouldn't survive a trip on foot. But after he'd rested and his breathing was somewhat restored, they would have to move quickly. Since Nombei's own cred was already transferred to Marla, they would have to try for Omar's.

# Chapter Thirty

It was evening, planet-time, when Sonja, Reanna and the other able-bodied refinery workers, dressed in security uniforms and armed with stunners, arrived at the mine buildings.

Sonja presented her credentials, but when the guard suspiciously picked up his speaker unit to communicate with his superior, Reanna put a stunner to his head and took the speaker from him, handing it to Sonja.

Sonja said to the official on the other end of the line, "Investigator Shankar here. Just a security check." She handed the instrument back to the guard. He said a bit shakily to his superior, "All OK here, Sir. Yes, signing off…Sir." Sonja took it and replaced it in its cradle. One of the refinery workers took over as guard and Reanna and her team went to secure the buildings.

Chalmers' few security people were rounded up and confined and were replaced with armed refinery workers in borrowed security suits. There were few management and staff left after the blasting and those were locked up with the security force.

She left Reanna to secure the facility and went into the dormitory. There were a few mine workers and the beggars. Why hadn't the sentients—Pella—been here already to help them? Was it because they were so few that were pearl addicted?

It was very quiet there. Most of the able-bodied miners gladly joined the refinery workers. Sonja sat down on the floor and placed her hands against bare concrete, feeling foolish. She missed the liveliness of the little dog left safely at the refinery. It was absurd to think she could call up Pella, like calling a spirit from the dead. How would the sentients possibly know she was here, close as they might be?

There was nothing—the floor did not warm, Pella did not appear. Sonja laughed at her flight of fancy. The stress of the last few days must be getting to her.

Sonja left Reanna in charge of the mine and took her hovi out over the crater again. The white glow had faded to orange. The cooling black edges were pulling in—healing.

A terrifying sense of unreality almost overcame her. She imagined the sheer power of these sentients, commanding, perhaps even controlling the immense volcanic forces of the planet. She laughed at herself. She was letting her imagination run wild. Too many amazing things had happened.

Back at the mine she tried again to contact Julie. This time the service person at Julie's apartment in the Earthdome inquired who was calling. Sonja decided to lie; Chalmers' staff would be listening. She remembered the name of one of the people she'd met at Chalmers' dinner party and gave that name.

"The Contessa is too busy preparing for her trip to visit her family on Earth. She is not taking calls."

Yes, Julie might well have decided to go back to the bosom of her family on Earth, especially after Chalmers took Pet away. "She will want to talk to me. I have her dog."

There was silence. It worked; the system changed sound. Julie must not be there but they had contacted her. Julie's voice suddenly loud, furious, outraged. "Is this some sort of cruel joke? Did Chalm put you up to this?" But before Sonja could speak communication had been cut.

She contacted Chalmers' office. When he was on the line she said, "Shankar here. Both the refinery and the mine are secured, and it looks as though the crater has started to cool down. Standing by for further orders."

"What's your game, Shankar. I haven't been able to contact my staff at the mine? What's going on?"

"It's still early, Sir. I did check the mine. Your staff there and the miners were unharmed. The crater that was provoked by your…intervention was very atypical of volcanic activity. As I said before, there is no flowing magma on the surface, no…smoke or ash, and temperatures are not excessively high even in what is left of the mine—not nearly as hot as one would have predicted. But there's no equipment in the mine, organic or otherwise—no communication or mining equipment left. No one except Omar and his assistant seem to have been harmed. Too bad we don't still have Omar. He was getting close to an answer about what was in the caves."

Chalmers said, "I doubt that. Harold was suffering from delusions about his nonexistent archaeological intelligence. Probably a result of overexposure to the vapors. I trust you have recovered. Let me know when the mine area has cooled sufficiently." Then Chalmers was off the communicator for a few seconds. Were they trying to get her location? But why would he bother to send someone after her now that he believed he'd succeeded?

He came back on. "You're wrong. It seems Harold and his little earthrat assistant might have gotten out of the cave. The blast must have opened some new passageways to the surface. We have reports from the valley area that they have arrived at the earthrat's hut. Check it out, will you, Shankar?

Then bring them back to the mine so we can get an…evaluation."

Was it a trap? But his Earthdome staff wouldn't want to go into the valley after renegades. They must be really traumatized by what happened at the mine. Earthdome types!

Sonja tried to sound reassuring. "Right. I'm on it. By the way, Sir, when I called Julie, she wouldn't speak to me. Seems to think her dog is dead and I am to blame. Enlighten her, please, so I can return it."

There was a long pause. Chalmers finally said, "Don't try and fool me. You know very well Julie's gone. I sent her to the transport station on moonbase to go back to the Family compound Earthside, and she's disappeared. I'm sure you're aware exactly how annoyed the Family will be if she isn't on the transport when it leaves. They will still have to pay for her passage. I don't know what you two are thinking. She, at least, knows she can't survive long without her life support, which is on the transport. Rather an oversight on her part not taking it with her if she is not going home."

Chalmers sounded almost pleased. He must figure he didn't need Julie or the Family now that he was going to be so rich. Sonja felt like she was falling into a giant black hole. She tried to remain calm. "So, did you kill her or just dump her somewhere?"

"I take it that comment means you don't know where she is either. I'm disappointed. I thought you two had a thing going. I guess it's just Julie having a temper tantrum. That hovi of hers will have run out of life support by now. Poor twit, lying out there in the desert. I don't have the personnel to hunt for her in this crisis."

Sonja tried not to think about Julie. There was too much to do. She told Reanna to be prepared for the arrival of the staff. They could be locked in the dormitory at the refinery, at least temporarily.

Nombei and Omar were sleeping when Sonja arrived at Nombei's housedome. The assistant, Marla, who had drugged their tea, looked very relieved when Sonja showed her ident card. Marla left the house, her duty complete, confident she would have a lifetime's cred in her account.

Sonja finally managed to shake Nombei awake. When she opened her eyes and saw Sonja she tried to escape, but Sonja was too quick. She held Nombei against the wall. "Don't worry. I'm here to help you. I don't understand how you survived Chalmers' blast or how you got here, but we're on the same side now." When Nombei stopped struggling, Sonja let go and Nombei sat down on a chair rubbing her arm.

While Sonja tried to wake Omar, Nombei said, "Why should I believe you? Why would you help us? Why defy your bosses now?"

Sonja stopped shaking Omar. A profound sadness she recognized as partly hypno-induced training to keep her loyal to the Eminences seemed to overcome her. She did not resist it. "I was willing to give my life, when I believed the Eminences were…honorable." She consciously turned the sadness into anger and said, "Now I know better."

Nombei sat down next to Omar. "Have you contacted the League?"

Sonja shook her head. "Communication with them has been blocked since I've been here."

"But you'll help us get off-planet and go to the League. Omar says—"

"Said." Omar opened his eyes and sat up slowly. Coughing, he whispered, "No time for that now. That would take weeks. Chalmers may not have destroyed the sentients yet, but he'll keep trying. And why should we be so sure of the League's good will?"

Sonja took a deep breath. The terrible sadness was fading. "It may be the sentients we have to fear now. Chalmer's blast seems to have made them stronger. They burned into the refinery to take pearl from the workers there. It's possible they could burn into the Earthdome, especially if Chalmers doesn't figure out that he's lost. I don't know what will convince him. No doubt he has already sent off-planet for reinforcements."

Omar said sleepily, "But so far the sentients have done their best not to kill people. I believe they helped us."

Sonja waved her hand dismissively. "Yes, but if they really understand now how ruthless Chalmers is—"

Omar's breathing had improved but he was still wheezing. "We tried to explain a little about the human capacity for selfishness and greed to the sentients—how we humans can rationalize our behavior even when we understand the consequences."

Sonja leaned toward them. "Maybe they do understand. Pella said that there's no more pearl—that it has been transformed into something else, some other substance that is inaccessible to humans. She said that what the sentients want from us is the return of pearl still in humans. But Chalmers will never admit that he is dealing with intelligent and capable beings. And I'm afraid those who control the Consortium will agree with him."

There was an edge of panic in Omar's voice now. "We have to find a way to stop him, make him really understand how powerful the sentients can be, that they have changed pearl—before it is too late, before he provokes the sentients into destroying us all."

Sonja took in a deep breath. "I don't think they'll do that, but if we don't have time to persuade people to give pearl back voluntarily, the sentients might just start taking it."

Nombei said, "Killing people to get it?"

"There is no way to know whether people would die if the sentients take pearl involuntarily," Omar said. "But since the sentients haven't tried to do that, one suspects that people might."

"They killed Pella," Nombei said angrily.

Omar rubbed his face, exhausted. "You know very well Pella asked to join them. That's different; she says she's part of them now. They can manifest her and anyone that joins them."

Nombei shook her head. "That Pella is just an illusion."

Sonja was getting impatient. "Illusion or not, Pella now represents the sentients' raw power as well as their ability to learn. That no one else has died may just be an accident, an oversight, evidence of their indifference to us. Look how long it took them to decide to protect their pearl. Much of the human race all over the galaxy has tasted pearl. The task of recovering it is overwhelming."

Nombei shook her head. "The Consortium won't take on that task no matter what the Galactic League says. They would dissolve first."

Omar said thoughtfully, "I think if there's no active resistance to the loss of pearl, people won't be hurt. Once people understand there's no harm to them they'll cooperate."

Nombei laughed. "When have humans not fought to keep their favorite recreational drugs?"

Sonja nodded her head in agreement. "But the comatose workers in the refinery are recovering after pearl was taken out of their bodies even though they couldn't consciously volunteer. I'm convinced they'll fully recover with time. That will show people they can be saved from the worst effects of pearl."

"The people in storage?" Omar asked.

Sonja nodded. "So far the sentients have taken it without harming people."

Sonja told them about what had happened at the refinery, describing how the sentients burned through the floor at the refinery.

"We saw the sentients' raw power down in the mine," Nombei said quietly. "They cracked open a passage for us so that we could escape the aftermath of Chalmers' explosion."

"That could have been an accident, a crack opened by the explosion," Omar said. "If they were that powerful surely they would go after pearl everywhere. They could crack open the ground in the valley. There are black market stores of pearl on this planet. Places like Huniman's where people can still get pearl for very high prices."

Nombei said impatiently, "Maybe the sentients can get the unconsumed pearl, but most users aren't comatose. They wouldn't see any reason to volunteer to give up pearl. I'll bet there is plenty of pearl in the

Earthdome, not even including what's in the people. Why don't the sentients go after that?"

Sonja said soberly, "If there's no cooperation I assume they will."

Nombei looked at Sonja thoughtfully. "If Chalmers thinks you're working for him, what does he expect you to do about us?"

"You're too dangerous to him now, alive. You know too much. He still believes he can get more raw pearl to refine. I'm supposed to take you back to the mine. The safest place for you now might be there, now that the workers control it. He won't try to go back there until he's sure the blast area has cooled."

"Will the workers really be able to resist Chalmer's security force?" Omar asked, skeptically.

"Now that they had the audacity to take over a Consortium facility they don't have much choice but to try. They need to hold it until they can negotiate the right to join a colony on some other planet, if not be colonists here," Sonja said.

"Why would the Consortium negotiate with mere workers?" Omar asked.

"Since they are desperate for pearl, they think they need the workers," Nombei said thoughtfully. "Once pearl isn't refinable this planet has no value to the Consortium. All we have to do is to find a way to prove to Chalmers that the sentients are taking back their pearl and transforming it into something humans can't use and the planet is ours."

Sonja shook her head. "No, you have to convince the Eminences. They are desperate. They will make the planet uninhabitable searching for pearl."

Omar rubbed his eyes. "If he blows open the underground water supply— It wouldn't take much to destroy the environment."

"For humans." Nombei said.

"And for the water-based endemic life-forms," Omar said sadly. "If we could just get some evidence to the Galactic League, maybe then the sentients would be left in peace and people wouldn't be killed."

Sonja took a deep breath and felt herself flush as she admitted, "None of my attempts at communicating with the League have gotten through. I wouldn't be surprised if Chalmers has been sending favorable reports in my name." Sonja sadly looked away. "Eminences believe pearl is their ticket to eternal life. Somehow they have figured out how to avoid the comatose state people suffer with overuse of pearl."

Nombei said, "The sentients are strong. We've seen their power. Chalmers can't destroy them."

Sonja shook her head. "Sooner or later, the sentients will be destroyed or forced into destroying humans."

Omar whispered desperately, "We could try to buy a little time with the sentients, if we could explain the situation. But I've no way to communicate with them with my equipment destroyed."

Nombei said impatiently, "They don't seem to have any trouble communicating. If Shankar wasn't hallucinating they responded to her or Pet's presence in the refinery and melted a hole in the floor."

Sonja said, "I'm afraid we won't see the sentients unless we're in a position to help them get pearl back. We'll just have to stop Chalmers ourselves."

With that statement Sonja felt free of her programming. Now even the thought of her death didn't worry her. After all, wasn't her death guaranteed one way or the other? She, of all of them, was the least likely to survive because of her betrayal of the Eminences.

Again she imagined herself running off to the desert with Julie—a strong Julie healed by the sentients. It would have to be a Julie changed so she could eat, so that she could live like other humans. Sonja imagined the sentients unravelling Julie's genetic code and changing her body. They would know how a stomach was supposed to look and function. She wanted that badly. She would still love the woman changed, even if she ended up with all the human imperfections, a real person, more like Nombei than like the Julie she'd fallen in love with. The two of them would join the Godong. They would find an underground lake.

She laughed out loud at the strength of her desperate fantasy. Julie would be amused, wouldn't she?

On the way to the mine Sonja left a message for Chalmers assuring him that all was well. It said she was taking Dr. Harold and his assistant to be confined at the mine. Ironically it was true that all was well, if only at the mine and refinery, though not in any way Chalmers would appreciate. The workers had them under control. There had been a few squabbles in the beginning over the scant resources, but the workers had settled their differences and were taking turns dressing in uniform in case any of Chalmers' employees showed up.

Sonja, Omar and Nombei found Reanna who told them that some of the armed workers had taken the beggars and a few of the mine staff—those with pearl addiction—at laser-gunpoint near the edge of the crater in the floor of the cave with red hot magma far below.

She found them and they told her what had happened. The recalcitrant beggars and staff had said they would rather die than give up their pearl. The workers claimed they had meant only to threaten, but that one beggar had fallen screaming into the hole. When they had looked over the edge all they saw far below was the glow of hot magma, but after a while a small pearl appeared at the edge of the crater. The pearl rolled toward them slowly as if pulled by an invisible force.

Then Pella had appeared in the cloud of vapors above the hole and reached down to pick up the pearl. In a voice that could barely be heard, she had said, "We are grateful for this of our history and substance returned. We regret we were not prepared to receive it without the destruction of the human entity. It is hard to reconstruct and record that individual's sentience when the contact is so precipitous. We partially reconstructed the essence of the individual who has just joined us, but not his corporeality."

A worker described her surprise when a lean shadowy figure had appeared behind Pella, translucent and blurry but recognizable as the man who had just fallen. The image had faded and reappeared slowly, then disappeared again.

The other beggars and staff had been frightened. Pella had spoken to them in a soothing, whispering voice as she became a swirling soft vapor that surrounded them.

Finally one of the beggars had reached a hand out to Pella and then crumpled, curling up. The other beggars watched wide-eyed as pearl was drained from him. Finally he got up and said in an excited tone, "It's all right. I feel fine." After a few minutes some of the others had begun reaching out their hands. Then when all who volunteered had been drained of pearl the vapor had disappeared.

But when Sonja went down into the cave to peer down at the swirling magma below she felt no presence. She even tried to visualize Pella but felt nothing but heat and fatigue.

Some of the workers had loaded the mine's security people, mine officials and staff into one of mine's shuttle cruisers, and were trying to figure out how to send it into orbit. Sonja got them to compromise and they put a month's worth of food and water on the cruiser. After destroying the communication and manual override equipment, they sent the cruiser out into an unoccupied part of the planet on automatic. It would land when the fuel ran out, too far away for anyone to walk back. If they were lucky they might land near one of the squatter settlements. If they were smart they would stay there. Chalmers could do nothing about it unless reinforcements came from offplanet.

While Omar and Sonja talked about what they should do, Pet ran up to Nombei. After a few minutes she laughed and said, "Do these animals— communicate—some sort of implant?"

Omar shook his head.

Nombei said, "But I think it's talking to me, and I can't understand."

Sonja turned to Nombei with a sigh. "What did you say about Julie's dog?"

"Maybe the sentients are trying to communicate through it. Is that the reason that you haven't returned it to the Contessa yet?"

Sonja was startled. They must be feeling something, too, seduced by that vain hope that there was some way to communicate. Pet was an animal, without words, without ordinary language. Why pick a dumb animal to communicate? It was their desperation speaking.

Nombei said, "Wasn't the dog there when Pella come though the floor? You can take over the main Earthdome with your workers. They can go in as security. Pet can call—"

Sonja thought about it. The Earthdome itself was a few miles from the mine. The volcanic vents might well make it possible. Maybe they—Pella—could get through, enter the Earthdome. But taking over the Earthdome so they could bring volunteers to Pella would be a daunting task.

Dismissively, Sonja said, "That wouldn't work. The security system at the main Earthdome is too sophisticated—too multilayered. There aren't enough workers to take over the Earthdome and they aren't trained to fight."

"We could recruit the squatters and some people from the farms and the valley," Nombei said, disappointed.

"Investigator Shankar is right," Omar said, "We might get into the service sector, but the residents are protected by artificial intelligence. An attempt to invade even the service sector would trigger the failsafe locking system. We would need to have someone on the inside who could give us permission to enter."

Sonja shook her head. "There isn't time for that, even if we could get them on our side. If the failsafe system were to be activated at the Earthdome, no one could get in until reinforcements got here from off-planet."

"You could get in there, Investigator." Nombei said.

"Maybe the sentients will figure out what to do with Chalmers," Omar said.

Sonja sighed. "He isn't the only one. Nobody in the Consortium is interested in giving up on pearl. But you're right, we have to get inside the Earthdome. Help the sentients get at pearl without destroying everyone."

"I know there must be pearl stores hidden in the Earthdome not to mention the number of people who are addicts," Omar agreed.

"I'll do what I can," Sonja said.

Nombei said, "Maybe we can persuade the residents to give up their pearl before reinforcements get there. That might be enough so the sentients won't destroy us all right away."

"I'd have to go there alone—now, before Chalmers makes another crazy attempt to destroy the sentients."

"Can you get in?" Omar asked.

"Chalmers still thinks I'm cooperating with him."

"If we can demonstrate that the sentients can reclaim pearl anywhere maybe he'll finally believe he's lost," Omar said.

"I don't think so, but you're right, it's time to do something. I'll go to the Earthdome, try to find Pet's owner, the Contessa. She might help us." Sonja picked up Pet.

Sonja got into Julie's apartment without any trouble because Julie really was gone; her apartment was empty and her service people had been reassigned. As Chalmers had indicated all the essential equipment had been loaded onto the transport waiting for her departure off-planet.

Julie's personal hovi was gone, too. The hovi staff said she left in it days before with as much food and water as it could carry. She couldn't eat the food so she must be taking it for someone. The Godong? Sonja checked the monitors and records. Julie had headed out into the desert toward Godong settlement, but her hovi had disappeared behind some hills and not reappeared. The staff had assumed she had landed and that she would check in again when she was ready to return. The monitor had been changed then to follow another craft. Chalmers hadn't authorized a search, though the staff had informed him that she hadn't returned.

Without Julie she had little hope of accessing the comatose residents of the Earthdome without raising suspicions. Already her movements were being monitored by the staff. And she was worried about her. She couldn't last long in the harsh conditions of the desert. Sonja left the earthdome while she still could and flew her hovi over the hill where Julie's had disappeared. Searching the surface, she finally found marks left by a hovi landing tracks, but nothing else. She and Pet got out and Pet sniffed around the tracks, his tail beating an excited rhythm round and round. Julie had been here.

Sonja began a methodic survey of the surrounding land beyond the hill with her hovi in a wider and wider arc. Finally she saw it off in the distance—Julie's hovi parked under a rocky overhang.

# Chapter Thirty-One

Most of the food and water and some of Julie's emergency equipment and the supplies for it were still in the hovi, but there was no sign of Julie. Had the Godong found her? Why hadn't they taken the rest of the food? Sonja sat staring at the desert, hoping desperately to see her. She could bear any amount of anger and rejection if only Julie were still alive. Finally she noticed Pet looking out her hovi window, watching her. When she set Pet down she immediately started off away from the hovi, nose to the sand. Without much hope Sonja followed. There was not much chance that Julie could have survived more than a few hours away from the hovi.

After a while she began to see traces of Julie—a dropped water bottle, a wrapper. Then she found some of Julie's emergency equipment in a neat pile, deliberately abandoned. At the brow of a hill Pet stopped and began to bark. Sonja hurried over to her. Below, on the other side, was a small Godong settlement. Had Julie known it was there and come to find it?

She hushed Pet and called out. No answer, no movement below. But Pet's barking would have frightened them. She hurried down the hill.

As far as she could tell there was no one left in any of the huts. But they'd been here recently. Hearths were still warm. Their meager food was still on the shelves. It looked as if they had left in a hurry. Were they afraid that Julie would be followed? Where could they have gone? Julie must be with them. Did she have some of her survival equipment with her? Without it she could be dead by now. Desperately Sonja searched. Finally, Pet led her to the entrance to a cave. They must be hiding there.

She did not find the Godong, but she found Julie. She was lying with an arm dangling down, reaching out and touching the red pearl she had seen when she first visited the Godong. Pet rushed over to Julie and licked her face and she opened her eyes—she was alive. Sonja picked her up, a leaf, light and dry. Julie protested softly.

Sonja carried her back to a hut and made her as comfortable as possible, pouring water on her lips and face till she opened her eyes again. Pet lay down next to her and Julie whispered, "Chalm told me you were bringing Pet back…dead. That's part of why I left. Nothing to keep me there. I should know better than to believe him; he always lies."

"I'm going back for the equipment you left in the desert. It won't take long."

"I don't need it now, just a little more clean water. It feels so good."
Julie had not meant to survive. Sonja poured more water on her lips and
hands and placed the canteen next to her.

It took her so long to find the sterile water attachment and emergency
nutrient package Sonja was sure she would find Julie dead when she got
back. But, to her shocked surprise, when she entered the hut Julie was sitting up, a bowl of vile-looking soup on the low table in front of her. Julie
lifted a spoonful of it to her lips and tasted it with her tongue before Sonja
could get it out of her hand.

She smiled at Sonja. "It's all right. It won't hurt me. I ate some already.
I'm not a good cook yet, but I'm learning. Mammon taught me a little, but
she and Babe have gone with the others to the mountains. The tribe no
longer feels safe here. They wouldn't take me with them, but they said I
could stay in this hut. Babe took me to the cave. I touched the red pearl,
Gawaya. She is making me better. I am learning to eat now."

Sonja wanted to weep with sadness at the intensity of Julie's wishful-
ness. Instead she said, "This is crazy. You need your equipment. You have to
go back."

Julie said nothing, just turned her back.

"Even if you survive a bit longer, what makes you think Chalmers
won't find you here?"

"By the time he gets around to it, I'll be gone."

"Dead, you mean?"

Julie said defiantly, "Gawaya *is* making me better. I can eat a little. I
won't starve now. Not that it would matter."

"To me it does." Sonja surprised herself at how much she meant this.
"And to your dog."

Julie rubbed Pet's fur, investigating her body, looking into her eyes and
talking directly to her. "You naughty girl. You shouldn't have let them take
you away. You should have barked to wake me up so I could stop them." She
turned to Sonja. "Chalm tell you to bring me Pet?" She asked suspiciously.

Sonja shook her head. "I have been trying to bring Pet back to you for
days. Now you have to return to the Earthdome for your own survival.
There is no Gawaya with power to cure you. What the Godong believe
doesn't apply to you. You need modern science to survive and there isn't
much time. You are dehydrated—"

Julie listened skeptically, pressing her face to Pet's warm fur and sitting
quietly for a few minutes. Then she looked up at Sonja startled. "She feels
different. What have you done to her." Julie's teal blue eyes were unusually
wide and staring. "She's, she's…talking back to me." Julie frowned and

shook her head, then she bent her head down next to Pet.

After a minute she looked over at Sonja, fear and excitement in her wide eyes. "Is it true? What I am…understanding…that she can talk to my mind? Or is she some sort of fancy robot now? I'll be very angry if you've tried to fool me."

Sonja took a deep breath. Should she really add to Julie's illusions? …add to her fantasy about being healed? But maybe the truth would help her bring Julie back. She finally leaned closer, almost whispering, "I don't really know, but I felt that somehow your dog was 'talking' to me, too."

"Is it right what she says, that they—the things down in the mine, the ones Chalm is trying to destroy, can help people?"

She took a deep breath. "There are sentients—beings on this planet that are clearly very intelligent. I don't know all they can do now, but they seem to be learning fast—"

Julie looked up, her eyes wide. "Go," she said, interrupting Sonja's speech imperiously. "Go outside and wait until I call you."

Sonja reluctantly sat outside the hut in the glare of the cold sun her back against the rough surface of the hut, wondering why she'd obeyed the command. Even the minimal oxygen augmenting equipment began to irritate her and she wanted to rip it off. She should be on her way. There was so much to do. She worried what the workers might do without her supervision. Chalmers might already know— She needed to get Julie back to the Earthdome where she could be properly cared for.

Then she heard Julie's call and hurried into the hut. Julie was smiling and holding the little dog. "We are going back to the Earthdome. I'll go in your hovi. Don't let Chalm know you found me. We'll send my hovi out in the desert so the security people can trace it and find it out there, but not me. He'll think I'm wandering about out there dying and be glad to be rid of me." She smiled. "I'm supposed to help you get pearl out of people," she said importantly, "You're to tell me what I need to do."

On the way back, Sonja told Julie about her experience at the refinery—the image of Pella coming out of the floor taking back pearl from the comatose workers and restoring them.

Julie listened carefully.Then said, "What can I do?"

Sonja took Julie's hand and said, "You could start by telling me if there are people at the Earthdome who are unconscious because of pearl and where they might be."

Julie looked puzzled. "I suppose you mean those in retreat in deep mediation, the ones who haven't returned. They're down in the sanctuary. Why?"

"So pearl can be taken out without harming them and they can be revived. The addicts who aren't yet unconscious can be helped too. But we will need to convince them to volunteer."

"Why would they do that? They like their state. They just want more pearl."

"If they don't agree to having it removed nothing will happen. First we must find that sanctuary. Any pearl removal, like everything else at the Earthdome, will be recorded on the security visualizer. Maybe Chalmers will finally see he has failed, that there will be no more pearl."

Julie took the little dog up in her lap and put her cheek against Pet's fur. After a few minutes she nodded to Sonja, kissed her and whispered, "That's what he says too."

Sonja frowned. "Just be…careful."

Julie smiled. "Don't worry; no one takes me seriously there, especially Chalm." Julie came close again and kissed her gently on the mouth, whispering, "You will go with me when I leave this planet?"

Sonja wanted to very badly. She nodded. "If I can."

"You can," Julie said matter-of-factly, as if she were talking about some holiday outing.

They entered the Earthdome through the service area so Chalmers would not find out right away that Julie was back. Once inside, Julie hurried to find the unconscious pearl addicts in their sanctuary. She collected a crowd that followed her to watch.

Sonja went to confront Chalmers. She found him in his lab. When he saw her he motioned her to follow him. In his office he turned to her his face flushed with rage. "You thought you fooled me, but I know what's going on with the workers. They won't get away with it. You know once the security force the Consortium has sent arrives, I'll have everything under control again. And that won't take weeks. You see I planned better than you gave me credit for."

"It doesn't matter. You won't need them. There is no more pearl to refine—no more pearl in the caves. It's gone. It's been dissolved, removed, changed."

"I don't know what you mean. No pearl has left the mines, or been taken offplanet."

"Not only have the sentients changed the pearl in the caves, they are taking back the pearl that is in the addicts. Julie is gathering them now. We'll demonstrate for you the uselessness of your plans. What must be done now is to convince the sentient not to destroy—"

"You've gone mad, talking about sentients. You sent the poor confused child on a pointless mission. It will amuse me to watch her struggle, but it will accomplish nothing. I've already informed the Eminences of your betrayal. The fate of the workers is in my hands. I'll offer the them pardon if they give up and agree to go back to work. You will be held responsible for their little rebellion. The Eminences will decide your fate. Once I have pearl back in production I'll decide what to do about the workers' impudence."

Sonja wanted to buy time for Julie. She hoped Omar Harold was right—that Pet was a vehicle to reach the sentients and that Julie would be able to handle the situation when Pella appeared even if Sonja couldn't be present. "Why are you bothering to tell me about it? Why not vaporize me and get it over with?"

"As you very well know, League employees of your level require a hearing witnessed by their peers."

"So now you are going to start going by the rules? I don't think so. You want something from me."

"I might intervene on your behalf if you give me some information."

"If you've been monitoring all my activities, what could be left for me to tell you?"

"Where is the pearl you removed from the comatose workers and how did you extract it?"

Sonja laughed. "Anything to keep from facing the truth."

"You can let me in on the joke," he said angrily.

"I told you they took the pearl—the sentient beings you are trying to destroy. They ate it, or vaporized, or turned it into electronic impulses. It's gone into some other form so you won't want it. All remaining unrefined pearl in the caves is gone."

"Very clever, Shankar. Have you joined the thieves? I wondered how you got away from that renegade Mark Star and his dirty little accomplice. You made some sort of deal with them. They won't help you now. They're in an asteroid mine digging their lives away. You're on your own here and might as well give up."

"Check the caves yourself. There's no pearl there."

"You want me to believe it's gone so I'll abandon the planet. That would leave you and yours in charge of pearl. When reinforcements get here—"

"You're not listening. Julie—"

"Is that why our little Julianna is so eager to help you? Not a flirtation at all. You sent her to find our unconscious users so you could extract pearl from them. You must already have amassed quite a reserve of pearl from the workers. With what you can get here in the Earthdome you could have a tidy profit while you wait until it's safe to start up the refinery again.

Sonja shrugged. "Whatever you say."

Chalmers looked almost disappointed, as if he'd hoped to have to use some stronger measures to persuade her to cooperate. Finally he leaned forward, trying to look sincere. "Look, Shankar, I'll share the profits and smooth your way to market with the Consortium if you share the pearl and the information about how to extract it from people."

Sonja tried to sound resigned. "Let Julie and me have unrestricted access to the comatose pearl addicts here, and I'll show you how it's done. Bring staff, anyone you want— even invite the Eminences to appear, holographically or in person. I'll give a demonstration. Even the Earthdomers might be desperate enough by now. We'll meet in the sanctuary below the failsafe area; we don't want to trigger that system. It would alert the Galactic League that there really is something wrong here."

He nodded hesitantly.

"Now let me go help Julie gather together the residents who want to cooperate. You'll have to call off your reinforcements. Don't want to share with them." She waited.

Chalmers looked at her uncertainly. "I knew you'd see reason, Shankar. You can't do it alone. I don't know where you got your extraction method but the records I saw from the refinery were impressive. Harold probably came up with it. Very clever. I don't know how we missed his research. Must have gone on before he went into the mine."

Sonja tried to keep the sarcasm out of her voice. "Yes, a very clever scientist, Harold; it might be best if he and his assistant were present when we…extract pearl." She looked into his eyes with her best sincere wide-eyed stare. "Not too many security people, either. You don't want to share the information any more than you have to."

"You'll be accompanied by security robots at all times."

"Of course."

# Chapter Thirty-Two

Julie, Sonja and a few skeptical Earthdomers gathered in the sanctuary chamber for the Earthdome's comatose pearl users, built deep in the rock beneath the Earthdome. Here the comatose were not on shelves with little maintenance equipment like the comatose workers at the mine and refinery. Here each was in a separate bed-capsule with their family crest and caste credentials imbedded at the head. There were a plethora of robot medics, who stood back, protective. Julie's audience were showing their amusement by laughing and joking about crazy Julie who thought she could bring the zombies back to life. They were always ready for a spectacle, especially when it included embarrassing a member of an elite family.

Julie was confident, but Sonja wanted to make sure they could make contact with the sentients before she alerted Chalmers. She sat with Julie and Pet in the middle of the floor. Julie held Pet tight and placed her hands over the little dog's paws on the rock floor to hold them still. One of the addicts Julie had invited tittered. Omar and Nombei were stationed to one side with recording equipment.

By the time Julie lifted her hand and Pet moved, some of the spectators had left in boredom. At first Sonja saw nothing. Then instead of the large hole that burned through the floor in the refinery, a tiny red-hot pinhole appeared with a narrow stream of vapor and smoke rising from it, bringing a sulphur smell. After a few moments a faint image of Pella began to appear in the vapor.

The few remaining spectators laughed at what they believed was a holographic image as Pella's vaporous hand reached over and touched the nearest comatose figure. The purple tinted skin began to change as pearl was withdrawn from the prone figure. Medical robots suddenly rushed forward when the person began to stir and sit up, her face flushed, her eyes wild.

Then the group of Earthdomers became silent and watchful, still not really believing what they were seeing. It wasn't until the second person was revived that there was a buzz of astonished conversation.

Sonja tried to contact Chalmers, but the electronics did not work. The medical and security robots also were disabled. She sent Nombei to find him and tell him what was happening. It was time to convince him that he'd finally lost.

More and more Earthdomers gathered as all the comatose addicts in the room were relieved of their pearl. Pella turned to the group of silent spectators and said, "We have transformed pearl so that it is no longer a substance that your life-form can ingest. Whatever pain you now suffer because you can no longer get pearl can be relieved. As with your compatriots here who have been revived, that will be done by touching me and allowing me to take back pearl that still exists in your bodies."

Finally, one of watchers, a woman with the opalescent lavender skin tones of a long-time user, reluctantly went up to touch Pella's hand. As her skin faded to a normal flushed tone she collapsed onto the floor. Other watchers rushed to her side, but she slowly got up, her eyes wide with astonishment.

Pella had just turned back to the crowd and held out her hand when Chalmers came in the chamber with his security people and surrounded Pella and those near her. The crowd moved back as he said to Sonja, "You can turn off your hologram now. I've seen enough. It's time to show me the pearl you have collected and tell me how you extracted it."

Pella said, "It is illogical to continue your quest for pearl in any form. We have removed what pearl remained in the caves as well as any that is freely offered by humans who have ingested it. It has been reincorporated into our being in a form not accessible to humans. There is no longer any reason for conflict between us. Your chemicals, explosive or otherwise, only provide us with fuel. They are amusing and interesting to taste but they will do us no harm."

Chalmers walked over to Omar and turned off his equipment, obviously assuming it was projecting a hologram. He turned, but finding Pella still there he looked further along the walls, gesturing to his people to help him. Finding no further source for a holographic projection he said, "Very well, leave it; it is amusing."

He turned back to Sonja. "Show me how it's done." Sonja took one of Chalmers' people who had the lavender cast to her skin and led her to Pella. The woman resisted, but with Chalmers' nod let Sonja put her hand in Pella's. The pearl drained from her leaving her with a healthy flush. The sentients must be getting better at it because the woman didn't even collapse, but simply turned to Chalmers, her eyes bright, a puzzled look on her face.

Chalmers went over to her and looked at her skin, had his techs test it and shook his head, puzzled at the results. He motioned to one of his people who was also lavender-tinted and tested his skin. Then he walked him up to Pella's image and he and another tech checked the area with hand-held instruments. The lavender-tinted man did not wait for Chalmers' nod, but reached out for Pella's hand. Chalmers tried to pull him away, but let go with a start when his color began to change. Instead Chalmers tried to reach into Pella—into what he thought was a holographic image—but his hand would not penetrate and sparks flew off as he cried out with pain from a burn. He stepped back, pulling out his stunner with his other hand, and fired it at Pella. Instead of hitting the wall behind her as it would have if she'd been a holographic projection, the energy from the blast was absorbed by Pella's image and she brightened becoming slightly more opaque for a second. Chalmers' face paled, his eyes staring in disbelief.

Pella spoke. "We have had great patience with your skepticism about our existence. However we will not tolerate further interference. Should you attempt to further damage us or our environment and that of our neighbors, including those humans who choose to live here peaceably, we will vaporize any resources that you might covet—water, metal, even stone. If you persist, it will no longer be possible for humans to remain on this planet."

Chalmers shook his head indecisively, still staring. He looked at the people being attended to by the robots, some of them even sitting up in their beds. Was he finally beginning to suspect that he had been wrong and was losing?

Julie laughed and said in a satisfied, teasing voice, "Your precious pearl is all gone, Chalmy…sweetheart. How are you going to explain this to your bosses?"

Sonja said, "You've lost, Governor. It is over. Give me the gun. Even weapons can't hurt them, can't stop us."

Pella went on gently now, her voice remote, her image fading. "The remainder of our history that humans now possess and have scattered to other worlds must be returned to us. As you can see, life-forms and their consciousness need not not be destroyed in retrieving our history—what you call pearl—unless you leave us no other choice."

But instead of admitting his failure, Chalmers' rage and frustration boiled over and he told his people to shoot. He himself took out a gun with old-fashioned bullets. Bullet and stunner bursts ricocheted off the walls and off Pella who was reaching out with a protective barrier around those near her. But some of the recovering elite were hit as well as one of Chalmers' security people and some robot medics. The other security people, realizing what was happening, stopped firing and took cover at the chamber entrance. But Chalmers still fired at Pella, his face red, his chin quivering.

Julie picked up a stunner from the disabled man, and to Chalmers astonishment, deliberately stunned him, saying under her breath, "I hope you have a heart attack." Then she dropped the stunner and walked over to Pella. A wispy light floated up from her hand and Julie reached toward it. Mist surrounded her, pearly, faintly glowing. She stepped into Pella. Everyone gasped as Pella melded into Julie.

Julie opened her eyes. Pella had disappeared and a smiling luminescent Julie stepped toward the onlookers. They stepped back in awe.

Julie walked up to a man wounded by a ricocheting bullet and reached down into his wound. It was as if her fingers went inside. People screamed and the robot medics moved closer to intervene but could not. When Julie's hand withdrew there was a bullet between her fingers. She said to the wounded man. "You won't die now; you will heal slowly in a normal way."

Julie turned to the others and said, "This is a reminder to you all. You are mortal. You will age and die as is appropriate for our species." The luminescence was fading, but Julie's voice was strangely hollow. Sonja wondered who, what, she really was. She could not take her eyes off this luminescent being before her that had been Julie, surrounded by a sparkling rainbow aura. The apparition smiled and spoke to Sonja, but no sound came from her lips. The words echoed in Sonja's mind, "We send our thanks. You will help us gather pearl."

The luminescence faded and the old Julie turned to the security people. "As you can see, my husband, Governor Chalmers is incapacitated. Investigator Shankar will be in charge now. Then she turned to the medical robots. "Take the governor to his apartment. We will tend him there."

While the medical robots made the still unconscious Chalmers comfortable, Sonja quickly made use of Chalmers' private office. She contacted moonbase and, using the governor's official code was able to send a report to the GLIA about what really had happened. She left it up to the League to inform the Consortium. She certainly did not trust the League to be able to control them. But she hoped they would be able to send League staff along with whatever force the Consortium sent.

In next few days even some of those who had witnessed the recovery of the comatose addicts, still refused to let Julie touch them. But it didn't take long for the news of what Julie could do to travel and people came—from the other Earthdomes and, then, from the valley—first to observe, then to give up pearl. Each day more people were touched by her.

Sonja learned from the GLIA response to her report that the Eminences had not accepted that pearl was gone and were still greedy for it, They were sending an interventionary force scheduled to arrive soon. Fortunately the League had managed to have their own staff be included.

Chalmers remained unconscious, but his staff reluctantly accepted

Sonja's authority. She offered to take anyone down into the mine to show them that there was no more pearl. None trusted her enough to risk such a trip, but could not deny that Julie somehow could remove pearl from addicts. They asked to make tests to see what happened to the pearl while she worked. She laughingly agreed, but said, amused by their skepticism, "You'll find nothing. The sentients tell me your minds and your science are too primitive, too mono-dimensional." As she predicted equipment registered nothing as the pearl was drained from a volunteer.

Finally, in desperation an addicted researcher let Julie touch him. After his pearl was gone he got up laughing and shaking his head. He went to the equipment and turned it off, saying to the other researchers, "She's right, all this is useless. We'll have to start over, begin again, rethink our models of reality."

Sonja asked refinery workers to guard Chalmers and confined resistant staff when necessary. Everyone onplanet waited for the Consortium's interventionary force to arrive. Those who could afford it, hired a transport and got ready to leave the planet.

Sonja confiscated and gave Julie and the sentients any supplies of pearl she could find, but was not yet willing to use force to locate it.

Julie was lighthearted and unconcerned—almost ecstatic about her daily vigil with those being freed from pearl. She was full of energy and enthusiasm inspiring her recruits who took charge of those who needed care once the pearl had been withdrawn.

Sonja was listening to a woman who'd been one of the comatose and now spoke to a crowd of curious Earthdomers. She looked down at her hand sadly. "I know it is hard to imagine the horror of being frozen by pearl. Lying still forever, not in the peaceful sleep of death, but horribly awake, unable to move, even to blink an eye, hearing your heart beat so slowly, your blood moving like mud. Your mind alone moving, but with your thoughts trapped. But now…" She held up her hands and wiggled her fingers, then touched her face in wonder. "…like a newborn babe, I am free and I am healed and when I die I will sleep forever in peace."

At the end of the day they went back to Julie's apartment. Over a cup of tea Sonja showed Julie a message she had just received and decoded. It was from Jason. "He is offering a refuge. You could live there and the Consortium hounds couldn't find you. If you leave now on the transport to Calsor you can contact him. He would meet you there. It won't be hard. But you have to leave the planet before reinforcements arrive. With Chalmers out of commission you can still get away."

Julie smiled serenely and said, "We'll go when our task here is completed." She paused for a moment. "I might leave now if you went with me. We could find those on other planets that needed my help."

Sonja sighed. "You know I can't. I have a job to finish."

"You made your report. They know what the situation is."

"My mentor at the League assures me—"

"That he will keep you out of the recycler? Their protection, even if they risk giving it, won't keep the Consortium goons off you if they want you gone. You know too much. They will wake up Chalm and use him against you. You encouraged workers to resist. You—"

Sonja said once again, "If you don't go before the reinforcements arrive you'll never get offplanet. They might recycle you."

Julie danced across the room, singing, "Can't, can't, can't."

Then she came close and pulled Sonja into her dance. "We'll eat the recycler. We'll eat the laser guns. We'll eat the ships. Your reinforcements will be left naked on the sand." She giggled and even Sonja had to laugh at the image of naked troops and Consortium officials shivering in the desert.

"Even if you and the sentients could destroy their equipment, they will send more and you'll be arrested—"

Julie kissed her. "They'll take me back to Earth. There will be a hearing with my grands. I will convince them pearl is gone. If not…" She shrugged. "Going back to Earth—it's what I want—what we…want. The sentients have agreed to go with me."

"You and your sentients. And how will they go with you? Hot magma in the bottom of the ship? Sentients are dependent on the volcanic forces of this planet for their survival."

Julie shrugged. "Would you have believed that they could do what they have done, before you saw it yourself?"

Sonja wished it were true that Julie could find a way to sway the Eminences, and others in power in the Consortium, but it seemed unlikely. If there was just time—time for Julie to gather more recruits. Time to bring addicted from other planets to xj-21 to be cured.

Before the expedition arrived Julie sent a holographic message to the Eminences and the Family. Sonja thought it too cryptic, but Julie laughed and said, "If I say more, I might be inclined to tell them the truth."

In the hologram Julie stood alone, a small iridescent image of a pearl in her hand and said, "Grannies, uncles, aunties, all my dear family. I have found the source of pearl. I can bring it home to you, my special gift to thank you for my being alive and for who I am." Before the new expedition was to arrive, a message from the Eminence instructed Julie to board a transport heading for Earth.

When Julie stepped onto the platform on the interplanetary satellite circling Old Earth, she and the other passengers were greeted by Consortium officials. The others, all of whom no longer had pearl, were taken off to be questioned. Julie was escorted to a shuttle to be taken directly to the Family satellite.

On the way the official, a cousin of Julie's said, "Our grannys are anxious to see you. We know you have been removing pearl and have brought it to them—none too soon." He smiled, nervously. "I'm sure you will include me in your generosity."

Julie smiled winningly and kissed him gently on his lavender tinted cheek. "Of course sweet cousin, I will—in spite of your teasing me when I was little."

He flushed. "Sorry about that. We were so young."

Julie nodded, still smiling.

Five Eminences in their carts gathered around Julie. Behind them stood a silent group of Consortium and League officials. Some had the purple cast of pearl use, some did not. Julie walked up to each Eminence and kissed them on the cheek in a Family greeting. Then to everyone's eyes, Julie became fainter, out of focus, more than one Julie. The Eminences' agitation had quieted and they were silent as their eyestalks began to sag, the eye dilated and their flesh began to lose its purple opalescent tone but no medical alarm sounded. The android medics stood back helplessly. The crowd begin to whisper as multiple Julies walked up to other Family members and gave them each a kiss. The last was the cousin who escorted her there.

All the Eminences were quiet but still alive, veins pulsing through translucent skin. The rest were looking at their skin and at those around with growing puzzlement and agitation.

After a few seconds the fluttering Julie images reunited and she moved away from people, taking the cousin by the arm and leading him away from the crowd. She whispered to him, "The sentients are hungry. We must touch Earth itself. Will you please take us down to the surface."

He was staring down at his hand, a normal skin tone for the first time in years. He looked over at her, his eyes wide. "But where is the pearl?"

She patted his arm. "It's there. You must have heard that pearl has been transformed. Now it's transparent, invisible and you don't have to eat capsules anymore. A great improvement, no?"

"But I don't feel—"

"Don't worry; you will."

Before they could leave the satellite they were stopped by Family security people. Because Julie was a Family member she was locked in a Family compound, a dome on Earth specifically for the confinement of aberrant defective and recalcitrant Family members. The guards that escorted her were clearly all afraid of her.

The prison was a luxurious suite. It looked as though someone had anticipated Julie's confinement because there was the feeding equipment she had needed in the past. They intended all along to accept her offer and lock her up.

When her Family jailers finally made contact through the built-in communication equipment, it was the cousin that was visible on the monitor, although it was clear others were present out of sight.

"We are very disappointed in you, cousin. Instead of the gift of pearl you promised you have stolen—" He looked away. "The grannys are barely alive. We are all very…confused. What is it you want in exchange for the pearl you promised? Name your price and—"

Julie said, contemptuously, "The grannys are only as alive as they should be now." She smiled triumphantly. "I don't think they'll be running the Consortium any longer—without pearl, they'll lose consciousness. The rest of you will have to run things for them now. Don't worry—you won't die, for a long time, but you won't live forever either."

He looked confused and walked away from the viewer. He was replaced by an uncle. "You haven't answered our question."

"I didn't say I was bringing pearl, I said I was bringing the source of pearl. All I want now is the freedom to move about the planet without interference."

"And in exchange for that you'll give us…the source of pearl?" he said hopefully.

She smiled at him then. "Yes. The intelligence, the sentient beings that your representative, my husband tried to destroy. Investigator Shankar sent extensive reports. Everything you need to know is there. By now your expedition to xj-21 should have confirmed her report and you know there is no more pearl."

"Your cousin says you told him you have some sort of device that changed or removed the pearl in our bodies. If you volunteer information about that or allow a physical examination so we can determine what it is how it works—"

Julie continued, tiredness showing in her voice. "You chose to believe my little lie and let me come here to free my grannies from the pearl poison. I can and will do the same for any who comes to me. But I can't give you any more than that. They are living entities; the sentients do now reside with me but they can't be taken, owned, or used."

Her uncle looked away a minute, listening, and then said, "You have deceived us. You will remain where you are until this matter is cleared up and you release the pearl to us in whatever form you have it since you stole it from us." The uncle disappeared to be replaced again by her cousin, his eyes frightened and anxious. "Sorry Julie, but I had to tell them. They are very upset with you. You better tell them. You can't get out of there. That dome is in the middle of an old poisonous munitions dump—"

Julie smiled at him, sadly. "An easy way out for you if I try to leave. I'm gone. No embarrassing hearing. You can claim I escaped. Committed suicide. Everyone will be grateful."

He shook his head not looking at her. "You can't get out of there; you're being monitored at all times. You have just twenty-four hours to reveal to us what you've done with the pearl and how you took it." Then her cousin shifted his eyes to her and whispered his own question. "The report Shankar sent said that pearl couldn't be removed from people without their consent. How did you do it?"

Julie smiled with satisfaction. "The sentients have learned a great deal about humans. Sometimes what you need is not what you want."

"And you, cousin Julia, are not human?"

Now her tone was bitter. "Don't you remember what you and your buddies used to call me? Mutant, slime worm, android and worse. You never thought I was…human. And I never liked being the kind of human I was born anyway."

He flushed and said, "I told you I was sorry about that. I'm just trying to help now."

"It doesn't matter anyway. I've done what I came back to do. I'll help anyone who comes to me rid themselves of the pearl poison. Otherwise don't bother me. She threw her shirt over the monitor and curled up in the chair. She could not feel the sentient presence, only a gnawing hunger and sadness. Did she dare eat or drink anything here or would it all leave her unconscious or poisoned? But she had to stay alive for their sake, until they could strengthen themselves. She stumbled about the place until she was drawn to a wall. She lay against it and fell asleep.

The sentients gathered just enough strength from the suite's metal poor environment to disable the monitors and open a small hole in the wall of the dome just big enough for Julie to crawl through out into the dry, hot environment.

She crawled as far as she could and then lay down on twisted, dry grass, the only thing that could grow on the poisoned piece of ground.

When the Family found the hole in the wall, they informed the GLIA of her suicide and sent out a search party for her body.

Before the expedition landed on xj-21 Sonja sent the refinery workers and any miners who chose, out to the scattered squatter settlements and informed people still onplanet that they should get together a petition to the League to help them, either to be moved to another colony planet or help establish an official colony on xj-21.

The combined League and Consortium officials that arrived agreed that Sonja should be confined at the Earthdome until their investigation was completed. Sonja was turned over to the GLIA personnel and debriefed for days.

The League and Consortium scientists and engineers explored the caves and the deeper caverns and found no pearl. Finally the Consortium began the process of withdrawing and the League took over management of the planet. Omar and Nombei were made part of a League team trying to resolve the problems of the planet's future. Pearl addicts were arriving from other colonies clamoring for help relieving them of pearl. When the mine caverns finally cooled and with the help of Pet they had some success contacting the sentients and relieving addicts of pearl.

When reports from the Consortium and GLIA investigators confirmed Sonja's story, they released her, but suspended her from active duty and sent her back to Earth. She was to remain in her small apartment at GLIA headquarters until she was finally cleared for reassignment.

When Sonja received the news of Julie's suicide, she was allowed to go to the place where they said they found Julie's body. There was only a green grassy slope. She lay down and wept, taking off her helmet and expecting to breath poisonous air. When she found the air sweet and breathable, she dug into the soil and put her face against the blackened earth. Julie might be gone, but she had brought the sentients here. The Earth would recover now. Then she took a bit of soil to her apartment and put it in with a house plant. She was not surprised when her plant didn't die. She didn't tell anyone.

When she was finally reinstated she was allowed to choose from a list of least desirable assignments. One of them was to follow up on a report of an evangelical crank, a woman, that had appeared in some of the warren entertainment centers agitating for earthrats to leave the warrens and 'reclaim their heritage.' They said the woman claimed the Earth was cleaned up enough for resettlement. Some people had already left the warrens with her encouragement. No one had bothered to go after them. The description of the guru resembled Julie. It couldn't be her, of course, but Sonja had to find out for sure and volunteered. It was something to do.

When she told her mentor she wanted to go into the warrens to deal with the exodus, he said with distaste, "A waste of time in my opinion going after one crazy woman. It won't stop them. Happens all the time—a bunch of earthrats go outside and slowly get poisoned. Not that their deaths would be any great loss. Just find her as quickly as you can. I've more important things for you to do."

She went into the warrens for the first time in her life. It was not as easy as she had thought it would be. Few admitted knowing about the woman. Even the Agencies regular informants were reluctant. Sonja finally found her—a fragile shadowy figure surrounded by a few earthrats in a stinking hovel of an arcade of ancient game machines. When they saw Sonja with her environmental mask, the audience scattered and left the woman standing alone.

The figure, ghostly in the shadows turned and then walked up to Sonja and peered through Sonja's visor. "I thought it was you. It *is* me. I thought you would be locked up by now or memory deleted." When Sonja didn't respond right away, the Julie look-alike looked down and said, "Or maybe you are."

"Contessa…Julie?" Sonja managed to choke out. "How can you still be alive?"

Julie smiled. "We fed on the poisons and the volcanics. The Earth juices are different but we are learning about them. And how did you escape punishment?"

"Why should they punish me? I was telling the truth. It took them a while to figure that out. And I did some things that the League couldn't condone even in an emergency. That's why I'm on assignment down in the warrens. My punishment. And you did change things, before they stopped you, though there are still those in power who hang on to pearl. But why are you here?"

"When they found me I was still alive, barely. The sentients had gone from my body to learn about the Earth juices and to feed, so the techs could still find nothing that explained how I took pearl out of the Eminences or how I escaped from their prison. By the time they found me the reports from the investigation on xj-21, had come through and the authorities had finally begun to believe that there was no more pearl in the mines. But still they wouldn't believe I had nothing to tell them—no secrets that would let them find or make more pearl. They sent me down into the warrens to force me to give them information they thought they wanted."

Julie stretched out her arms and smiled. "Now the sentients have grown strong and have cleaned enough poisons from Earth that people from these warrens can live on the surface again. I just tell them about it. The exodus is beginning, but I'm glad you've come for me. We are ready to go to other planets where our essence, our history can be recovered."

In the privacy of her apartment, Sonja observed Julie and the sentients. One moment there was one Julie, the next there were many and they looked at each other and began to laugh. They began melting into each other and separating again in an hilarious dance.

When they had fused back into one, Sonja said, "How far apart can you be? Can we send separates of you to other planets?"

When Julie spoke now it was with many voices, as if they were all speaking in unison. "We would be lonely for each other, but space is one and all distance means nothing."

Sonja sighed. The human Julie had been difficult but this one—

Julie said to Sonja sadly, "I don't know if I can bear to be merely human now. The color, smell, erotic imagery that they-we experience—I might have to be part of it…forever."

"But before you didn't have a chance at what it is like to be fully human."

Julie laughed. "And now that I know what that is, I'm not sure it would be enough."

GLIA Agent Sonja Shankar took her prisoner to the Planet Calsor where there was a mining operation that would take earthrat criminals as workers. Once there she contacted those who were trying to get to xj-21 to rid themselves of pearl.

Julie stood before an assembled crowd of addicts. Sonja hadn't realized the extent of transformation the human body could tolerate and still be technically alive. Even those that still walked had iridescent purple-toned skin. In the center were those no longer mobile—some in wheeled chairs some on stretchers, their bodies so stiff that they had to be carried prone.

The crowd became silent and seemed to draw back as the luminescent halo wrapped Julie's body and translucent pink forms fluttered around her. Julie reached out her arms wordlessly to the crowd. With the help of their aides each came forward, some tottering on stick legs. Each in their turn was surrounded by mist as their flesh lost its pearl.

Those who had given back their pearl chose to wear simple white tunics and live simply, talking about their new freedom and joy in life with an enthusiasm that gave no one peace until they too went to Julie. With them she traveled to other planets gathering pearl.

# Epilogue

Without fresh supplies of pearl, addicts everywhere turned to Julie's recruits, begging for Julie to free them from the pearl curse.

Omar and Nombei stayed on xj-21. As more young workgrubs began to appear in the fields, Omar became their advocate with the farmers that remained, and, after a few years, got them protection from the Galactic League. Nombei took over her business and eventually she and Omar became family partners, taking in children from the Godong who chose to be educated in the valley.

Even with the care of the expedition's doctors Chalmers did not wake up. He was returned to his family on Earth for long-term care.

With the Galaxy League's help most of the refinery and mine workers found work on the farm or in the valley community. The Galactic League decreed that the Earthdomes must be dismantled and all who chose to live onplanet must accept the local environment as theirs. No more imitation-Earth environment. Very few of the elite stayed on; most left with the Consortium, so the planet was left to the true settlers, eventually to be recognized as a full colony by the League.

Reanna negotiated with the farm community and the squatters to put together a government of sorts. The rift valley preferred to be independent, but that was under negotiation.

On Earth the Eminences remained only technically alive. Even with all the artificial medical supports, they could not sustain consciousness, having been alive too long and too long dependent on pearl. Other younger Consortium managers took over and the Consortium looked to other enterprises for profit.

Julie became the sentients' representative with the Consortium and the Galactic League. She would remain their representative until all pearl was returned to the sentients.

Sonja no longer worked for the League. Her bosses agreed to release her from her obligation in exchange for her silence. She eventually found Jason and some other former agents on one of the least habitable of the planets. Most of them had removed all of the artificial enhancements that had been required by the Agency and lived simple, but comfortable, lives. Some, like Jason, preferred to act as independent agents, freelancing to support their colony. But instead of joining them Sonja continued to stay with Julie as she moved from planet to planet looking for pearl.

One day Sonja asked Julie, "When the sentients have all their pearl back will they do more to control us?"

Julie looked far away. "Yes, but only if we threaten them again. They didn't recognize humans as intelligent at first because of our destructive chaotic nature. Destruction is the action of mindlessness. The volcanic forces that feed sentients would be randomly destructive without sentient control. Meaningful control is a definition of mind to them."

Sonja argued, "It would be destructive to us if they control us even to protect themselves—if we are not free."

Julie's form seemed to become vaguer, surrounded by a fluttering red haze; only her eyes were bright with fire. "Human concepts like freedom mean so many things they're without meaning. Like the rest of human language—the sound-based means of communication—words are much too vague and incomplete. Human language sensitivity, human intelligence is not sufficient to express what humans need to understand—what humans need to know."

When Julie talked this way Sonja became anxious. Did the human woman still exist or— She reached out and pulled Julie close to feel her warmth. The human Julie sighed and held her close for a moment.

Sonja asked, "What will we do when all the pearl is recovered? Will you stay with me? I want to be with you always."

"Humans are always looking to beginnings and endings. You and I, Sonja and Julie, being human, will end." Julie sighed and turned away. "Sentients think it must be very lonely for us humans, separate for all time. They don't have the constraints of our species. But we, you and I will be part of their…memory."

Then she pulled away and danced across the room, while a slightly disembodied voice continued the conversation. "Humans caught our attention only when you threatened us, when you stole our history, our joyfulness. Then we needed to learn about you and exert the control that you were incapable of. We have recorded all we need about you. You are no longer a threat. We can occupy your planet's volcanic space without effect on you or other Earth-based life-forms. Our presence will enhance your species' survival because we will control those volcanic energies. However, when we have pearl back we will have no further contact with you."

"That's sad for us."

"Your species has much to learn."

Then the human Julie danced back again into her arms.